# THE PROMISE

## SOPHIE'S STORY

### A SOPHIE STAR PREQUEL PART TWO

## AUTHOR
# L. J. WEBB

# THE PROMISE
## SOPHIE'S STORY
### BY L. J. WEBB

eBook ISBN  **978-1-7330939-8-9**
Paperback ISBN  **978-1-7330939-9-6**

Library of Congress Control Number: **2021912442**

# TABLE OF CONTENTS

In the hope of eternal life which God,
who cannot lie, promised before time
began… Titus 1:2 NKJV.

# PROLOGUE
## ANNA

Anna had so much to catch up on after being missing for the past two years. Duke and CJ had changed so much; they were going to be twelve this summer. Anna still saw a sadness in the love of her life, David Scott. There was a hole in his heart that hadn't entirely mended from her disappearance. In time the new memories would replace the pain of the time they lost. Anna was determined to make sure of that.

Anna realized the missing years had been easier for her, in a way. She had lost her memory in an accident while trying to complete an extraction from Syria. She had gone to Syria with fake IDs and papers to get a Christian family out of the country. Her partner on this mission worked inside the government of Syria. He knew they were on the list of dissidents. Christians often got on that list for various reasons. Usually a vengeful neighbor or family member. Faiz was her contact; he worked in the Political Security Directorate. His position allowed him access to who on the list was going to be arrested and imprisoned.

The Christian Non-Profit Organization they were a part of was called Mission of Peace. Their declared 'mission statement' was to feed the hungry. Which they did; all over the world. But they had a more covert mission too. Mission of Peace smuggled out Christians who were on lists like the one in Syria. The members who took on these missions knew they were putting their own lives at risk. David's family ran the nonprofit; his father, Emmett Scott, was the founder.

Their mission went awry when a sandstorm derailed them. The van transporting them and their passengers went down the bank to the river. Anna was thrown from the vehicle. She woke up in the home of a local family who lived in the outer regions of Syria by the border with Turkey. Her only memory was her love of God and her skill as a physician's assistant.

Anna had no idea why she was in Syria or if there was anyone she left behind. David, on the other hand, remembered everything and continued to search for her. Losing Anna devastated him.

Now she was home and intended to catch up on everything she missed. She loved the new additions to their small group. Anna particularly wanted to get to know Duke and CJ's new friends. She heard the whole story of the kidnapping and how they protected and took care of one another. Anna wanted to encourage and nurture that relationship. Anna went all out on birthdays making up for the ones she missed. When Duke told Anna how the bus had left Sophie and Lizzy at school when Sophie was sick, it made her angry. She took the kids to and from school every day since. This year she and Zoey planned on sharing carpool duties.

The Sunday BBQs helped her catch up with the news, and Anna made sure there were more social events. They found fun things to do all around the city.

Once a week, Anna and Zoey tended to the sick in one of the neighboring more impoverished church communities in Adana. She involved the others in helping to supply and serve Thanksgiving dinner in the same area.

Christmas with Anna back was a whole new level of fun. One of the first things Anna did when she got home was rent a piano for their home. It made singing Christmas Carols sound so much better. She had started Duke and CJ on piano lessons before she went missing. Now she wanted to give lessons to all the kids. Luke Star was excited about that since his mother had been a concert pianist. He hoped Sophie might have inherited some of his mother's talent. It seemed it skipped his generation.

Anna had been home for a year now, and she loved her life.

# THE PROMISE

# CHAPTER ONE

Luke held Sophie's backpack while waiting outside for Zoey to pick her up for the first day of fifth grade. It was Liam's first day too; he was in first grade. Ricky, Lizzy's brother, started first-grade last year.

Luke looked at his daughter's face. She was usually so happy to go to school, but without Lizzy, every day was miserable for her.

Ruby Diaz got a call from her brother saying their mother, Elizabeth, Lizzy's namesake, was in the hospital. Leo told her if she wanted to see her, she better come right away. Manny took a month of emergency leave and took his family to Montana, so Ruby and the grandkids could see her again. Ruby's mother died a few days later. She had held on long enough to say goodbye to her family. Now they were dealing with funeral arrangements and settling her estate.

Even though Sophie Skyped with Lizzy every day, she still missed her so much. Duke and CJ took her to the movies and the arcade with them, but it just wasn't as much fun without Lizzy.

Zoey pulled up; it was her turn to drive this week. Luke could see that her SUV had a third row that pulled up in the cargo area. He planned on going to the motor pool and trade in his SUV for one like that. Luke helped Sophie with her backpack and squatted down to talk to her.

"Sophie, I know you miss Lizzy, but you need to perk up and enjoy your first day of school." He placed his hand over Sophie's heart. "Little girls have huge hearts, and those hearts have room for lots and lots of friends. You can give a big piece to your best

5

friend and still have plenty of room in there for others. You and Lizzy have other friends at school."

"I know, Daddy. But Lizzy is my best friend."

"I understand, princess, but being happy to see your other friends won't change that. The other kids at school will feel bad if you aren't glad to see them and want to be their friend too." Luke kissed her forehead and walked toward the car.

CJ could see how unhappy Sophie was, so he got out of the coveted front seat and let Sophie sit there. She smiled at him and got in. Luke closed the door after saying hello to everyone. He stepped away and waved as they drove off.

Luke received a call from the temporary receptionist at the Jag office. She passed on a request for a lawyer to come to the MP station. A Captain DaSilva was just arrested for a hit and run and wanted a lawyer.

Luke arrived at the MP station twenty minutes later, asking to see the captain. The receptionist, Private 1st class Sorensen, got on the phone. She called back to the holding cells and asked the guard to bring the prisoner to an interrogation room. She explained his lawyer was here.

Sorensen allowed Captain Star past the pony wall and swing gate that separated the reception area from the inner functions of the MP station. She directed him to the interrogation room DaSilva was in. Luke could see the captain was agitated when he walked in.

"Are you my lawyer?" Captain DaSilva asked.

"Yes, my name is Captain Luke Star. Why don't you tell me why you're in here, Captain DaSilva?"

"That's what you need to find out. I was pulling into my driveway, and the police pulled in behind me and arrested me."

"They didn't read you your rights and tell you why they arrested you?"

"Yes, of course. The MP said he was investigating a 'hit and run'. Then he asked me to take a breathalyzer test. Don't you think I would have known if I had hit something?" DaSilva said.

"I don't know." Luke could smell a faint odor of alcohol on his breath. "Have you been drinking?"

"Don't be ridiculous. It's only 9 am."

"Captain DaSilva, did you agree to take the breathalyzer test when they picked you up?"

"No," DaSilva replied.

"Captain, I can still smell alcohol on your breath. If you don't tell me the truth, I can't defend you properly." DaSilva bowed his head. Luke could tell he was debating whether to tell him the truth.

"Do I need to pay you a retainer or something? If I talk to you, is it privileged?"

"Yes. If you tell me you want me as your lawyer, then the attorney, client privilege applies."

"Ok then. You are my lawyer," he hesitated again. "I was out all weekend on a bender. I slept in my car last night in the Officers Club parking lot because I was afraid to drive home. But this morning, I needed to get home to take a shower and be at my office on time. I was still a little foggy, but I wasn't drunk anymore." DaSilva was still in handcuffs, his arms on the table. He leaned over the table and looked Luke in the eyes. "I didn't hit anything. It's the truth, Captain Star."

"Alright, Captain, I'm going to go see what charges are pending. I'll be right back." Luke stepped over to the MP standing guard outside the interrogation room.

"Corporal, do you know who arrested the captain?"

"Yes sir, it was Private 2nd class Noah Adams."

"Will you see if he is available to talk to me?" Luke asked.

"Yes sir." The Corporal went to find Private Adams.

Luke recognized Private Adams from a few years ago when he helped arrest a man, Corporal Krause, who had abused his wife, Amy. Krause had gone after Ruby when he found out she was hiding his wife. Sophie stayed with her to help distract him so the others could run.

Private Adams smiled and stretched out his hand to Luke as he walked up to him. "Captain Star, it has been a long time." Luke reciprocated the smile and the handshake.

"Yes, it has, Private Adams. It's good to see you again." He nodded over to a couple of chairs in the hallway so they could sit and talk.

"Private Adams, what precipitated the arrest of my client Captain DaSilva?"

"The switchboard got a call about 7:45 this morning. An anonymous caller said someone in a light-colored GMC was driving erratically. The man gave us the location, and I attempted to find him, hopefully before anything serious happened. As I was driving to that location, I came upon an accident scene. A white Honda Accord had slammed into a metal lamp post. I stopped to give aid and found the driver unconscious and his son in the back seat with a cut on his forehead. His head hit the window when the car collided with the pole.

"I called an ambulance, and they took the man and his son to the hospital. I had taken his license out of his wallet so I could contact his next of kin. I contacted his wife, and she went to meet them at the hospital.

"At first, I thought this driver was the man who was driving erratically. I saw no evidence there was another car involved. While I was waiting for the tow truck, I noticed damage to the car's bumper and checked it out. I called Base Security and asked them to see if their cameras picked up the accident; they sent me the footage. It was plain to see that a GMC Jimmy plowed into the back of the Honda, forcing it into the lamp post. The plate wasn't visible, but when I looked up who owned a vehicle like that on

Base, there were only three. The security footage is black and white and a little fuzzy, so I couldn't tell the vehicle's exact color. I went to the first address, and Captain DaSilva was getting out of his vehicle when I pulled up. I checked his vehicle for damage and saw a dent in his front bumper. He smelled of alcohol and I requested he take a breathalyzer. He refused, so I arrested him."

"Did he agree to a breathalyzer at any point?"

"No, he continued to refuse. I brought him in and requested a medic take his blood to test for alcohol. He hasn't arrived yet."

"Did he give you an explanation for the damaged bumper?"

"He refused to tell me anything until he had a lawyer."

"Private Adams, you would not have had enough to arrest the captain, except for the fact he refused the breathalyzer."

"Yes sir. If a man appears drunk and doesn't agree to a breathalyzer, our orders are to bring him in for a blood test."

"That gives you probable cause for the DUI but not for the 'hit and run'." Luke didn't say anything else. He got up, thanked the private, and went back to the interrogation room.

Luke sat down. Captain DaSilva had his head down on his folded arms. He thought he might be asleep, but DaSilva lifted his head as soon as Luke sat down.

"Captain DaSilva, what color is your GMC?"

"It's a light blue."

"And how long ago did you damage your front bumper?"

"About a week. I came out of the PX and found someone had backed into it, causing the dent. There was no note on my car."

"I don't believe they have enough to charge you for the 'hit and run' yet. However, by refusing the breathalyzer, the MP was within his rights to bring you in for a blood test."

"Can you get me out of here? I'm already late for work. They wouldn't let me use the phone to call the unit to let them know."

"I'm going to see if I can get you released to your commanding officer. You are lucky they are taking a blood test instead of an EtG (urine test)." Luke left the room.

Sophie was in line to pick up her hot lunch. When she headed to her usual table, she saw that it was full and no one had saved her a seat. She felt rejected. She went to sit at an empty table. Sophie placed her tray on the table and sat down, bending her left elbow on it, and leaning her head on her hand. She moved her food around on her plate with the fork in her right hand.

Duke had seen her in line. When she didn't come to the table, he looked for her. He saw that she was sitting alone. He got CJ's attention and said, "look, CJ, Sophie is sitting by herself." They got up, grabbed their trays, and went to sit with her.

The others at the table noticed, and the entire table moved to where she was sitting. Some dragged over chairs from another table to accommodate everyone. A new student, who had been invited to sit at 'Sophie's table', as they called it, asked why they were moving.

"That's Sophie." Figuring that was enough of an explanation. The new kid didn't get it but moved anyway.

The group started congregating around Sophie; she looked up as they greeted her. They asked her where Lizzy was, and then they all chatted about what they did that summer. Sophie smiled; her dad was right. Lizzy wasn't there, but she still had friends she could share her day with.

Luke went to talk to the Sergeant taking Manny's place while he was on emergency leave. He knocked on his office door, which was open.

"Yes?" The Sergeant stood and saluted when he saw it a captain standing there.

"As you were, Sergeant," Luke said as he reciprocated. "Can I speak with you about Captain DaSilva?"

10

efforte=11

"Yes, please sit."

"Sergeant, your MP wants to charge him with 'hit and run', but there is not enough evidence for that charge. The officer arrested him because he appeared impaired and refused a breathalyzer. But his blood won't likely show anything above the limit after this much time. I'm requesting you let him go and wait until you have sufficient evidence before you charge him with 'hit and run'," Luke said.

"Captain Star, while I might agree with you about the insufficient evidence on the 'hit and run'. My MP had more than enough reason to bring in the captain on the DUI. He pulled into his driveway, smelling of alcohol, and his eyes were bloodshot. I need him to remain here until a medic draws blood to test. Depending on how long ago he had his last drink, he might still be over the legal limit. We impounded his car, the crime scene lab will process it for evidence, and then he can pick it up."

"Alright," Luke looked at the Sergeant's nameplate, "Sergeant Clarke, but you need to get that done then release him. If he is over the limit, you can issue him a DUI citation and release him."

Private Sorensen knocked. "Enter."

"Sir, the medic is here taking Captain DaSilva's blood."

"Thank you, Private," Clarke said. Luke stood. Clarke did the same and saluted.

"I'm going to wait with my client until you release him," Luke said.

"Yes sir."

Luke went back to the interrogation room. The medic was still in there taking blood. Once the medic left, Luke sat down with him again.

"Captain, they do not have enough evidence to hold you on the 'hit and run'. However, they do intend to keep your car for processing. Now that they have taken your blood, we just have to wait for them to release you. If you are over the legal limit when the results come back, they will give you a citation. The matter will be handed over to your commanding officer to decide how to handle it.

They plan to continue the investigation on the 'hit and run', if you are re-arrested for that, give me a call." Luke leaned forward, placing his forearms on the table. He had more to say. "Captain, if you are having weekend benders, then you are most likely an alcoholic. How many DUIs do you have?" Luke asked.

"None," the captain could see the shock on Luke's face. "I am an alcoholic — a well-functioning one. I never drink at work and usually drink alone at home, so no one sees me; that way, I don't have to drive. This weekend was an exception."

"How long do you think you can go on like this?"

Captain DaSilva bowed his head. "I don't know. I've been a heavy drinker since I was sixteen. Back then, I didn't do it in private and got myself in a lot of trouble.

"After high school, I decided I wanted to change my life and joined the Army. I stopped drinking for a few years," he looked up at Luke. "But you know how it is. All my buddies went out drinking, and you can't drink club soda for long without someone noticing. All it took was one drink for me to be off the wagon. I didn't want to mess up my career, so I hid it well but continued to drink.

"It has ruined my relationship with every woman I ever cared about," he ended his story there.

"Captain, there are all sorts of programs now; you can get help."

DaSilva snickered, "sure, as long as it doesn't get out your seeking help. And the chances of that are slim. Once you get tagged as a drunk, your promotions stop. I'm a career Army man. I don't want to have my career stalled."

"I can understand that. But if you don't do something, your health may give out, or worse, you could hurt someone else."

Captain DaSilva nodded. "Look, Captain, if I can find you a program outside of the Base, would you consider going for help?"

DaSilva did not answer right away. "If the program is not attached to the Base in any way, I think I would."

A knock came at the door; Sergeant Clarke entered. He moved over to the prisoner and uncuffed him. "You are free to go." Everyone stood.

"Your blood has been sent to the lab. We will be in touch with you if the test shows you were over the limit or anything develops on the 'hit and run' case," Sergeant Clarke informed them, then left the room.

"Thanks for your help, Captain Star. Can you give me a ride home?"

"Sure."

Luke walked off the elevator on the second floor of the newly named Justice building. He went to Captain Jonathan Young's office; he wanted to discuss his new case.

The door was open, Luke knocked. "Good morning sir, do you have a few minutes for me?"

"Sure, Luke, come in."

"Jonathan, I received a call from the MP station this morning..." Luke went on to tell Jonathan the whole story.

Jonathan rocked in his new office chair for a moment. "Luke, if this man seriously injured someone in an accident while under the influence and didn't stop. He could be in serious trouble."

"I know, but he insists he was no longer drunk when he woke up in his car. And he is certain he didn't hit anything." Jonathan raised his eyebrows. Luke knew what he was thinking. "I know, you can't trust a drunk who says he wasn't drunk."

"Well, if he is telling the truth, then you need to make sure the investigation continues. If it wasn't him, they need to look for anyone driving a similar vehicle," Jonathan said.

"I agree. Normally, I would talk to Manny about it. Do you think I should go outside the MP's investigator and contact Agent Marquez at CID?"

"You could. What about DaSilva's blood test?"

"It will take a while to get the results."

"Well, then give Agent Marquez a call and see if he'll agree to investigate."

"Jonathan, there is one more thing. Captain DaSilva acknowledges he is a functioning alcoholic. He won't get treatment on Base for fear it will stall his career. Is there anywhere in Adana that might have Alcohol Anonymous meetings or the like, in English?" Luke asked.

Jonathon considered the question. "I wonder if Anna could find out from someone she volunteers with at that local church?"

"That's a good idea, I'll give her a call." Luke got up to leave. "Is the group still going Ice Skating Saturday? Sophie is miserable without Lizzy. I'm hoping that will cheer her up."

"I believe we are." They said their goodbyes, and Luke went to his office to call Agent Marquez.

When Sophie got home, she was in a much better mood. She ran to her dad when he walked in and hugged him. He bent and kissed the top of her head.

"How was the first day of school, princess?" Luke asked, putting down his briefcase by the door and hanging up his coat.

"It was great, Daddy. At lunch, I thought no one wanted to sit with me because the table was full and no one saved me a seat, so I sat at an empty table. When they saw me at a different table, they all got up and moved to sit with me." She hopped onto the couch and finished, "wasn't that nice of them."

"Yes, it was."

# THE PROMISE

# CHAPTER TWO

Sophie was back to her chipper self and the first week of school went by without any incidents. During early morning Skype calls, Lizzy and Sophie counted down the days till she left Montana.

Monday at lunch, CJ and Duke talked about their dad's tour of duty ending this summer.

"Duke, are you excited we're going back home?" CJ asked.

Duke didn't get a chance to answer before Sophie interrupted them. "What do you mean, you're going home? Home where?" Sophie asked.

"Our dads joined up on the buddy program, so their tours end at the same time. I heard them talking about it, and now that mom is back, they want to return to the States," Duke answered.

"What about Lizzy and me. You're going to leave us?" Sophie was getting upset.

"Sophie, you know that these tours only last four years. Our folks were going to transition out after their last tour in Germany was up. They only stayed because mom was still missing, and dad wouldn't leave without her," Duke said.

"But you can't leave without us."

"Sophie, you need to talk to your dad and see what he plans on doing at the end of his tour," CJ suggested.

The lunch bell rang, and the kids all dispersed to their classes, but Sophie couldn't concentrate. Her dad had explained to her they would likely only be in Turkey for four years. She hadn't thought about what would happen when it was over. If Duke and

CJ were going to leave her, that meant Lizzy would be leaving soon too.

By the end of the day, she had made herself miserable thinking about it.

"Hello?"

"Agent Marquez, Captain Star here. I was calling for an update on the 'hit and run investigation."

"Good morning, Captain Star. I do have some news. I located the other two vehicle owners. One belongs to an enlisted man who works in the procurement office. I found his car in their parking lot and took pictures; there wasn't even a scratch on it. The other GMC belongs to a private who works in supply. I asked to see his vehicle, but he said it's missing. He said his son used it last; he dropped off his brother at the preschool on Base and drove himself to school. He said when he went to get in it after school, it was gone."

"He's saying someone stole it?"

"Yes. I asked if a police report was made. The Private said he reported it. I looked it up, and he was telling the truth."

"That sounds a little suspicious to me. What day did it go missing, Agent Marquez?"

"Last Monday, I think, the father believes his son's explanation, but I want to talk to the young man and see for myself. I have an appointment with him today."

"Can I sit in?"

"I don't see why not. I talked to Sergeant Clarke, he told me DaSilva's blood did show alcohol present but not over the limit."

"That's no surprise, but he needs to get a handle on his drinking, or this won't be his only run-in with the law," Luke said.

"The young man is coming in at 3:30 pm. Right after school."

"I'll be there. Thanks, I appreciate you letting me sit in."

"See you then."

Luke was leaving his office to sit in on the CID interview. Before he got out the door, his cell rang.

"Hello?"

"Daddy, when are you coming home?" Sophie seldom called her dad at work unless something was bothering her.

"I should be home by 5, sweetheart. I'm on my way to sit in on an interview. Is something wrong?"

"Yes, Daddy. Duke and CJ are leaving us, going back to the States. You have to do something, Daddy. If they go, that means Lizzy will be gone soon too." Luke could hear her voice crack.

"Sophie, we can talk about it tonight. Don't worry; we'll figure it out. Ok?" Luke asked.

"Ok, Daddy, but don't be late," Sophie said and put down the phone.

Luke had been thinking about this for weeks now. He knew David's and Jonathan's tours were up about the same time as his. Manny's tour would be up a few weeks earlier. It wasn't just that he didn't want Sophie to lose her best friends. The group was good for both of them. He wasn't sure how to broach the subject with the others.

Luke arrived at CID twenty minutes early. Agent Marquez came down to the lobby to escort him up.

"Lance, thank you for letting me sit in," Luke said.

"I'm happy to do it. If you have any questions when we get in there, I don't have any problem with you jumping in."

"Thank you."

A guard from the lobby called up and told Marquez, Master Sergeant Martin Rolle and his son were in the lobby. Lance headed down to escort them up.

As they entered and sat in the interrogation room, Agent Marquez made introductions. He was trying to keep the interview casual.

They shook hands and sat. Luke could see that the young man was scared, the whites of his eyes visible. The young man clasped his hands together on his lap. No doubt, to keep them from shaking.

Luke could empathize. Walking into an interrogation room intimidates men twice his size and age.

Agent Marquez started the conversation, opening the file he had in front of him.

"Master Sergeant Rolle, you reported your car stolen last Monday, right?"

"Yes. As soon as Logan called me after school and said the car wasn't in the school lot."

"I see. Logan, can you tell me everything that happened that day concerning the car?"

"I'm not sure what you mean, sir," Logan said.

"Let's start with what time you left the house and go on from there."

"I leave the same time every school day, 7:15 am. I go on Base and drop off my little brother at preschool. It's the only way I get to use the Jimmy," he looked directly at the man sitting across from him. "Then I headed to school, parked, and went inside," Logan finished.

"Did you see anything unusual on your way to school?" Agent Marquez asked.

"What do you mean, unusual?"

"Like an accident or someone driving recklessly?"

"No, sir," he answered while turning his head away.

"Can you tell me what route you take on Base every morning?"

"I come in the gate and take a right on Patten Street, go past the Commissary and PX. Then I turn left on Tank Rd. and right on Battalion St. The preschool and kindergarten are on that road. Then I take the same route back off the Base and head to school."

"What time did you drop off your brother at preschool?"

"If I don't drop him off by 7:40, I'm late for school."

"Were you running on time that morning?"

"No, there was a long line at the gate; it took me ten minutes to get onto Base."

"So, you had to hustle to get to school on time."

"Yeah, I guess." Logan was having a hard time looking at Agent Marquez while answering his questions. He moved his hands to the table and was picking at his fingernails.

"Even in a hurry, don't you think you would have noticed an accident on Tank Rd. at the exact time you would have been there?" At that point, Logan's father started to see where this was going and interrupted.

"Agent Marquez, what is it you are getting at. Are you suggesting my son has done something wrong?" Rolle asked.

"I'm trying to get some answers, Master Sergeant."

Luke decided to take a shot at it. "Logan, look at me." He looked up. "Logan, having an accident is not a crime. We've all had them. And I can understand panicking at your age. But it's time to come clean." A tear rolled down Logan's cheek, he laid his head on his arm. His dad put his hand on Logan's back and spoke softly.

"Logan, what are these men talking about. Did something happen last Monday?" Martin waited for his son to answer. "Son, tell me. We can work this out together."

Logan lifted his head and looked at his father. "Dad, I'm sorry I lied to you. I didn't know what to do. I was changing the channel on the radio and when I looked up a car was stopped right in front of me. I slammed into his rear end, and his car bolted into the lamp post." He bowed his head again. "I just panicked. I was afraid to stop. So I drove off and went to school."

"What did you do with the car?" Martin asked.

"I knew I couldn't take it home with a crashed front end, so I took it out behind the school in a wooded area and walked away. I'm sorry, Dad!... Once I left the scene, I didn't know how to make it right." He wrapped his arms around his dad and cried.

"It's alright son, you're doing the right thing now. That counts." Rolle turned to Agent Marquez. "What happens now?"

"Master Sergeant Rolle, luckily, the driver and his son's injuries were minor. You have insurance, I'm sure, or you couldn't drive on Base. I suggest you and your son contact the other driver and give them your insurance information. And it might go a long way if your son apologized," Agent Marquez answered. Logan sat up wide-eyed.

"Was someone hurt?" He looked horrified.

"Yes. Which you would have known if you had stopped," Marquez admonished. Logan's eyes dropped to his hands again.

"I know. I don't know why I didn't."

"Agent Marquez, we'll go check in on them. Are there going to be any charges brought against my son?"

"I don't make the final determination. I will talk to the MP who is handling this case and explain the circumstances. He might let it go with a reckless driving ticket. You know this will cause your insurance to skyrocket for at least three years. And that ticket carries a hefty fine."

"I understand. Actions have consequences. Logan might have to get a part-time job for a while to pay for the ticket, but he'll make this right. I know my son; this had to be eating him up inside."

Agent Marquez stood up; the others followed. "Master Sergeant Rolle, I believe you, and I'm sure your son regrets his actions. The MP will get in touch with you."

Rolle put his hand on his son's shoulder and said, "we need to go retrieve the Jimmy and get it fixed so your mother can use it. You won't be driving for a while."

Agent Marquez stepped out and asked one of the other agents to escort them down to the lobby. Then he stepped back into the room.

"Do you think the Jag office will want to press charges?"

"We don't generally get involved with accidents. The victim might want to press charges. But that's unlikely." Luke had another thought. "Lance, I don't understand. The caller said they saw a reckless driver. From what it sounds like, Logan only took his eyes off the road for a moment."

"I traced the caller's number back to a Private who was on his way to work that morning. He said he was turning onto Officers Club Circle when a car came barreling down and nearly hit him. He said the driver was all over the road. He called it in then tried to follow and get the plate number, but the vehicle was nowhere in sight."

"Are you saying it's a coincidence? That it was two different vehicles on the same morning that just happened to be almost identical?"

"I never have put much stock in coincidence, but in this case, I believe that's exactly what happened."

"I will let Captain DaSilva know he is no longer a suspect. Thanks for getting to the bottom of this."

"Happy to do it. Jonathan invited me to the BBQ Sunday. I'll see you then."

"Great. I'll be there." Agent Marquez escorted Luke out and went back to work.

Luke headed home; he promised Sophie he wouldn't be late. When he pulled in, she was sitting on the porch waiting. Luke sat next to her, putting his briefcase down next to him.

"Hello, princess." Sophie turned her head to look at him.

"Daddy, how are you going to fix this. Everyone is going to leave us."

"I don't know yet. But I'll figure it out. You don't need to worry about it."

"You promise?"

"Yes." That must have satisfied her because she stood up and grabbed her dad's briefcase and headed inside.

The fact that Sophie trusted him so completely that all he had to do was make a promise was a heavyweight on him. He had no idea how he was going to keep that promise.

Deniz had dinner on the table by the time Luke had changed and washed up. He thanked her and handed her an envelope with her paycheck in it. After watching her get into her car, he went into the kitchen to eat with Sophie.

Sophie didn't bring up them leaving again; instead, she told him she had a letter from the school. She ran to get it.

The American School had a sister Turkish school. Every year the 5th through 8th graders from the American school spent a week at the Turkish school. They taught in both English and Turkish so that the children could learn together. The Turkish schools all taught English to their students from second grade. Teaching a second language was a practice he wished the American schools would adopt. The letter was a permission slip he needed to sign.

"Well, this sounds like fun. The letter says you will have to bring a sack lunch that week. We can go to the Commissary and get you things for lunch on Saturday." It was the first smile he saw on his daughter that night.

"Yeah, I'm excited, but Lizzy is going to miss it."

"I know, that is a shame. But you can tell her all about it."

They watched a movie together, and then it was time for her to go to bed. Luke brushed her hair exactly fifty times and wrapped a ribbon around it. One of Sophie's prayers that night was that Jesus would help her dad with his promise. He tucked her into bed and kissed her forehead.

Luke decided to call Manny, even though it would be early morning in Montana. Luke knew separating the kids had to be on Manny's mind too.

"Hello?"

"Hi Manny, sorry to call so early; how are things going there."

"Hi Luke. I'm glad you called. This has been pretty hard on Ruby. She loved her mother; she thought she would have many more years with her. The funeral was two days ago. We had to wait for some family who lived out of state. Now she and Leo are working on the estate. They are going through the house to see what they want to keep for themselves. They plan to bring in a company specializing in estate sales. The company will price everything left and handle the two-day sale.

We've been staying at her mom's house. It's a lot of work to get the estate in order, but it has to be done. After the estate sale, they plan on selling the house. Neither of them has an attachment to it since they didn't even move into it until they were in high school. The two of them will split whatever profit might come after all the bills are paid. Her mother had medical and life insurance, so there won't be a big medical bill or hefty funeral expenses."

"Wow, I know this has to be a big stress on your family. When my parents died, my dad's lawyer helped me do all that. And my father's Will was detailed. People don't realize how much it helps those left behind to have a Will."

"What's going on at home. Lizzy wants to get back to school. Her teacher has been sending the assignments every day. At least she won't be behind too much when we get back. But Lizzy misses Sophie and Ricky misses Liam."

"That's part of what I wanted to talk to you about. Sophie came home today upset. Duke and CJ mentioned that their families are moving back to the States after this tour. She said everyone was going to leave us. She wants me to fix it."

"I've been thinking about this, too. It was never an issue before because the kids were so young. But the relationships they have forged are strong, and it's not just them. Ruby and I don't want to lose any of you either."

"I was hoping that you felt the same way. I want to call Jonathan and see if he and David would come and talk to me tonight. Were you planning on re-upping after this tour?"

"Originally, yes, but I'm rethinking that. What are you going to do?"

"I don't know that I want to sign up again. I think it's time to go home. But I'm flexible. I know Jonathan and David signed up years ago when they had the Buddy plan. That allowed them to stay together no matter where they were stationed. The rest of us can't guarantee that."

"You said the boys think they are going back to the States?"

"That's what Sophie said. I'll call you after I talk to them. If there is a way for us all to stay together, are you interested?"

"Yes. I'll wait to hear from you."

Luke's next call was to Jonathan. Jonathan said he and David could come over in half an hour. Luke put some of Deniz's homemade cookies on a plate and set them on the table for his guests.

Sophie was almost asleep when she heard a knock on the door. She recognized the voices, but their words were muffled because her door was shut.

The voices moved into the kitchen. Sophie needed to know what was said, she slipped into the hall and sat against the wall to the kitchen.

# THE PROMISE

# CHAPTER THREE

L uke placed cups of coffee in front of David and Jonathan on the kitchen table. Then he poured himself one, took it to his chair, and put it on the table as he sat down. Luke was staring at it, not sure how to start the conversation. He looked up to speak, but David spoke first.

"Luke, I have to apologize to you that Duke and CJ told Sophie we were going back home before we had a chance to talk to you."

"You have no reason to apologize. I know you and Jonathan have had your future laid out for years."

"That's true, but we planned to talk to you when Manny got back. Jonathan and I intended to transition out of the Army when our tour in Germany was up. But as you know, we wouldn't leave without Anna. God had a different plan for our lives, and like always, His plans are always better than ours.

I believe the relationships shaped over the past four years were divinely appointed. So I said all that to say, we have a proposition to offer you. Are you interested?"

"Yes," Luke responded.

"Jonathon and I want to open a practice together in our home state of Texas. We would like you to work with us on a salary basis until you decide if you want to become a partner."

"A partner. David, I don't have that kind of money."

"That can all be worked out," Jonathan said, then added. "Luke, you are a great lawyer; you would be an asset to our firm."

"What about Manny?"

"We want to offer him a salaried position too. We will need an investigator, and I know he passed the CID investigative classes he took. The business would pay for his PI license and any other classes he would like to take," David said.

"Do you think he'd be interested, or is he planning to stay in the Army? He would be offered a partnership too," Jonathan added.

"Yes, I think he would definitely be interested."

"What about you, Luke. You interested?" Before he could answer, Sophie came around the corner.

"Say yes, Daddy." She moved over to him and put both hands on his cheeks. "Say yes." He smiled and turned to the other men.

"Yes." Sophie hugged him, said goodnight to Uncle David and Uncle Jonathan, and ran off to bed. Her dad had kept his promise; now she could sleep.

"Where in Texas?" Luke asked.

"Austin. But we can talk details when Manny gets back. I didn't want you to make other plans."

"To be honest. I had no idea what I was going to do. I don't care where I live as long as our group can stay together."

Luke refilled their coffee cups, and they visited for a while. After walking them to the door, Luke called Manny.

"Hello?"

"Manny, it's Luke. I'm sorry if I'm interrupting your day."

"You never have to worry about that with me. Do you have news?"

"I do. Can you put me on speaker so Ruby can hear?"

Luke heard Manny call out for Ruby.

"We are both here now."

"David and Jonathan came over tonight. David apologized; he had no idea Duke and CJ had overheard part of their conversation. They had planned on talking to us when you got back. He made us an offer."

"What kind of offer, Luke?" Ruby asked.

"They are transitioning out at the end of their tours next summer. Jonathan and David have planned on opening a practice together for years. He asked if I wanted to join the practice."

"That's a great opportunity for you, Luke. Are you going to accept?" Manny asked.

"That depends."

"On what?"

"On you. They made an offer to you, too. They want you to be the firm's PI. He said he would pay for the license and any other classes you would want to take. You would be on salary, to the firm."

"That's a great offer. Did David or Jonathan say what the salary would be? Ruby and I are only making it now because she works. I'd like her to be able to quit sometime," Manny said. Luke could hear Ruby talking to Manny softly.

"Manny, I don't care how long I have to work as long as we can all stay together. And it would be a dream job for you."

"That's true."

"And you know how generous the Scott's and Young's are. I can't imagine them not making you a good offer," Ruby added.

"There is one more thing. They offered us a buy-in to be partners. The offer is good any time we want to take the leap."

"That would be amazing." Manny was almost speechless.

"I want to do this. But I want to do it with you. Are you in?" Luke asked.

"What do you think, Ruby?"

"I love the idea. I imagine the plan is to open the practice in Texas. I know that's where they are from. Anna told me David's family history one day at lunch. Anna said David's father was an

Air Force Jet Pilot. Some of his friends died when their jets went supersonic. The stabilizers couldn't keep up with the nanosecond-by-nanosecond adjustments needed. The planes went into nose dives the pilots couldn't recoup from. Emmett invented a stabilizer that corrected every nanosecond. As you know, anything you develop or design in the Military belongs to the Military. All he received for the invention was $350 in government bonds.

"When Emmett left the Military, he designed a better stabilizer for Commercial Airplanes. Boeing bought it and paid him a fortune. That's how he funds his non-profit, Mission of Peace.

"When his two sons turned 21, he gave them a portion of their inheritance. He wanted them to have the freedom to stake out any kind of future they wanted for themselves. His brother, Jared, started a private airline, mainly moving cargo, but he flies people too." Ruby finished the story.

"WOW! That explains a lot. I wondered how they could afford to open a practice with their Officer's pay," Luke said.

"Manny, I don't think we can pass this up. Even if the salary is smaller, then we need. Once mom's estate is settled, we should have a nice nest egg. We can supplement our income with it until you make partner," Ruby said.

"I agree, Ruby. Luke, we're in."

"I'm sure glad because I don't think Sophie would have ever forgiven me if we didn't find a way to keep us all together."

"Lizzy too. Thanks for calling tonight. It's news that will take a weight off us."

"Goodnight, you two."

"Goodnight, Luke."

The following day Luke was waiting with Sophie for Anna to pick them up. It seemed as though all the little things that had been annoying her had faded away. All that mattered was that they would all be together.

Sophie gave her dad a big hug and hopped into the car. She looked at Duke and CJ and said, "Lizzy and I are going with you to the States." She had a big smile on her face.

"Of course you are Sophie, you're family," Anna said. The boys smiled at her. She sat in her seat, satisfied.

Saturday morning Luke took Sophie shopping at the Commissary for her school lunch. Sophie decided on bologna sandwiches, Lunchables, apples, and small bags of Fritos. Her mom had sent her a fancy lunch box from Paris. She insisted her dad buy duplicates of everything so she could share with her sister-school partner.

Sophie spent a lot of time on Skype with Lizzy, talking about moving back to the States, together.

Sunday, they went to the BBQ at David's after church. Lance introduced Sally, the woman he'd been dating for a couple of years. Everyone greeted them then Lance went to help the men grill the steaks and chicken.

The women welcomed Sally and encouraged her to tell them about herself. They could see the obvious; pretty, height 5'8", hair color bleached blond, and a figure you only see in the movies.

"As you know from Lance, I'm a Corporal. I work as a supply clerk. Lance thinks we met by accident, but I asked one of my friends at work to introduce us. I noticed him one day when he came in for supplies for the CID," she chuckled. "My friend knew him well enough to invite him to a party she was having."

"Sally, where is home for you?" Anna asked.

"I lived in California before I joined the Army."

"Do you come from a Military family?" Zoey asked.

"No, I joined because I knew I could travel, and there were lots of men to choose from. If I find an officer I like well enough to marry, I could transition out and have a nice comfortable life," Sally said. She was open with her motives.

"Well, Lance is a very good man," Anna said.

"He'll do for now. He's generous and fun, but I don't think he is ambitious enough. He's happy in his current position. Moving up the ladder doesn't seem to matter to him. Now, if he were a Jag officer, he would have all sorts of potential."

Zoey saw her eyes move toward Luke. It was apparent she had hooked up with Lance to find someone higher up on the food chain.

The men brought over the grilled meat, and the conversation was over. Anna called the kids, who were playing soccer on the grass.

After everyone got comfortable, the men started their bantering. It was always fun to listen to them. The ladies managed to get in the conversation off and on.

Sally had positioned herself between Lance and Luke at the table. Sophie was sitting across from them next to Liam.

"Sophie, you're a very pretty little girl. Are you 7?

CJ, Duke, and even Liam snickered. Sophie responded.

"I'm nine!"

Luke's hand was on the table, and Sally reached over and laid her hand on top of his. "She may not appreciate the fact she looks younger now. But when she gets older, she will." Luke moved his hand as discretely as possible. Anna had noticed the exchange.

After cleaning up the remains of lunch, the kids went back to playing soccer, and the adults sat and visited. Sally found ways to stay in a conversation with Luke and often found excuses to touch him. If Lance noticed, he didn't react. Finally, Luke asked the guys if they wanted to join the kids' soccer game.

"What can you tell me about Luke?" Sally asked Zoey.

"Sally, Lance is Luke's friend. If you think he would ever ask you out, you are mistaken. If you are leading Lance on until he introduces you to someone with a higher rank, you need to rethink that. There is no one in Lance's circle of friends who would betray him like that," Zoey responded.

Sally turned and looked Zoey in the eye. "You are so naive. There is not a man on this Base that can't be tempted."

"You are right; every man can be tempted. But men that have any substance will walk away from it," Zoey replied, sitting up straight in her chair.

"Well, I have never met one. You just watch; Luke will be asking me out before you know it."

Sally was done talking, other than a few responses to questions from Anna and Zoey. She spent the rest of her time watching Luke play soccer.

**Monday**

Sophie was excited about going to the Turkish school. She picked one of the new dresses from the wardrobe her mom sent her last month. Luke put Sophie's hair in a ponytail and wrapped it in a fancy ponytail holder. She had her lunch packed and was hurrying Luke up so they wouldn't make Aunt Anna wait.

After being ushered off the bus at the Turkish school, each class hooked up with its counterpart. The girl's and boy's classes were separated. The Turkish teacher spoke English with an accent but were easy to understand. Each child picked a partner that they would spend the week with.

# THE PROMISE

Sophie looked around the room and saw one little girl staring at the ground. She was in the back row; no one sat close to her. She looked lonely, so Sophie picked her.

"Hello, my name is Sophie. What's yours?" The girl didn't look up but spoke.

"My name is Jael Rossi."

"Can I be your partner?" Sophie asked.

"I don't think you want me. My classmates don't talk to me; you will be an outcast," Jael said.

"Why would they treat you that way?" Jael did not want to answer, so she shrugged.

"I don't care. I would still like to be your partner." Jael finally looked up at her and smiled.

"Really?"

"Yes, of course," Sophie said. She noticed how pretty Jael was. She had pretty brown eyes, and her chestnut-colored hair was in a ponytail like hers, wrapped by a rubber band. When she smiled, her face lit up.

The girls worked together on their class assignments. When the lunch bell rang, Sophie grabbed her backpack, and Jael grabbed her sack lunch. Jael took Sophie to the milk cart, then they made their way to the covered playground, sitting down at an empty table.

Sophie noticed no one else would sit with them. Jael must have been used to it because she didn't act like she noticed. Jael pulled her sandwich out of her sack and laid it on top of the brown bag. Sophie pulled her fancy lunch sack out of her backpack and opened it up. As she pulled Lunchables, apples, bags of Fritos, and sandwiches out, Jael's eyes got big. Sophie handed her one of each.

"Sophie, I have nothing to share with you." Jael lowered her voice.

"Of course you do, Jael. You are sharing your school and your friendship." Jael lifted her eyes to Sophie and smiled; they ate, giggled, and enjoyed each other.

After they ate, Sophie asked if Jael would like to play Jacks. They moved over to the sidewalk area and laid down their coats to sit on. Before Sophie sat down, she took the pretty cover off her ponytail and wrapped it around Jael's.

"That looks much prettier on you than me, Jael."

While playing Jacks, some bigger boys ran up behind Jael and yanked hard on her ponytail. Sophie was stunned; at first, she thought they were playing. Then another boy came and yanked it hard enough that it pulled Jael back; her head hit the sidewalk. Sophie stood up, screaming at them.

"Stop that! Get away from her." Another boy came up and grabbed the pretty cover off of Jael's ponytail.

"Give that back!" Sophie screamed. Jael had pulled her knees up to her body, wrapping her arms around her legs. She put her face down on her knees, trying to be invisible.

Duke and CJ were playing soccer with a group of boys when he heard Sophie yelling. There was no mistaking her voice. Duke and CJ ran over to see what was going on.

"Sophie, what happened?" Duke asked. Sophie was crying.

"Those boys are hurting Jael."

Duke turned to his school partner. "Peter, what's going on? Why are they doing this?"

"Her father is in prison," Peter answered.

"What has that got to do with her?" CJ asked.

"It makes her a target," CJ's partner, Emel, said.

"What is he in prison for?" CJ asked.

"Printing Bibles," Peter answered.

"That can't be right. No one goes to jail for printing Bibles." Duke couldn't believe it.

"That is what my dad told me," Emel shrugged.

"That boy took Jael's scrunchy." Sophie pointed to a boy that was laughing in a big group of other boys.

"Emel, you tell that boy to give it back, or I will come to get it from him," CJ said, angry at what happened.

Emel went to talk to the boy and brought back the stolen item. Sophie dusted it off and put it back in Jael's hair. Jael was still sitting on the sidewalk crying.

The school bell rang, and everyone filed back into class.

At the end of the day, Sophie stood outside with Jael, waiting for the bus to transport them back to their school.

"Do you live close by, Jael?" Sophie asked.

"Yes, I walk to school. I only live one block, that way." Jael pointed in the direction of her house.

"Will you be alright walking home by yourself?" Jael lowered her head.

"Sometimes boys follow me home and throw rocks and sticks at me," Jael said. "Thank you for being so nice to me." She took the scrunchy off her ponytail and handed it back to Sophie.

"What are you doing? That's for you."

"Thank you, but someone will just steal it again. I'd rather you keep it," Jael said.

"No, Jael, you keep it. If someone steals it, I'll bring you another one."

Duke and CJ came up to the bus line after saying goodbye to their school partners.

"Duke," Sophie said. "Boys follow her home and throw rocks at her."

"How far away do you live?" She pointed down the block.

"CJ and I will walk you home." He turned to Sophie, "you have to have them hold the bus for us."

Jael gave Sophie a hug, and the trio walked away.

The bus came, and everyone filed on. Sophie wouldn't move. Her favorite teacher, Mrs. Coulter, said, "Sophie, it's time to go."

"We can't go yet, Mrs. Coulter. Duke and CJ had to walk Jael home. They are not back yet." Mrs. Coulter's husband works with Lizzy's dad.

"Why would they do that?" She asked.

"Because the boys in the school hurt her." Mrs. Coulter was surprised by the response.

"Ok, I will talk to the bus driver. Then I want you to tell me what's going on."

As Sophie finished telling Mrs. Coulter what had happened, the boys ran up and hopped on the bus.

On the ride back to school, Sophie was sitting across the aisle from CJ and Duke. Duke turned in his seat, putting his legs in the aisle. He looked at Sophie; a tear had slid down her cheek.

"Sophie, CJ, and I will protect Jael this week. I'll talk to Peter and Emel about making sure those boys don't hurt her," Duke said, touching her arm to get her attention. Sophie turned to look at him.

"Why would someone go to jail for printing Bibles?"

"I don't know, Sophie; there has to be more to it than that."

"Can our dad's get him out of jail? They're lawyers."

"I don't think so, Soph. Our dads don't have jurisdiction in Turkey. They have their own lawyers."

"Someone has to do something. It isn't right. It just isn't right, Duke!" She bowed her head again, another tear finding a path down her cheek to her shirt.

"Look, Sophie, my grandpa, helps people like this. I'll talk to him about it," Duke said. Sophie sat up and turned to him.

"You will?"

"Yes, as soon as I get home."

"I'll talk to my dad too; maybe he can find out the truth about Jael's dad," Sophie said.

# CHAPTER FOUR

When Luke drove up to his house, Sophie was waiting for him on the steps. He got out of his car and sat next to her, putting his briefcase on the step. Sophie always waited for him on the porch if something was bothering her.

"What is it, Sophie? Did something happen at school?"

"Yes Daddy. You have to do something about it."

"Why don't you tell me what happened," Luke said. Sophie told him the whole story. She cried a few times, but she managed to get through the entire story of her day at the Turkish School.

Luke stood up. "Let's go inside. I'll get changed, and we can eat dinner. I need time to think about this."

"You'll do something to help them, won't you, Daddy?"

"I can't promise that Sophie. I have to get more information." Sophie nodded, trusting he would do what he said. She looked up at him, stood, and took his briefcase in the house.

Duke walked into his house and went to say hello to his mom. When she asked how school was, he didn't give her an answer. Anna placed a freshly baked muffin and a glass of milk in front of him.

"Mom, I need to talk to Grandpa Emmett."

"Ok, honey. Do you want to call now?"

"Yes," Duke answered while pulling off a piece of his muffin and putting it in his mouth. Anna dialed Emmett's number on the landline and handed it to Duke.

"Hello?"

"Grandpa."

"Duke, my favorite grandson. How are you, my man?"

"Grandpa, I'm your only grandson."

"And my favorite." They made the same exchange every time Duke called, a tradition that made him smile.

"Grandpa, I need your help." Duke went on to explain what happened at school.

"Duke, Turkey has a tolerance policy for religious freedom. At least on paper. There has to be more to this; I would need more information. There is one other problem. Our team usually gets people out of a hostile situation before they are incarcerated. I don't know what we can do now, short of breaking him out."

"Grandpa, there has to be something you can do?"

"The organization could pay for an attorney, see if we can't challenge the judge's finding."

"Can you do that, Grandpa?"

"I still need more information. Have your dad call me when he gets home. We will see if there is anything we can do."

"Thanks, Grandpa. I love you."

"I love you too, Duke."

Duke hung up and went out back to sit on the porch.

Anna stepped over to David as he walked in the door and gave him a kiss.

"How was your day, sweetheart?" Anna said. David held onto her.

"Not as good as coming home to you." David kissed her again.

"Something is going on with Duke," Anna said.

She nodded to the back porch. "He called your dad when he got home from school, but he wouldn't tell me what it was about."

"Let me change out of my uniform, and I'll go talk to him."

"I'll hold dinner for a while." She kissed his cheek and went back to the kitchen.

David came out to the back porch and saw Duke sitting on the bench swing. He sat down next to him.

"Hi Dad."

"Hello, son. Your mom said you called grandpa. Is everything ok?"

Duke told his father what happened at school and what his grandpa told him.

"Dad, we have to help Jael's father, but we can't tell mom. If this turns into a mission, you and I can take care of it. I don't want her in on it."

David knew exactly what Duke was feeling.

"Son, I still look for her the minute I walk in the door, just like you do; to make sure she's still here. The joy of having her home gives way to the fear of losing her again. I get it. But we can't live like that. We won't live like that."

Duke turned his face away and stared blankly at something beyond the fence. David could see the tears dripping down his cheeks. He wrapped both arms around him and let him cry. When Duke calmed down, David said, "Your mother's disappearance was not God failing us. It was more like our plans did not match up to His.

The Bible says, 'For My thoughts are not your thoughts, nor are your ways My ways,' (Isa. 55:8). God had a plan, and he used your mom to accomplish it. I won't say it was easy on any of us, but I will always trust Him, through the good times and the bad times." David moved so he could see his son's face. "And your mom did not abandon us. She had amnesia, or she would have done anything to get back to us." Duke nodded his head.

"Do you think we can help this girl, dad?" Duke asked.

"I don't know. We'll try. And I promise you this. If it does turn into a mission, we will discuss it as a family and decide how to handle it. You are old enough now to be a part of that conversation."

"Thanks, Dad. I love you."

"I love you too, son."

After dinner, Sophie went to her room to do her homework and watch 'Saved by the Bell'. Sophie would Skype with Lizzy in the morning to talk about the show. More importantly, she wanted to talk to Lizzy about Jael. It was worth getting up early to speak to her; a 10-hour time difference made it challenging to communicate.

Luke had to wait until 9 pm to talk to Manny about what Sophie told him earlier. It would be early in the morning in Montana, but he knew Manny wouldn't mind. He was hoping Manny could convince Captain Demir to allow Lance to look at Jael's father's file and court transcript. Manny had a good working relationship with Captain Metin Demir of the Turkish Polis. Luke knew there was no way the file could leave their station. What Luke wanted Lance to do was outside of the guidelines of both their jobs. He decided to call Lance while he waited for a decent hour to call Manny.

"Hello?"

"Lance, it's Luke. Do you have time to talk?"

"Sure. What's up."

"Do you mind coming over to my house? I'd rather not talk on the phone."

"Sure, I can be there in twenty minutes."

"Thanks, Lance."

Luke had just bought a new Keurig coffee maker with lots of pods. He got out several pods and some of the muffins he bought at the Commissary's bakery.

Luke answered the knock on the door expecting Lance.

"Sally?"

"Hi, Luke."

Luke looked for Lance, thinking he brought her with him. "Are you with Lance?"

"No, just me." She started to move toward the door expecting to be invited in. Luke pulled the door partially closed as he stepped out.

"What can I do for you?"

"I felt bad that I insulted Sophie by saying she was seven. I thought I could make it up to her by taking you both out for ice cream."

"It's almost 7 pm, Sally. Sophie has school tomorrow," Luke said.

"Oh. Well, since I'm here, can I come in and visit with you?"

"I don't think so. I don't entertain other men's girlfriends."

"Lance and I are just friends." She smiled and moved closer to him.

"Does he know that?"

"I think he likes me more than I like him. But he's not my type."

"What is your type?"

"You." Sally reached out to touch his arm. Luke moved away.

"I'm sorry, Sally, but even if you weren't Lance's '*friend*', I'm not interested." Luke saw Lance out of the corner of his eye walking to his house. He didn't want him getting the wrong idea.

"You need to go."

"Come on, how do you know I'm not your type unless you give it a chance?" She reached for him again.

"I don't want to be rude, but the fact you are stringing Lance along is reason enough."

"Alright, I can take a hint. But if you tell Lance about this. I will tell him you made a pass at me."

"He won't believe you."

"He'll believe whatever I tell him."

"Really?" A voice came from behind her.

"Lance?" Sally turned to face him.

"Luke invited me over; I didn't want to be rude to one of your friends, so I came. He said Sophie wanted to say hello, and I believed him. Obviously, he had ulterior motives."

"Really? If he invited you over, why are you standing outside."

"I just got here."

"Sally, do you think I don't know your reputation. You string men along until you find someone you think can do more for you?"

"What!?" Sally responded.

"When you made a play for me, I didn't have anyone else I was interested in, so I thought, why not."

"So you were leading me on!"

"No, I thought there might be something there. But by the looks of it, I was wrong."

Sally pushed him out of the way and walked to her car, speeding off for dramatic effect.

"She's going to get a ticket from one of the MPs if she doesn't slow down," Luke said.

"Maybe she can flirt her way out of it," Lance said. Luke didn't mean to, but he laughed.

"I'm sorry, man. You know I didn't invite her over. I would never do that to a friend."

"I know; I saw her flirting with you at the BBQ."

Luke opened the door and invited Lance in. They headed for the kitchen.

"I have a new Keurig. You want some coffee?"

"Sure. I bought one of those too. The PX just got them in. Do you have a Hazelnut pod?"

"You bet." Luke put a pod in the coffee maker and placed the plate of muffins in front of him. After brewing both of them coffee, he sat down. Lance was looking down at his cup.

"Lance, I know you liked her. I'm sorry about Sally."

"It's better I find out now than after I have too much invested. I look at how great Manny's marriage is. David and Jonathan's too. I've been looking for someone for a long time; I thought the rumors about Sally were just that; rumors."

"Lance, take it from a man who has been divorced. It's better to wait for the right woman. I was raised Christian; I knew better than to marry someone who didn't believe like I did. Having a common set of beliefs and moral standards goes a long way in making a successful marriage. The Bible is the most recognized and accepted standard to live by. Without absolute right and wrongs in one's morals, people will do by nature whatever feels good at the time. My wife hooked up with one of her clients. I was blindsided, Lance. It was devastating."

"I'm sorry, Luke. My parents divorced. I saw what it did to our family. I don't want to do that to my kids."

"Have you committed your life to Christ, Lance?"

"No, Jonathan has been talking to me about what it means to be born again, but I have never been religious."

"I'm not religious, Lance. I have a personal relationship with my Savior. I didn't understand it when I was a kid; I was raised going to church. But one day, when I had gotten myself in a bad situation with some friends in high school, I had to make a choice. They wanted me to take ecstasy with them. I was faced with a dilemma. Did I believe the Word of God or not? It was the moment of truth for me. I believed there was a God in heaven, and he saw everything I did. I knew I could walk away from all that and choose a different life. I'd seen how these boys lived; they were unhappy, angry, jealous, and lost. I loved my life; why give it up for something less.

"I walked away from them and made a decision. I would serve the One who loved me enough to sacrifice His life on the cross for me, for the rest of my life." Luke finished.

"I have always believed there is a God. There is no way this world was some cosmic coincidence. And where did the singularity that supposedly created the 'Big Bang' come from? Jonathan gave me a Bible. If you believe in God, it isn't much of a leap to then believe His Word. But I don't know that I could live the life. The last thing I want to be is a hypocrite." Lance took a sip of coffee.

"It's not like that, Lance. It's not about rules. When you decide to ask God to forgive you for your sins and live your life for Him, Jesus helps you do the rest. When you are truly saved, the way you look at things change. Your mind is renewed; you choose differently. If you stumble, He is faithful to forgive you. You don't need to rely on your own strength, but His. But being saved is more about having a relationship with the ultimate Parent. Someone who wants the best for you, so much so, He would give up His own life."

"I like that analogy. The ultimate parent," Lance said.

"Why don't you come to church with us Sunday. We all try to make the 10 am service at the Base church."

"Maybe I will." They sat a moment quietly, eating muffins and drinking coffee.

"The reason I asked you over is that I have an off the books case. Normally, I would ask Manny to do it. But he can't do the leg work from Montana. I need your help, but I don't want you to do anything that may get you in hot water with your department. So if you don't feel comfortable, please say so." Luke watched Lance for a response.

"Luke, why don't you tell me what is going on, and I'll see if I can help." Luke told Lance all he knew.

"I'm going to call Manny tonight and see if he can get ahold of Captain Demir. He has a good working relationship with him. We need to see what is in the file. This idea he was arrested for printing Bible's just doesn't make sense. Turkey has a tolerance policy."

"Well, yes and no. Turkey has a policy, but they don't always stick by it."

"If Demir agrees to let someone come look at the file, will you do that?"

"I can't see any harm in that."

"Thank you, Lance. I know something is missing from the story we have right now. If we can figure out what, maybe we can help this family."

"Luke, you have no jurisdiction in Turkey. Even if there is something off about the conviction. There is nothing you can do about it."

"Maybe not on the books. We'll have to see," Luke responded.

Before Lance could respond, Sophie came into the kitchen.

"Mr. Lance, hello. Is that lady with you?"

"Sophie!" Luke rebuked her. Sophie dropped her eyes. "Sorry, Mr. Lance."

"It's alright. I get it." Lance smiled at her.

"Daddy, can I have some milk and a muffin?" Luke got up and grabbed some milk from the fridge and filled a small glass. He took a muffin from the plate on the table and put it on a paper towel.

"Here you go, princess," Luke said. Sophie thanked him and turned to go. She stopped at the door and turned to Lance.

"Mr. Lance, are you going to help Jael and her father?"

"I hope so, Sophie."

It was 8 pm when Lance left. Luke called Manny earlier than he planned.

"Hello?"

"Manny, hi, it's Luke."

"Hey Luke, we got some good news last night. A neighbor down the street contacted Leo and said his in-laws retired and want out of California. They want to come here and help their daughter with the newborn triplets. He said they would pay whatever the appraiser values the home at."

"I guess coming from California, any price would seem reasonable to them," Luke laughed.

"Yeah, I guess. That means I will be able to take my family home with me when my emergency leave is up."

"That's great news, Manny. We all miss you guys."

"What's happening with you?"

Luke relayed the whole story. He mentioned Lance was willing to look at the file if Manny could convince Captain Demir to let him see it.

"Captain Demir and I have done favors back and forth many times. I don't see why he would object. He is the second watch captain in his precinct. He didn't have enough seniority to boot the guy on the first watch out," Manny chuckled. "But he was too high profile, after the Sandalli takedown, to put him on the graveyard shift. He should be there now. I'll give him a call."

"Do you think he might want Lance to come tonight?"

"Maybe, I'll call you right back."

Luke called Lance to see if he was willing to meet Demir this time of night. A call blinked in on his landline.

"Lance, hold on, that could be Manny." Luke clicked over.

"Hello, Manny. What did he say?"

"Demir said the station was slow tonight, which doesn't happen that often. If he wants to see the file, it would be best to come now."

"Thanks, Manny; Lance is on the other line. I will let you know what he finds." Luke clicked back to Lance. "Lance, Demir said the station was quieter than usual; tonight would be a good time to come. Are you up for that?"

"Yes, I can go right now. Is Demir still in the Downtown district?"

"Yes. Call me no matter what time you get done."

"Alright."

Lance walked into the Downtown district. He waited for the officer behind the glass to acknowledge him.

"How can I help you, sir?" The man spoke Turkish, but it wasn't hard to figure out what he was asking.

"I'm here to see Captain Demir." The man nodded and picked up his phone. He pointed to the chairs in the lobby once he finished his call. Lance nodded and sat down.

# THE PROMISE

# CHAPTER FIVE

L ance watched the activity going on around him until he noticed Captain Demir coming his way. Lance stood and walked to the door as the captain opened it and extended his hand.

"Agent Marquez. Nice to see you again."

"Please call me Lance; I'm off duty." He followed Demir to his office.

"Please, have a seat. Manny called in a favor, and since I owe him one, I agreed. But I would like to know what interest you have in this case." Lance decided it was best to be upfront.

"Captain, it has come to our attention that there has been a gross miscarriage of justice..." The captain interrupted him.

"Even if that is the case, you would have no authority to address it."

"That's true. But if we can find something actionable, it might be possible for *you* to do something about it," Lance said. Demir flipped through the file to familiarize himself with it. The case was four months old; officers from his district went out on the call.

"Lance, I do remember this case. One of my officers raised some questions about the arrest with the sergeant. I contacted the Cumhuriyet savcısı (Prosecutor of the Republic), but he told me to keep my nose out of his business. I heard later there was no trial; the man went straight to prison."

"May I look through the file?"

"It is pretty thin," the captain handed it over and motioned to the small table in his office for Lance to use.

Lance read every page; the few there were anyway. An anonymous tip led officers to the small printing business of an Emir Rossi. The informant said the owner was printing seditious and insurrectionist materials. The officers raided the place but only came up with Bibles. Lance read Emir's written statement. It stated that a man named Mateo Borg offered to buy the business. Emir did not want to sell. He just purchased new equipment that would allow him to take on larger projects with a higher profit margin. After that, Borg did everything he could to ruin Emir's business. Emir told the Polis that this was another attempt by Mateo to take his business.

The Polis officer wrote that he felt Emir was telling the truth. He did not find anything that could be classified as seditious in his printed material.

The officer called his sergeant and said the tip was bogus and they were leaving. As the officers were getting in their patrol car, they got a radio call from headquarters. The Prosecutors office ordered Rossi arrested. So they followed orders.

The only other paperwork in the file was a court document saying Emir confessed.

Emir was sentenced to 20 years, and his business was confiscated.

"Captain, have you read this file?"

"Yes."

"I have a few questions. Do you know this Mateo Borg?"

"Yes, he is a wan-a-be mobster with a small operation. He can get away with it because his brother is a judge." Lance looked back in the file.

"So, his brother was the judge on the case?'

"Yes."

"The file says he confessed. Where is the confession?"

"If it is not in there. I do not know."

"You can't possibly think this is a legitimate prosecution?"

"I have no reason to get involved," Demir said.

"How about because you're supposed to be a purveyor of justice," Lance responded. Then realized he had no right to speak to him that way. "I apologize, Captain. This is not your fault."

"I understand your response. But there are few avenues in our system to question a judge's findings. I am sorry, Lance." Lance stood and handed the file back to the captain.

"Thank you for letting me look at this." Lance headed to the door, then stopped and turned. He thought of one more question. "The file says the property was confiscated. Do you know what happened to it?

"Confiscated properties get sold off, and the money goes in the government coffers," Demir relayed.

"Do you know who purchased it?" Lance asked. Demir got on his computer and looked it up.

"A company owned by Mateo Borg," neither the captain nor Lance were surprised by the finding.

"I'll pass on the information. Goodbye, Captain." They shook hands, and the captain walked Lance back to the reception area.

By the time Lance got back in his car, the injustice of it all was boiling inside of him. He called Luke and asked if he could come over. It was 10:15 pm when Lance knocked on Luke's door.

"Come in, Lance," Luke said as he opened the door. "David called earlier. He said he and Jonathan want to be a part of this."

"Talk about a corrupt prosecution, Luke..." Luke stopped him.

"Let me get Manny, David, and Jonathan on the line, so you only have to repeat it once." Luke put the conference call on speaker. "Ok, Lance, tell us what happened."

As Lance went through what he learned in the file, his voice got more and more agitated.

"It's a horrible miscarriage of justice, and Demir said there was nothing he could do. Even though one of his officers reported from the start, the tip was bogus."

"We can't blame Demir for not getting involved; I'm sure this isn't the only miscarriage of justice he ever came across. Without some political clout or a ton of money, there isn't much he could do," Manny said.

"Ok, now we know what happened, what can we do about it. We have no standing in the Turkish courts?" Jonathan said.

"We still need more information. Luke, you said this man, Emir, has a sister?" David asked.

"Yes."

"She will know what is not in the file. One of you needs to go see her tomorrow," Manny said.

"I'll go. Sophie might know where she lives," Luke volunteered.

"Duke and Jonathan walked Jael home; one of them may be able to direct you," Jonathan added.

"We also need to know why that Borg fella wanted that business so badly. There is no way it's for a legal purpose. Emir's statement said he had purchased the most advanced digital printing equipment. I have no doubt that was why he wanted that place," Lance said.

"Why not just buy his own?" Jonathan asked.

"One reason could be that Emir's business was well established. It's the perfect front for illegal activity. My guess is he hasn't changed a thing, inside or out," Manny said.

"Lance, was the address of the business in the file?" David asked.

"Yes. I remember it."

"You interested in doing a little late-night surveillance?"

"You bet I am."

"I can pick you up at Luke's in ten minutes," David said.

"I'm coming with you," Jonathan insisted.

"I'm sorry, guys, I wish I was there to help," Manny apologized.

"I can't leave Sophie here alone, or I would go with you," Luke said.

"No problem, we have this. I'll pick up Jonathan and head over now." The group said goodbye and hung up.

Luke could see Lance was still agitated at the injustice of it all. "Lance, I don't want you getting involved with this and ending up getting in trouble with CID. You've already done plenty." Luke had given him some coffee when he came in and watched him take another sip.

"I'm already invested. I have no idea what we can do about it, but I'm not walking away until we've tried," Lance said.

Luke didn't have time to respond; a knock came on his door. Luke let them in. After a short discussion, David said.

"Ok, if Mateo is doing something illegal in Rossi's shop, he is likely to have some sophisticated security. Let's not end up in jail tonight. We'll take pictures and go from there."

The building was lit inside and out, making it easy for the men to locate. David pulled behind the shop into the alley. They could see people were moving around inside. Jonathon took out his binoculars and looked for cameras.

"I see one camera," Jonathan said.

"It's a little late to be working, isn't it?" Lance asked.

"Maybe, unless he has a legitimate deadline, or what he is doing is illegal," David said.

"We came all this way. What do you say we stay a while and see if they leave? Maybe we can get some pictures of them," Jonathan said.

David could see there was nowhere to hide his vehicle in the small alley. He pulled into the small parking lot of the building next store and turned off the engine and lights. Jonathan was still looking at the place through his binoculars.

Jonathan read off the license plate numbers of the two black SUVs in the back lot.

"There is a keypad by the back door. Do you think that's for the security system or to open the door?"

"Maybe we'll get a chance to see," Lance said.

Forty minutes later, the lights inside went off. The security light out back clicked on, adding light to the already lit backlot. The back door opened, and two large burly men came out first. They were wearing black slacks, button-down shirts, and leather jackets. They looked around then held the door for two other men.

The man who appeared to be in charge was maybe three inches shorter than the shortest bodyguard; he wore a suit. The other man was much older, maybe 70 years old. He was shorter, wore a fedora, an expensive suit judging by the fit, and was carrying a leather briefcase.

The two men in suits both got in the second SUV with one of the bodyguards. The other SUV led the way.

David used the zoom-in function on his camera to get good pictures of the men. Jonathan watched the keypad as one of the bodyguards punched in a key code. He said the numbers out loud for Lance to write down.

The men waited to be sure the SUVs were nowhere in sight before they left.

"David, can I see your camera? I need a better look at the older man. He looks familiar." David handed Lance the camera as he pulled out into the alley.

"I know that face. I just don't know from where. We see over a hundred international wanted posters a month at CID." Lance took a picture of the face on David's camera and sent it via his cell phone to Manny. "Manny gets the same alerts I do."

"The man in charge has to be Borg," Jonathan said.

"Most likely. Lance, can you see if Captain Demir will run these pictures? They are likely local criminals."

"Yes. I'll go back to Demir's office tomorrow after work." Lance's phone rang. "It's Manny," Lance said to the others. "Hello."

"Lance, where did you get that picture?"

"He looks familiar to you too?"

"Yeah. The classes I took to qualify for CID did a two-week course on forgeries. That man is considered the best forger in the world. He provides provenance with everything he forges, so that they have never been able to pin anything on him."

"That's right! It's Pierre Dupuis. I thought he was retired living in Sweden on the millions he earned."

"Is he one of the men involved in this?"

"Yes, David took his picture tonight coming out of Rossi's business."

"Man, there is a lot more to this than we thought," Manny said.

"Who is this guy?" David asked, waiting for a light to turn green.

"Ok, Manny, I'll talk to you later." Lance hung up and answered David's question. "Dupuis is an international forger. He became infamous about thirty years ago. He forged a letter from Lincoln to General Winfield Scott Hancock. The letter came out of nowhere. For that reason, it was widely considered illegitimate. But the forgery, the paper, and the writing were so perfect, no one could disprove it. He even forged provenance papers. They were convincing enough that it sold at Sotheby's for a quarter-million dollars."

"WOW!" Jonathon said.

"Yeah, wow. Scotland Yard knew it was Dupuis, but there was no way to prove it. They tagged him for almost a hundred other forgeries they couldn't prove either," Lance said.

"What on earth is he doing with a small-time criminal like Mateo Borg?" David asked.

"If Dupuis is involved, it's anything but small-time."

After dropping Lance off at his house and calling Luke to update him, they all headed home.

**Tuesday**

Sophie was excited to see Jael again. Luke waited on the porch with her for Anna to pick her up. When Sophie got into the SUV, Duke said.

"CJ and I will stay with you and Jael at recess and lunch, so no one bothers you."

"Thanks, Duke. Everyone is so mean to her. I hate that," she said, "I brought extra lunch and some new ponytail holders for her."

"I'm sure she will love those," Anna said as Sophie showed them to everyone.

Luke had appointments all day. He expected that Jael's aunt also worked, so he decided to see her later in the day. He planned on talking to Major Scott about it when he arrived at the office, but he was on the phone when he went to knock. It was over a year now since the Army sent a commissioned Judge Advocate General to the unit. That freed David up to do what he liked; litigate.

David was talking with his father.

"Dad, we went last night to look at the print shop that was confiscated from Mr. Rossi. It was late when we got there, but the lights were on, and there were people inside. We decided to wait to see if we could get some photos of the men. There were two bodyguards and a man we assume to be Mateo Borg. There was another man we found out was an infamous forger named Pierre Dupuis. So there is something illegal going on in there."

"That is definitely suspicious. But why did Borg need that particular print shop is the question?"

"Lance read Emir's statement. It said Emir had just purchased the highest end digital commercial printing machine."

"Yeah, but a machine like that can't produce quality counterfeit dollars or euros to fool anyone. So why that equipment?"

"I don't know, Dad. We need to find a way to get in there to check it out. They have a security system, lights, and cameras outside; it would be hard not to be detected."

"No, David, don't try that. Maybe you can hack into the security system to get a look inside. If they have cameras outside, maybe they have cameras inside too."

"It's worth a try. We have to do something. This poor man was railroaded and has lost everything. We have to help him."

"I agree, son, but you guys getting put in jail in a foreign country is not a good plan. Who would help him then?" Emmett said.

"You are right, Dad. Pray we can come up with an answer," David responded.

"I will pray, son. As soon as you come up with any way we can help, let me know. Be careful, David."

"Ok Dad. Goodbye."

As David was hanging up the phone, Luke poked his head in the door again.

"Major, do you have a minute?"

"Sure, come in."

"After work today, I'm going to go over to Jael's house and see what her aunt knows about the whole situation. She may be able to give us information that wasn't in the file," Luke told him.

"Agent Marquez called earlier. He set up with Captain Demir to take those pictures over. Demir agreed to run them. We need to know for sure who we are dealing with."

"How much is he going to tell Captain Demir?"

"We talked about that. We are not telling him anything about Dupuis. It would be too tempting for him to immediately arrest him to get notoriety. But that would leave us with nothing to help Rossi. We agreed to ask the captain to trust us for now and not ask too many questions. When we have something concrete, we will turn everything over to him so he can get the collar," David said.

"Do you think he will go for that?" Luke asked.

"I have no idea."

Lance waited until he knew Captain Demir would be on duty and drove to the Polis station. The same officer was at the desk. Lance asked for Captain Demir once the officer acknowledged him.

Captain Demir came down to reception to escort him to his office. Demir directed Lance to a chair and sat behind his desk.

"Agent Marquez, do you have those photos?" Lance placed the pictures they took outside Rossi's business on the desk in front of the captain.

"Can you identify these men for me, please?" The captain did not look at them but kept his eyes on Lance.

"Why are you involving yourself with a matter not in your jurisdiction?" Lance leaned back in his chair. He could see the captain did not want to do anything that could put a blemish on his new position.

"Captain, I know this puts you in a precarious situation. But a little girl is being ostracized and assaulted at school because her father is in prison. It's not right, Captain, and you know it." The captain picked up the pictures.

"This is Mateo Borg," he threw the picture back on his desk. "These two are his bodyguards, Burak Abdou and Duman Traore." He tossed the other photos with the first.

"How did you get these?" He gestured to the pictures.

"We drove by Emir Rossi's business late last night; the lights were still on. We decided to wait to see who came out."

"Agent Marquez, Mateo Borg has reach beyond what you can imagine. There is nothing you can do to help Rossi. If you try, you are likely to get him killed."

"Are you telling me there is not a judge in Turkey that would overturn a wrongful conviction? That they are all corrupt?" Lance asked.

"No. Of course not. But like in your own country. judges do not like to overturn a finding of another jurist."

"Captain, if we find enough evidence to prove Judge Borg and his brother are corrupt, can you find us, one honest judge?" Lance asked. Demir leaned back in his chair and rocked a minute, keeping his eyes on Lance.

"I can. My sister's best friend's husband is a judge. One of the most honest men you would ever meet."

"What kind of proof would we need to satisfy him?"

"I would have to ask him. But you realize if this gets out, Mr. Rossi will be dead. Then your inquiry will mean nothing."

"I know. That's why we will only work with you. Sergeant Diaz and I know you to be an honest man. We trust you."

"Is Manny back at Incirlik.?"

"No, he is still in Montana. But he is helping us remotely."

"Alright, Agent Marquez, I will talk to Judge Bulut and give you a call." Captain Demir stood, making an obvious end to the conversation. Lance stood, thanked him, and moved to the door.

# CHAPTER SIX

**D**uke drew a map so Luke could find Jael's house. He drove slowly down the road that bordered the Turkish school. Luke looked for a light-yellow house with a composition roof. As Luke spotted the house, he also noticed a black sedan with heavily tinted windows. He had intended to pull in the driveway behind the blue sedan but thought better of it. Instead, he passed the black sedan to see if anyone was in it and drove down the street. Two men were sitting in it watching the house.

Luke turned left on the next street. He pulled far enough up the road to ensure the sedan could not see his vehicle pull over. There was an alley between the back-to-back houses on that block. He walked to the back of the little yellow house's wood slat fence, unlatched the gate, and walked in.

The yard and fence needed some minor repair and a coat of paint, but the house looked to be in good repair. Luke walked up to the back door and knocked. A woman's face appeared in the triple vertical glass windows in the door. She spoke through the window.

"Ne istiyorsun?" She asked.

"Hello, Ms. Rossi. My name is Luke Star. I am Sophie's father. Jael's friend." The woman looked around through the window to see if anyone else was around, then opened the door.

"Forgive me, Mr. Star, I have to be careful," she said in accented English.

"I understand, Ms. Rossi."

"No, my name is Haleh Ersoy; I moved in with my brother when my husband passed away a few years ago." Haleh hesitated a moment, then directed him to sit at the kitchen table. She walked over to the front picture window and closed the curtain.

Luke noticed the house was well kept. Haleh was attractive, even without makeup. Her hair and eyes were dark brown. Haleh's slippers scuffed across the floor as she came back into the kitchen. She was still in what appeared to be her work clothes, a skirt, and blouse.

"What is it I can do for you, Mr. Star?"

"Is Jael here?" Luke asked before he started.

"No, she is down the street with the only classmate that will talk to her, doing homework."

"Ms. Ersoy, Jael told Sophie her father is in prison. Sophie asked me to see if there was any way to help him."

"No! Mr. Star, you must not inquire about this," Haleh said.

"Don't worry, we are being discreet."

"We?"

"Yes, there are a few of us. Can you tell me how your brother ended up in prison?"

"Emir opened his print shop twenty years ago and worked hard to make it successful. Earlier this year, he bought a machine that would allow him to get large corporate contracts." Haleh took a kettle of hot water off the stove and poured two cups of hot water. She placed one in front of Luke, pushing a jar of assorted teas toward him. She put some chocolate tea cookies on the table and sat down with the other cup.

"He got his first big order a few months ago for one thousand Bibles written in Turkish. He gave them such a discount that he will barely break even, but printing Bibles was something he always wanted to do." Luke listened while picking a teabag from the jar, dunking it in his hot water, and then reaching for a cookie.

"He had made the complete run and was binding them in their covers when a man came in and offered to buy his shop. He thanked the man for the offer but told him he had no intention of selling." Haleh shook her head, taking a sip of her tea. "He should have sold to him."

"What happened when he wouldn't sell."

"The windows in his shop were broken, nasty graffiti was sprayed on all the walls. His clients were afraid to come in because of the large men standing outside telling them to leave.

When Emir still wouldn't sell, they beat him up. He was in the hospital for two days."

"Why didn't he call the Polis?" Luke asked.

"He did, but when Emir identified the man doing this to him, the Polis refused to pick him up."

"Why?"

"Because Mateo Borg's brother is a judge and a lot of the Polis get payoffs from him."

"I see. So how was it your brother ended up arrested?"

"Mateo Borg called the Polis anonymously and said Emir was printing seditious materials."

"When they didn't find any in his shop, how could they prosecute? Or did they plant something?" Luke questioned.

"No, they didn't plant anything. The prosecutor claimed the Bibles promoted hate and discontent. No one really believes that, but he was paid off to press charges. They were able to get the case tried in his brother's courtroom."

"Why didn't he get a lawyer and fight the charges?" Luke questioned. Haleh stared into her tea; Luke thought she might not answer.

"Because of me and Jael. They said if he fought the accusations, they would arrest me as an accomplice and put Jael in an orphanage." She looked up at Luke, "Jael's life in an orphanage would be brutal. He couldn't let that happen. That's why you can't ask anyone questions, Mr. Star."

"Do you have other family?"

"Yes, a brother in Germany. He has been trying to get us to move there, but Emir wouldn't leave his business." She took a sip of tea. "When he bought that new machine," she smiled, "I hadn't seen him so happy since before his wife died of cancer eight months ago. He would sit right where you are at breakfast, like a kid with a new toy. He would open his laptop and start a print run so when he got to work, he could start the process of binding the books..."

"Wait. Are you saying Emir could control his printer from his laptop?" Luke asked. Haleh looked at him, confused.

"Yes, the printer is digital; he could do all sorts of things with the machine from home on his laptop."

"Where is his laptop?"

"He kept it with him always. They arrested him here, so it's probably in his room," she said.

"Could you go check for me, please?" Haleh was hesitant, not sure if she should do it.

"I promise you this could help him," Luke said. Haleh got up and walked down a hallway. She came back a few moments later with the laptop.

"Mrs. Ersoy, do you happen to know the password?"

"Yes, but what do you want with his laptop?"

"If we can figure out what those men wanted with his business, then we can turn the tables on them," Luke said.

"Turn the tables?"

"If we find they are doing something illegal and get them arrested, we might be able to get Emir's conviction overturned."

"You can't do that, Mr. Star. If they find out, they will take Jael from me. Emir would not want that. He loves her more than his own life."

"What if I can help get you to your brother in Germany?"

"Mister Star. I know you mean well, but if Jael and I leave town, they will kill Emir. He is alive because they have us as leverage to keep him from talking to defend himself. Once we're gone, they will simply kill him."

"Mrs. Ersoy, not everyone in the judicial system is crooked. Some people are willing to help. Will you give me a chance?" Luke sat with one hand on the laptop, waiting for an answer.

"I would need to get permission from Emir. It's his life," she finally said.

"How often do you see him?"

"On Wednesdays and Saturdays. Jael goes with me on Saturdays."

"Can you ask him tomorrow if he will give me a chance? I promise I won't do anything with the information on this computer until you agree."

"I am very tempted to do this, Mr. Star. I would love Jael to have her father back. I will ask him. You can take the computer, but you have to keep your promise not to do anything until Emir agrees. I'll go see him in the morning."

"I promise."

"Alright. The password is Cansujael. He used his wife and daughter's names together."

"My daughter loves Jael. Would it be alright if she came to visit sometime?"

"Yes, Jael spoke of how kind Sophie was to her. I would love to meet her."

"Thank you for trusting me." Luke pulled a card and pen out of his pocket and wrote on the back, handing it to her. "My cell number is on the back. Call me after you talk to Emir." He stood and went to the door.

"You know you have men watching your house?"

"Yes, they follow me to and from work every day." Haleh opened the door for him and said goodbye.

Luke watched to make sure no one saw him leave her yard and went back to his car. He drove away more burdened than ever about the situation Jael was in.

Luke called Lance on his way home and asked if he could come over in an hour. He wanted to spend a little time with Sophie first.

When he walked in the door, Sophie ran over to him and gave him a hug.

"Daddy, I had so much fun with Jael at school today. And no one bothered us because Duke and CJ stayed close." Luke bent down to hug her.

"Have you gotten Jael's father released yet? I told her you could do anything."

"Not yet, Sophie, but you shouldn't tell her that. What if I can't do it?"

"Daddy, you will, I know it. Deniz made spaghetti tonight; you're just in time."

Luke thought of the scripture that said we should become as little children. He understood why. They never doubt; they simply believe.

After dinner, Luke helped Sophie with her homework until a knock came on the door.

"Sophie, that's Lance. Do you mind finishing your homework in your room?" Sophie grabbed her books and went to her room. Luke answered the door.

"Thank you for coming, Lance. I wanted to tell you what I found out at Emir's house." Luke told Lance everything Haleh told him and opened his briefcase to pull out the laptop.

"You have the password?"

"Yes. But I don't know if we should open it. What if there is a way for them to know someone else is logged on?"

"Do you remember Agent Pamela Hill? She played David's date up on the rooftop takedown of Oguz Sandalli."

"Yes, I remember."

"Pam is a genius with computers; that's a big part of what she does for CID. The pentagon offered her a job, but she wanted to follow in her father's footsteps and enlisted. CID scooped her up immediately."

"But this is way outside the CID's jurisdiction. Do you think she will want to get involved?"

"I don't know. Let me call her; she lives across from the park in a duplex. Maybe she will let me come over and explain what we're doing."

"If she won't, maybe David's father has a contact that can help us," Luke said. Lance called Agent Hill and headed over to her house.

Luke called David and Jonathan and asked if they wanted to come over to discuss the new developments.

Luke answered the door to find David and Jonathan had walked over together. As they were walking in, Lance pulled up with Agent Hill. She was shorter than Lance by about five inches, had pretty blond hair just past her shoulder, and blue eyes. There was no doubt she worked out, but she kept her feminine figure.

Luke offered them all coffee as they sat down around the kitchen table.

"Agent Hill, how much has Lance told you about what we are trying to do?" David asked.

"Please, call me Pam. Not much, but I told him I would help if I could."

Luke told her everything they knew about Emir's situation. He handed her the laptop.

"Ok, let me get into the program's database. I'll be able to see if anyone is using it at the moment." Her fingers flew over the keyboard, and in a moment, she had her answer. "No one is on it. Do you want me to see the last item printed on the machine?"

"Yes." The group said in tandem. Pam hit more keys, and an image of a bearer bond popped up.

"Is that a bearer bond?" Luke asked.

"It's a Euro bond with coupons." Pam studied it carefully. "It's not complete. It doesn't have a denomination, a date of purchase, interest rate, or country of origin."

"What does that mean. What good is it without that information?" Jonathan asked.

"We know Dupuis is involved, so there has to be a way these are usable."

"They have a list of authorization numbers. Those can't be faked. If they are not legitimate, the bond won't be honored."

"How could anyone get ahold of those numbers?" David asked.

"I have no idea, but I'd bet my paycheck they are authentic," Lance said.

"Ok, so they are forging bearer bonds, but they have to be complete to cash them in. These are worthless," Jonathan said.

"Not necessarily. If they work backward, they can get the missing information," Pam said.

"They can cash in a coupon, and the information for the bond will come with the payment," Lance added.

"How do they know someone hasn't already cashed in the bond?" Luke asked.

"It's a risk, but one they are apparently willing to take. It's a brilliant fraud. So many bearer bonds have been lost or destroyed over the years; thousands of them. Those can be forged and redeem without the worry of being caught. Once lost or destroyed, they cannot be replaced. The ones that are still in someone's possession are another issue. But if they just use one coupon off a thousand bonds and get those funds, they are likely to make close to a million dollars. There are at least ten thousand numbers on this list. But they must plan on doing more than that, or Dupuis would not be involved. Once they have all the information, I'm sure they plan on cashing in the bonds too. If the forgery is good enough, no one will know the difference until the real owner tries to cash his in," Pam said.

"Wow, that's quite an operation, but how will knowing any of this get Emir released?" Luke asked.

"When I talked to Captain Demir, he told me he knew a judge he could trust. He might overturn Judge Borg's finings, but only if we have proof of corruption and collusion. This proves corruption on Mateo's part. What we need is proof of collusion with the prosecutor and Mateo's brother, the judge," Lance offered.

"If we can catch them in the act of trying to redeem one of these bonds, we could hand that over to the captain," Jonathan said.

"That still doesn't incriminate the prosecutor or the judge," Lance stated.

"No, and it's not likely Mateo would turn on his brother. But I bet the prosecutor would. If we make him believe we have proof of his part in this fraud, he is the weakest link," Luke said.

"We have no authority to do anything. If we get the proof and tell the captain about Dupuis, maybe he will let us help take them down," Lance said.

"Dupuis would be a great collar for anyone. If CID finds out we handed him over to the Turkish Polis, instead of turning the info over to CID, we could get written up." Pam said.

"There is no we, Pam. You can't be involved any more than you are. I'm not willing to let you put your career in jeopardy," Lance insisted.

"That's very chivalrous, Lance. But you don't get to tell me what I can get involved with. I want to see this through. Besides, you need me to monitor this site without letting them know it's being watched. Unless one of you know how to do it?" Pam answered.

"I apologize, Pam. I wasn't trying to tell you what to do. I just don't want you to get in trouble for helping us."

"It's alright, Lance. Your heart was in the right place." She looked at Lance and smiled. Luke noticed the little sparkle in her eye and glanced over at Jonathan, who was holding back a chuckle. Maybe, Pam had an ulterior motive for sticking around.

"Are bonds printed on special paper?" Luke asked.

"Yes. Not paper as sophisticated as currency. But not readily available to the public," Lance answered.

"Pam, can you fill the entire screen with that image?"

"Yes."

"Luke, can you hook up your printer to this computer?" David asked as he got up from his seat and stepped closer to the computer. Pam enlarged the image. Luke took the laptop to his office and connected it to his printer. The image of the incomplete bond printed out.

"I know we can trust the captain, but we can't say the same for those around him. If anyone gets wind of what we are doing, Judge Borg will have Haleh arrested. Then they will put Jael in the orphan home," Luke said.

"We can get them out of the country," David responded.

"Yes, but then they will kill Emir. Whatever we do, we have to coordinate it to get Emir in protective custody before there are any arrests. And we have to give a new judge time to overturn the conviction. Which he can't do until we have the prosecutor ready to confess."

"Ok, Luke, how do we do that?" Lance asked.

"I'd like to talk to the captain tomorrow," Luke held up the printed bond, "and show him what is going on. Then maybe he can figure a way to get Emir into protective custody. Lance, could you come with me?"

"Yes."

"If the captain can't help, I will call my father. He has all sorts of contacts all over the world. Maybe he can," David offered.

After everyone said goodbye, Luke locked up and went to bed. He prayed God would pave the way for Emir to get released.

**Wednesday**

After Sophie drove off with Anna and the others to school, Luke headed to the office. He had one appointment he needed to keep. His phone rang on the drive to the office.

"Hello?"

"Hi Luke, do you have a minute?"

"Of course, Manny."

"I just wanted to check in and see what you found out about Mr. Rossi." Luke told him everything that had happened since they last talked.

"The captain is ambitious. I wouldn't tell him who the forger is, only that there is one. And I would meet him somewhere other than at the precinct," Manny offered his advice.

"We were thinking the same thing. Do you think we should go with Demir to meet the judge?"

"Yes, Luke, but you can't go in a group. If the captain lets you accompany him, it should be just you and him. And meet him away from the precinct too."

"Thanks, Manny; I sure wish you were here. Don't get me wrong, Lance has been terrific, and he brought Agent Hill in to help with the computer. I think she likes him."

"What happened to Sally?"

"They broke up. I'll tell you about it when you get home. Do you have any idea when that will be?"

"The house is sold; we are moving everything that Leo and Ruby want to keep to Leo's garage. He told us we could keep her things there until we get back in the States. The estate sale is this weekend. So we think we will be home the following Saturday."

"Sophie is going to be thrilled. Call me with your airline arrival, and I'll pick you up. Have a good night, Manny, and tell Ruby and the kids hi for me."

"I will, Luke. See you soon."

# CHAPTER SEVEN

Luke met with a young, enlisted man needing to make a will after recently getting married. After writing up the will and calling in a notary, he made a copy and gave the original to the young man. He got up to get some coffee from the break room when his phone rang.

"Hello?"

"Captain Star, this is Haleh Ersoy."

"Yes, Ms. Ersoy."

"I talked to Emir. At first, he was against it. He didn't want to take the chance Jael would end up in an orphanage. But I told him I trust you. That I believe God sent you to help us."

"I believe that too, Ms. Ersoy," Luke agreed.

"My brother told me to do what I feel is right. I am willing to trust in the Lord, Mr. Star. Just tell me what you want me to do," Haleh said.

"Keep praying, and I will be in touch," Luke said.

"I can never thank you enough," Luke heard Haleh's voice crack.

"If this works, the only one you will need to thank is God, for it will be a miracle." They said goodbye, and Luke praised the Lord.

Before he left, he stopped at the unit secretary's desk to ensure he had nothing else on his schedule. He called Lance as he got on the elevator.

"Hello?"

"Lance, can you call Captain Demir and see if he will meet us somewhere. I don't think we should go to his precinct?"

"I agree. Demir works second watch, so he should be home. Where would you want to meet?"

"Would he come to my house?"

"When?"

"As soon as possible."

"I'll call and let you know."

With that, Luke walked to his car to wait for a call back as he headed home. His cell rang. Before he could say Hello, Lance spoke.

"Luke, he said he could be there in an hour."

"Can you be there, Lance?"

"No, we have a fluid situation here. I told Demir that, so he's expecting to meet with you alone."

"Thank you, Lance."

"Let me know how it turns out."

"I will."

Luke picked up some donuts at the small drive-through donut shop on Base. They always sold out by the time he got off, so this was a treat for him. He got out of his uniform, wanting to make it clear this was not an official request.

Captain Demir knocked on his door; Luke welcomed him in and led him to the kitchen.

"Captain, thankfully, it has been a while since I've seen you," Luke said. The captain laughed.

"Yes, in our business, that is a good thing."

"Please have a seat; I bought some donuts," Luke laughed. "I guess that was a little cliché of me."

"It's alright; I like donuts."

"What kind of coffee do you like."

"Ah, you have a new Keurig."

"Yes, I'm getting quite spoiled."

"I'll take a French vanilla; thank you." The captain said as he sat down. He too, was out of uniform. He sat back in his seat and laid one arm on the table.

While Luke was letting the coffee drip, he put a small plate and some napkins in front of Demir. He took the donut box and placed it on the table for him to choose what he wanted. He took a glazed donut and a coconut and chocolate bar.

"Captain Demir, I know how unorthodox this all is. The last thing I want to do is jeopardize your new promotion, but I can't let this go." Luke handed Demir his coffee, then took his cup and sat down across from him.

"I have spoken with Judge Bulut. He does not wish to overturn another judge's finding. However, he is willing to hear you out. You would have to demonstrate there was gross misfeasance. So far, all you have given as evidence is the fact the Bible was used to say he was printing seditious materials."

"Well, that alone is outrageous, Captain, but there is much more."

"It is outrageous to you because you are from a Christian country. Not everyone sees things as you do. What other proof do you have that there was corruption?" Luke got up and grabbed the folder he had placed on top of the refrigerator.

"Please, Captain, look inside." The captain opened the folder, took out the sheet of paper inside, and looked at it.

"What is this?" Demir threw it back on the table dismissively.

"That is why Borg wanted Rossi's machine. It's what he and his men are printing."

"This? This is worthless. It is incomplete and not even on the right kind of paper."

"I understand that. I printed that off Emir's laptop. His laptop still has access to the machine; Borg has no idea. And that's not all. The night Lance surveilled the property, he recognized a forger walking out with Borg. This," Luke lifted the paper off the table, "is worthless now, but it won't be soon." Demir took the paper from him and looked closely at it.

"Complete and on the right paper, I can see this could pass as a legitimate bearer bond." Demir placed it back on the table, his fingers strumming over it as he took a moment to think about it.

"This is a crime, but how will it release Mr. Rossi. His conviction has nothing to do with this?"

"You told Lance your friend the judge would need proof that Mr. Rossi was convicted falsely. I'm trying to show you that Borg wanted that particular printer and needed Rossi out of the way. He colluded with the prosecutor and his brother, the judge, to fabricate a case against him."

"It is compelling evidence, but it is not proof of collusion. Even if Mateo had bad motives. Maybe the prosecutor believed the Bible actually has seditious materials in it."

"Really?" Luke's eyebrows lifted. Demir raised his hand.

"All I'm saying is, it does not prove collusion. If we pick up Mateo on this, he will never admit he was in collusion with his brother to get Rossi out of the way."

"You are right. They will never turn on each other, but the prosecutor might." Luke noticed Demir's coffee cup was empty. He got up and took it off the table. "Would you like more French Vanilla?"

"Do you have Hazelnut?"

"Yes." Luke brewed him some more coffee and placed it on the table in front of him. Demir took a sip after blowing on it and then a bite of his glazed donut.

"We need to talk to the judge. Let me call him," Demir finally said.

"I don't think we should speak with him in public," Luke suggested.

Captain Demir was driving. Judge Bulut had the day off and had just left the country club. He said his wife was out with her friend's shopping, so no one was at his house.

The judge lived in a part of Adana Luke had never seen. The homes were modern and expensive, the type of homes that have *grounds* rather than yards. It took forty-five minutes to get there.

Demir drove through the open gate and down the long driveway. They walked up to the large oak double doors and rang the bell. Luke was surprised when the judge answered the door himself.

"Welcome," Judge Bulut said as he stepped aside to let them into the large marble-floored foyer. He closed the door, and Captain Demir introduced Luke mentioning he was a Jag officer. Then the judge led the men into a study that was in the back of the house. Large windows were overlooking the groomed backyard.

"Please sit." The judge directed them to two Christopher Knight club chairs. The Judge sat on the opposite side at his black Kingstown Admiralty Executive Desk. After they all sat, he said.

"It is good to see you again, Captain. How is it you would bring an American Jag officer to my home?" The judge said to Demir in Turkish.

"He has brought to my attention a terrible miscarriage of justice, sir," Demir answered in kind. Judge Bulut sat looking at Luke for a long moment, then turned back to Demir and spoke in English.

"Captain Demir, what is it you think I can do for you?" Demir explained everything Luke and Lance had told him.

"Captain Demir, you decide who and when to arrest someone. I have nothing in that."

"Yes sir. What I need from you is a commitment to overturn Judge Borg's findings. That is, of course, when I get the Savci (prosecutor) to admit the collusion."

"Who is the Savci?" The judge asked.

"Yükse. I believe he will testify if Bassavci Ozkan will give him a deal." The judge kept his eyes on Captain Star even though it was Demir speaking.

"Is Emine agreeable to this? Bulut asked.

"I have not approached him yet, sir. But I believe the chief prosecutor to be an honest man."

"I believe he is," Bulut responded. "But you want me to risk my career to overturn a verdict by Judge Borg? That is political suicide, you know that."

"I do, sir. But I am willing to do the same. I will admit, the first thing I thought of was how it would affect my future promotions if this didn't turn out well. But I did not sign up to be a politician. I joined to be a purveyor of justice. I want to expose corruption," Demir said.

"You feel our justice system corrupt?" Judge Bulut said, furrowing his brow.

"There is corruption in every system in every country. Our country is no different. But I do not want to be a part of it. I want to do what is right. Getting this man out of prison and making sure Mateo and Judge Borg cannot keep doing this is the right thing to do."

"As I understand it, Mr. Rossi signed a confession. He refused a lawyer. If he was innocent, why not fight the charge in court?"

"I can answer that, sir," Luke spoke for the first time. "Mr. Rossi was told if he did not comply, they would arrest his sister as an accomplish. Then they would place his daughter in an orphanage; he believed them. Mateo Borg has men watching Rossi's house every day."

"Is that true, Captain Demir?"

"Yes sir, and there is no confession in the file."

"What are you asking me to do?"

"Sir, I need an order from you to allow me to get Mr. Rossi out of prison and in protective custody. I plan on getting Savci Yükse into an interrogation room and get him to confess. I need your word you will overturn Rossi's conviction once I have that." The judge didn't say anything. He opened his drawer, pulled a sheet of paper with his official letterhead and seal on it, and wrote out the order.

"Here," he handed it to Demir. "Do what you need to. I will overturn the conviction if you can prove what you say." The judge stood up. He was finished with this conversation.

"Thank you, sir," Demir said and extended his hand to him. Luke did the same.

Luke and Demir road for a while in silence as they left the judge's home. Finally, Demir said.

"I am jumping off a cliff here, Mr. Star."

"I know that Captain."

"What is our next step?"

"We have to coordinate a way to protect Emir's family before we approach Yükse. It will be hard to keep this secret once you talk to him. Do you have men you can trust?"

"I do."

"You trust Bassavci Ozkan?" Luke waited for an answer.

"I do. I am not friends with him. But I have heard he refuses to take bribes from criminals or make deals with the judges. My guess is he is the most honest of the prosecutors."

"We need to know if he is willing to give Yükse a deal to testify against Mateo and Judge Borg. And that Ozkan is willing to charge and prosecute them after you get Yükse's confession," Luke insisted.

"Savci Yükse is out of town until Saturday; he is at his sister's wedding in Istanbul. I will talk to Ozkan before he returns," Demir said.

"Once you have Rossi in protective custody, we will get his sister and daughter out of the country."

"How do you plan on doing that, Mr. Star."

"I don't know yet. But the minute we do, Emir Rossi's life will be in danger."

Luke called the office to see if he had any more appointments come in for the day. When there were none, he decided to go home early. He let Deniz go home and sat outside to wait for Sophie.

Luke stood up when he saw Anna's car pull in. Sophie hopped out of the car and ran to hug her father.

"Daddy, Aunt Annie asked if I wanted to help her make dinner and cookies at her house tonight. Can I go?"

"Of course you can." Sophie smiled and clapped her hands. "Why don't you hurry and change, so you don't make her wait." Sophie started to run inside. Luke stopped her. "Take your backpack." He handed it to her; she had put it down when she hugged him.

Anna stepped out of the SUV to speak with Luke.

"David told me what you all are doing for Sophie's friend. Duke won't talk to me about it. He is afraid I'll get involved, and something will happen to me." She turned to look at Duke in the car when she made that statement. "But I talked it over with David. I'm available to do whatever you might need to help this family."

"Thank you, Anna. And thank you for all you do for Sophie. She loves her piano lessons and spending time with you, Zoey, and Ruby helps her not miss her mother as much."

"We all love Sophie, Luke. There is no need to thank us." Sophie ran back out of the house and hugged her dad again.

"You won't be lonely eating by yourself, will you, Daddy?"

"No, of course not. Have a good time and bring me home some cookies." Sophie giggled and hopped in the car.

"Anna, will you see if David and Jonathan will come over after dinner. I have lots to tell them."

"Sure." Anna turned and got back in the SUV. Sophie waved as they drove off.

After Luke finished off some leftover spaghetti from a few nights ago, he called Lance.

"Hello?"

"Hey Lance, can you come over?"

"Sure, do I need to see if Pam can come too? Lance asked. Luke smiled.

"Yes, we need her to see what the printer has been doing."

"I'll be there shortly."

Lance knocked on the door fifteen minutes later. Luke ushered him and Pam in and offered them some coffee. He placed some of Deniz's homemade peanut butter cookies on the table with mugs of steaming coffee.

Luke took Emir's laptop off the top of the refrigerator and handed it to Pam.

"Can you see if anything has changed?" Luke asked.

"Sure." Pam opened the computer to the machine's program. "It looks like they have printed over a thousand bearer bonds coupons. They must intend on redeeming them soon. The bonds are almost complete except for the amount and the maturity date."

"How do they know where to send the coupons?" Luke asked.

"The issue number reflects the country of origin and whether it is a government bond or a company bond. A company bond has to be registered with their countries Fiscal Responsibility Department. They do that by sending in the issue or identifying number on each bond." Lance explained.

"I had no idea. So when a bond's coupon is redeemed, the number tells the trustor the value of the coupon. The person redeeming it gives them an address where they want the money sent?"

"Yes," Pam said. Luke heard a knock on the door and opened it to David and Jonathan.

"Come in, please. Do you want some coffee?"

"I would like some. Anna said she would bring Sophie home when I get back," David said.

"I appreciate that."

"No coffee for me, thanks," Jonathan answered.

Luke asked Pam to repeat what she had just told him.

"So they have over a thousand coupons ready to redeem?" Jonathan asked.

"Yes, but it's still a long game. The process will take weeks," Pam answered.

"Our immediate problem is coordinating Mateo's arrest with the protection of Rossi's family. Captain Demir will be picking up the prosecutor in Rossi's case, Kiral Yükse, on Saturday. He is out of town at the moment.

When the prosecutor is picked up, Mateo will send the Polis he has on his payroll to pick up Haleh and Jael. Taking them will be a sign to Emir to keep his mouth shut and warn the prosecutor that he can do the same to his family," David said.

"Mateo has men outside Haleh's house. I parked around the corner and went in the back to keep from being seen. When they realize they are gone, they will try to kill Emir," Luke said.

"Luke went with Demir to Judge Bulut today. Bulut gave Demir an order for the Warden to release Rossi to the Captain, " Lance relayed.

"So, you are saying the minute Yükse is picked up, Rossi has to be out of prison, and Haleh and Jael must be gone?" Jonathan asked.

"Yes, exactly," Luke answered.

"Alright. Then let me make some suggestions," David interjected. "If we take Haleh and Jael out of harm's way early Saturday morning, no one will notice. But they need to travel separately. Where are they going?"

"Haleh says her brother in Germany has been trying to get them to move there for years. That is the most logical place. Even if Mateo finds out they are there, his reach is not long enough; he won't be able to hurt them," Luke answered.

"We won't have time to get them new names and passports. They will have to travel on their own papers. But if we time this right, they will be out of reach before Mateo's organization even starts to look for them."

"That makes sense, David, and I think having them travel separately is a good idea too. But Jael can't travel by herself," Pam said.

"That's true. If Anna is willing to take the boys, Sophie, and Jael, they could travel as a family on the train. I could purchase them a compartment in the sleeping car. Jonathan and I could drive Haleh; we can all meet in Izmir. My dad has a contact there. Emir can catch up to them in Izmir. Then they can get on a fishing boat in Cesme and go to Rafina, Greece, across the Aegean Sea."

"That leaves me and Luke available to take Emir. We will have to wait for Judge Bulut to overturn his conviction before we can leave," Lance said.

"Yes, and Demir said he has a prosecutor he can trust. He plans on talking to him before Yükse gets back in town. We need him to charge Judge Borg and his brother if Yükse turns states evidence on them," Luke said.

"Ok, then we set everything up as planned and pray that God makes way for it to all fall into place," Jonathan said.

"I will talk to Haleh tomorrow after work. Let her know what the plan is. She won't be able to tell her brother what's happening. The prison records conversations on the phone and in person."

"Ok, Luke. I will call Captain Demir. Hopefully, he will go along with our plan," Lance said.

"What if Mateo isn't at the business when Demir sends his officers out to arrest him? Mateo has been arrested before, according to Demir. He must have a record of where Mateo lives in his file. But we know he has no idea where Dupuis is staying or even that he is here."

"You're right Luke, I'll sit on the business tonight. If they are there, I'll follow them and find out where Dupuis is staying."

"I'll go with you Lance, you'll need backup," Pam volunteered.

Lance and Pam headed out, and the others finished their coffee and said goodnight.

Lance pulled in the alley behind Rossi's printing shop and saw that the same black SUVs were parked in the back. He pulled into the parking lot next store and parked in a spot where they could easily see the back of the building.

Lance reached in his back seat for his camera and handed it to Pam.

"You can take shots of them as they come out. Last time Mateo and Dupuis got in the same SUV. If they are creatures of habit, we will be in good shape. If they get in different cars, we will follow Dupuis."

"Sounds like a plan to me," Pam said with a smile.

For Lance, it was the best two-hour stakeout he'd ever been on. He enjoyed talking and laughing with Pam. When the men walked out the back door, Pam started taking pictures. Mateo and Dupuis got in the same car, and Lance gave them plenty of space before he followed. There were few cars on the road at this time of night, and he had to be careful not to get too close.

Lance followed them to Turhan Cemal Derrike Blv. They got off at Dr. Ali Mentesoglu Cd. And turned again on 61004 Sk. Then the SUV pulled into the driveway of the Ibis Adana Hotel and pulled to the front doors. The driver got out and opened the back door for Dupuis. Dupuis walked into the Hotel's revolving door.

"I'll follow him to his room and get the number. You follow Mateo. I'll wait in the lobby until you get back."

"Are you sure, Pam?"

"Yes," she said as she hopped out of the car; she didn't want to lose Dupuis. Lance continued following Mateo to his home.

Pam saw Dupuis get on the elevator. She was too far away to get on with him. Pam watched to see what floor the elevator stopped at and ran up the three flights. When she opened the stairwell door, she saw him use his key to get into his room. When he stepped in, she went down the hall to see the number on the door. Then went down to wait in the lobby.

Lance followed the SUV onto E 90 for ten minutes; the SUV took the exit to 86037 Sokak and turned again on 86045 Soka. The SUV pulled into a driveway of a four-story fancy stucco apartment building. It was a nice place, but not one Lance expected a criminal with the money the Borg's had accumulated, to live in.

He took down the address and the apartment number. Then he headed back to pick up Pam. He would give this information to Demir in the morning.

# CHAPTER EIGHT

**Thursday**

Lance called Captain Demir the following day; he wanted to catch him before he went to the precinct. He told Demir of the plan they laid out the night before.

He finally spilled the beans that Pierre Dupuis was the forger working with Mateo. Demir was excited to hear that. He knew it would be a notable collar for him. Lance gave him the name of the hotel and room number that Dupuis was staying at, if needed. Lance also gave him Mateo Borg's address, but the captain already knew it. Captain Demir agreed with the timeline the men had in mind.

Lance decided to go to the Jag office to talk to Luke. When he got there, he found Luke and David were both in court. Jonathan was there, so he knocked on his open door.

"Hello Major, can I come in." Jonathan stood to greet him.

"Sure, have a seat."

"I wanted to come by and let you know about our stakeout last night. I gave Captain Demir the run down this morning," Lance said. Jonathan couldn't help but smile.

"How was the stakeout?" He said it in such a way it made Lance smile.

"Fine," Lance said, unable to look Jonathan in the eyes.

"Just, fine?" Jonathan baited him. Lance grabbed a paperweight that had the seal of the Army embedded in resin off the desk and fiddled with it. Jonathan could see he was embarrassing him, but what else are friends for?

"Agent Hill goes to the same Church service we go to on Sunday. She's in the choir."

"Really?"

"Yes, how would you like to come with us Sunday?"

"Luke has invited me before; I've considered it. I wouldn't want to come just to see Pam. If I go, I want it to be because I want to change my life."

"Is that something you have been thinking about? Changing your life?"

"I appreciate you telling me how you came to have a personal relationship with Christ. Luke told me his story too. As I told Luke, I've always believed there was a God. I don't know why it has been so hard for me to make the leap to give my life over to Him. I just don't know that I can live the life, and the last thing I want to be is a hypocrite. But Luke said something that made sense to me. He said it isn't about following rules but about a change in one's heart and mind. He said when you get saved, you look at things the way God sees them; your mind is renewed." Lance looked down at the paperweight he was turning in his hands.

"That's right, Lance, you want to do things to please the Lord. But if you make a mistake, Jesus is always there to pick you up and forgive you if you ask Him.

"I'm not sure your motivation for coming to the service matters. When you hear the sermon and feel the Spirit of God, you'll know getting right with God is the only thing that matters."

"Thanks, Jonathan. I'll think about it."

"Why don't you tell me about the stakeout and what you told Captain Demir." Jonathan knew God was dealing with Lance. It was a choice only he could make. Lance would either accept or reject the call to salvation.

"We followed the SUVs this time and found out where Dupuis and Borg live. I gave that information to Demir since we don't know where they will be when he decides to send his officers to arrest them. Demir was pretty excited that Dupuis was the forger."

"I bet. I hope you don't get a reprimand for not turning that information over to CID."

"Hopefully, they will never find out. But it's the right thing to do. The Polis are the only ones who can make things right for Rossi. If CID were involved, their only concern would be arresting Dupuis. Rossi's needs would be irrelevant."

"I agree. Luke is going over to tell Rossi's sister about the plan tonight."

"Yes, he mentioned that." Lance put the paperweight back on the desk and stood up. He started to the door then stopped, "thank you for caring, Jonathan. You know, about me being right with God."

"We all care about you, Lance. Thanks for coming in."

It was 5 pm when Luke got out of court, so he didn't go by the office but went straight home. When he walked in, Sophie ran to him and gave him a hug. Luke put down his briefcase and walked into the kitchen.

"Hello, Mr. Luke," Deniz said.

"Hello, Deniz. Are those tacos you are making?"

"Yes."

"Do you mind staying late tonight?"

"No, Mr. Luke, that is not a problem."

"Daddy, where are you going?" Luke stepped to Sophie. She was back at her seat at the kitchen table doing her homework.

"I have to go see Jael's Aunt."

"Daddy, can I go with you?" Luke thought about it for a moment. There was no reason she couldn't.

"Ok. Deniz, just put the taco makings in the fridge. We'll assemble them when we get home. I won't need you to stay."

"Alright, Mr. Luke." Deniz put the taco makings in the fridge, and Luke went to his room to change.

Luke drove past the front of Haleh's house to see if Mateo still had men watching. The black sedan with tinted windows was still sitting across from her home. He pulled around the corner.

"Daddy, you passed her house," Sophie said.

"I know, sweetheart, men are watching her, so I go in the back." Sophie turned in her seat to look for herself, but they were already out of sight.

Sophie grabbed her backpack. Luke told her she didn't need to bring it, but she said, "I brought some of my clothes for Jael." Luke nodded his approval.

They opened the back gate and stepped up to the door. Haleh was surprised to see them.

"Mr. Star, and this must be Sophie?" Haleh smiled, "come in, please." Jael came out of her room when she heard her aunt talking to someone.

"Sophie!" Jael ran up to her and gave her a big hug. They ran off to her room.

"Mr. Star, what brings you to my home?" She asked.

"There is a plan in play to get your brother out of jail. You will all have to leave the country. But at least you will all be together again."

"A plan, what are you talking about?"

"We have a judge who is willing to overturn the conviction if we can get the prosecutor to confess to the collusion. But to keep Mateo from harming you and Jael, we have to get you out of town. Emir will follow after he has been vindicated," Luke knew Haleh was confused. She directed him to the kitchen chair and moved to the stove to turn on the water for tea.

Luke explained everything to Haleh. "Are you willing to leave everything behind?"

"Will Emir get his business back if they expose Borg?"

"I don't think so. If your government is like ours, they will confiscate it because of the criminal activity."

"Then there is nothing to leave behind, except this house. Maybe we could hire someone to sell it for us. But it wouldn't matter. What matters is that my brother gets out of jail so he can raise his daughter. We can start over. Our brother in Germany will help us."

"Good. I will pick you and Jael up early Saturday morning and take Jael to the train station to meet the others. David and Jonathan will take you by car." Haleh sat staring at the hot water she just poured for herself and Luke. He knew how hard it was to walk away from everything and start over. "Will you be alright, Haleh?"

"Yes." She looked at Luke and smiled.

"I don't know how to thank you and your friends."

"No thanks..." Luke didn't finish the sentence. There was a screech of tires in front of the house. Haleh ran to see.

"It's the Polis. They have come for Jael and me. Please leave and take Jael."

"No. Stall before you answer the door." Luke ran to Jael's room. "Sophie, you need to take Jael and run. Deniz lives three blocks that way." He pointed north, "then turn right. You will recognize her house when you get there." Sophie and Jael's eyes went wide.

"Daddy, what's wrong?"

"Don't ask questions. Here, take my phone if you get lost, call Deniz. Her number is in it." He gave the phone to Sophie, went to the window, opened it, and took off the screen. "Hurry.

Stay hidden." He grabbed Jael's arm, helped her out the window, and then helped Sophie out, handing them their backpacks.

"Daddy, I'm scared."

"Go!" When he saw they were running to the gate, he closed the window, leaving the screen off, and closed the curtains. He could hear the Polis banging on her door. She couldn't stall any longer.

"Open the door; this is the Polis." One of the men yelled in Turkish. Luke went back to the living room, and Haleh opened the door.

"Evet? Ne istiyorsun?"

"Mrs. Ersoy, you are under arrest." They stepped into the room. Luke grabbed a pen and paper sitting on an end table and wrote down the names on their uniforms. Korkmaz and Sahin. Luke didn't understand Turkish, but there was no doubt they were there to arrest her.

"Ask if they have a warrant," Luke told Haleh. She translated and asked the officers.

"Hayir."

"Tell them they can't take you without a warrant." Haleh translated. The men moved toward her; one took her arm.

"Siparislerimiz var."

"They say they have their orders," she translated. She leaned closer to Luke and whispered in his ear. "Jael's passport is in the drawer of my night table. Please send her to my brother." One man took out a pair of handcuffs, placing them on her wrists. They took her arms and led her to their patrol car. Luke followed. He wrote down the cars identifying number.

"Where are you taking her?" Luke shouted. Haleh translated. One officer was putting her in the back seat; the other turned to Luke and said.

"72." Luke assumed that meant the 72nd precinct.

As they were leaving, another car pulled up. A woman stepped out and spoke to Luke in Turkish. When she realized he didn't speak the language, she repeated herself in English.

"I am here to take Jael Rossi."

"Take her where?"

"To the orphanage. We were notified her aunt was being arrested."

"She is not here," Luke replied.

"Where is she?"

"I have no idea." The woman stepped into the house to look for herself. In a few minutes, she stepped back outside, got into her car, and left. Luke stood there watching the car leave. He turned to go into the house, just as he saw Mateo's men driving right at him. He jumped out of the way, and they kept going.

Luke called Captain Demir as he hurried to get Haleh and Jael's passports out of the nightstand. He saw Emir's was there too, so he grabbed it along with a change of clothes and shoes for Emir. Emir wouldn't be able to come home after his release, and he couldn't travel in his prison uniform. Luke then locked up and headed to his car, waiting for Demir to answer.

Demir answered his cell. "Alo?"

"Someone leaked our plan. The Polis arrested Haleh without a warrant."

"What!? When?"

"Ten minutes ago. I was there telling Haleh our plan when the Polis came. They are taking her to the 72nd." Luke gave Demir the car's identifying number and their names.

"That's Captain Polat's district. I know him. I'll take care of it."

"You have to get Emir out of prison. They will kill him now. Our plan has been exposed."

THE PROMISE

Sophie and Jael ran as fast as they could, past the gate. They were afraid to walk along the street. They found a house on the alley that didn't have a fence and cut through to the next road. Sophie stopped; she wasn't sure what to do.

"Let's keep cutting through the yards," Sophie said. The sun was going down and casting big shadows. They started walking by another house. Sophie didn't see the chain-link fence until they were right up next to it. They turned to go back when a large dog ran up to the fence and jumped on it, barking and snarling. The girls ran scared back to the street and down the road. When they finally stopped, Jael was crying.

"I have to find out what happened to my aunt. I have to go back."

"No! I'll call my dad when we get to Deniz's house." Sophie grabbed Jael's hand and started toward another yard when she noticed a car moving slowly down the street. They ran onto the porch of the closest house. The two girls crunched down in the corner and waited for the vehicle to pass. When they felt confident it was gone, they got up to leave. The light on the porch came on, and the door opened. A woman, tall and thin, came out and caught the girls leaving her porch.

"What's going on?"

The girls froze in their spots. Jael turned and started to cry. She spoke Turkish, "I'm sorry, ma'am, we meant no harm. We just got scared. We thought a car was following us." The woman stepped out into the street and looked both ways.

"It's getting dark. Why are you on the street alone?"

"We are on our way to a friend's house but got lost," Jael said. The woman waved them in. Sophie hesitated, but Jael told her to follow.

The lady directed them to her couch. "What is the address of the house you are trying to find?" Sophie looked to Jael to translate.

"She wants to know your Deniz's address."

"I don't know it." The woman understood English and responded.

"You don't know where you are going? Have you two run away from home?"

"No, I know where she lives; I just don't know the address." The woman looked like she didn't believe her. Sophie was afraid she would call the Polis or children's services. She got up to leave. "We have to go; she is waiting for us."

The woman said to wait, "let me get you something to drink. Then I will help you find your friend's house." Sophie saw her pick up her phone on the way to her kitchen.

"We need to get out of here. She is turning us in," Sophie whispered and grabbed Jael's hand. They ran out the door and down the porch steps. There was no fence, so they ran through the back to the alley and through the adjoining yard to the next street.

"We have to stop and call someone, Sophie. We are lost," Jael said. Sophie agreed. They went behind a bush, and she pulled her dad's phone from her pocket and found Deniz's number.

"Alo?"

"Deniz, it's Sophie." She started crying; the stress was finally catching up to her. "We can't find your house."

"Where are you?"

"I don't know."

"Go to the corner. Look for some numbers on the curb." The girls left their hiding spot and went to the nearest curb. Sophie read off the number.

"Now go to the connecting street and read that number." The girls walked until they saw another number and read it off.

"Alright, stay right there. I'm coming."

Captain Demir grabbed his uniform jacket off the coat hanger and his gun out of his top desk drawer. *Who could have betrayed us? I told no one of this except Judge Bulut. I can't believe he would do this. He is too honorable.* Captain Demir was wrestling with these thoughts as he took the stairs down to the lobby. He couldn't believe it was the judge. He stopped cold. *The warden was the only other one I told. I gave him a heads up I would be coming. He must be on Judge Borg's payroll.* He moved faster, dialing Chief Bozkurt, deciding he wasn't sure he could trust Captain Polat. Bozhurt was Demir's former boss and friend. It was his personal line Demir called, Bozhurt answered himself.

"Merhaba."

"Merhaba, Chief." Demir continued in Turkish, "Captain Demir here; how are you, sir?"

"Good, my old friend, good."

"I need your help," Demir told him everything. "Two officers from your precinct arrested Rossi's sister about ten minutes ago."

"Nothing has come over my desk about an arrest. Who did this?" Demir gave him their names and the patrol car number."

"I need you to stop them wherever they are. I will send men that way to put her in protective custody. But more than that, this whole thing is bigger than me; I need your help. I'm on my way to the Cezaevi to pick up Rossi. I could sure use some backup. I don't know who I can trust anymore. And if you want to work with me on this corruption case, I'm more than happy to share the collar."

"I'll help you, but this collar is yours. I'll meet you at the Cezaevi in twenty minutes."

"Thank you, sir."

The Chief stopped at his sergeant's desk on the way to his assigned vehicle.

"Sergeant." The man stood at attention.

"Yes, sir."

"Who gave the order to have Haleh Ersoy arrested." The sergeant looked down at his desk.

"I received a call from Judge Borg, sir."

"Since when does Judge Borg give the orders around here?"

"He is a judge, sir."

"Are you on his payroll?" The sergeant puffed out his chest with indignation.

"No, sir"

"I need you to tell officers Sahin and Korkmaz to pull over in the nearest parking lot. They are to wait for a car from the downtown district to pick up their prisoner."

"But sir, what about the judge?"

"If he calls again, tell him you have ordered your men to pick her up, nothing more. If he argues, have him call me."

"Yes sir."

"Call me with their location."

Captain Demir grabbed two of his officers coming on shift, men he felt he could trust.

"I need you to head toward the 72nd precinct. One of you give me your cell phone number. Do not answer any radio calls or respond to any requests for your location. I will call you with an address to meet one of their patrol cars. You are to take custody of their prisoner. Bring her back here, through the secure Sallyport. Take her directly to an interrogation room and stay inside with her. She is in protective custody. I don't care who orders you to do differently; you do not leave her side or hand her to anyone else. Is that clear?"

"Yes sir."

"I will call you with the location of the pickup."

"Yes sir."

# THE PROMISE

# CHAPTER NINE

Chief Bozkurt called Demir with the location of his officers. Demir, in turn, called his men and reiterated the necessity to protect Mrs. Ersoy.

Twenty minutes later, Demir was at the Cezaevi. He pulled into a parking spot reserved for law enforcement. Demir waited until the chief pulled in and got out to meet him.

"Do you have the order from Judge Bulut with you, Captain?"

"Yes sir."

"Give it to me." The captain hesitated, taking a long look at him, then handed it over, following him through the gate.

Chief Bozkurt walked into the administrative offices of the Cezaevi like he owned it. He told the sergeant at the visitor's registration desk to take him to Warden Tekin's office. He ordered the two guards to stay where they were and not to make any calls. He asked Demir to stay there and make sure of it. Luckily, it wasn't visiting hours, so no civilians were in the lobby.

The sergeant used his key code to take Chief Bozhurt into the prison proper and up to the warden's office. Chief Bozkurt didn't wait to be announced; instead, he walked right in with the sergeant in tow.

"Warden, I would like to know how long you have been on Judge Borg and Mateo Borg's payroll." The warden stood up as if horrified at the accusation.

"I am no such thing, Chief."

"I can get your telephone records, Warden. I have no doubt they will show a call from Captain Demir about coming for prisoner Rossi. My guess is your next call was to Judge Borg."

Tekin sat down hard in his chair; his male secretary was standing in the doorway. Bozhurt turned to him.

"Get Assistant Warden Yildiz in here, now!"

"Warden, who else is on the payroll?" The warden looked at him then glanced over to the sergeant. The assistant warden came in as the chief slammed his hand on the desk, hard. Everyone in the room jumped. "Who else, Warden?"

"The sergeant and the captain of the guards." The chief turned to the assistant warden. "Arrest the warden, the sergeant, and the captain of the guards and take them downstairs."

Bozhurt turned back to the warden, "I want to know where Emir Rossi is?" Tekin looked at his sergeant. The chief turned to him. "Where is he?" Assistant Warden Yildiz spoke up, but Bozhurt kept his eyes on the sergeant.

"The warden had the captain of the guards put him in isolation in the basement a few hours ago."

"He better be alive!" The chief said. He asked Yildiz to call in one of his guards to get Rossi out of isolation. "Have him brought downstairs for transport."

"Sir, I can't just release a convicted felon." The chief showed him the order from Judge Bulut. After reading it, he complied with the chief's orders. Assistant Warden Yildiz cuffed the sergeant and Warden Tekin and marched them downstairs.

Emir Rossi was brought up in chains twenty minutes later. The chief requested transportation for the warden, sergeant, and captain of the guards. Yildiz asked where Chief Bozhurt wanted them transported.

"The 72nd precinct," he turned to the prisoners. "If you tell me what you know about the Borg's criminal activities and confess to your part in it. I will ask the prosecutor to give you a deal."

"Sir, what about Rossi. Where do you want him transported?" Yildiz asked.

"He will go with Captain Demir to the Downtown District."

The assistant warden handed Chief Bozhurt papers to sign for the men he was transferring. Then went to Captain Demir to sign for Emir Rossi.

After securing the Rossi home, Luke went to pick up Sophie and Jael at Deniz's home. Mr. Kaya answered the door and greeted him inviting him in.

"Mr. Star, how nice to see you again. Please come in; we just sat down for the evening meal. Please join us." Luke knew it would be rude to refuse, so he agreed to stay. Sophie ran over to hug him.

"Daddy, what happened?" Luke shushed her and said he would tell her later. Jael appeared.

"Where is my aunt?" Luke knelt down in front of her.

"She will be fine. Don't worry," Luke tried to calm her, but Jael started crying.

Luke hugged Jael and told her his friend was getting Haleh released. Jael calmed down, and Mr. Kaya directed them to the kitchen.

Luke pulled into his driveway an hour later; Sophie and Jael went straight to Sophie's bedroom. Luke called David and Jonathan and asked them to come over. David said he would bring Anna. He called Lance next.

"Hello?"

"Lance, can you come over?"

"Luke, I just got off the phone with Captain Demir. He wants me to drive by the print shop to see if Mateo is there. Then he wants me to take Haleh somewhere safe."

"He has Haleh?"

"Yes, he intercepted the arresting officers before they got to the 72nd."

"Are they getting ready to arrest Mateo and his crew?"

"Yes, Pam is going to stake out the print shop with me until they can get a raid organized."

"Alright. Keep us in the loop while it's going down. And be safe."

"10-4 on that." Luke hung up and made himself a cup of coffee. He pulled the muffins he bought from the commissary off the shelf to share with his guests.

Lance and Pam pulled into the lot next to the shop. They saw the same black SUVs in the parking lot behind the print shop. Lance called the captain.

"Alo?"

"Captain Demir, the crew is here."

"Thank you, Agent Marquez."

"I'll stay here while you get your men ready. I'll let you know if anyone leaves."

"Teşekkürler."

After Lance hung up with Demir, he reached between the seats for something in the back. He could smell a soft fragrance of lavender. He took a deep breath; embarrassed, he hoped she hadn't noticed.

"I brought a lite snack for you this time, Pam."

"Really?" Lance handed her a small bag. She opened it. "Oh, you're kidding me; how on earth did you know I loved these cookies. I buy them at the Cookie Place in the PX mall, on occasion. It's my guilty pleasure." She laughed at herself and turned her head to smile at him. Pam reached into the bag and brought out a large chocolate cookie. She bit through thick chocolate icing, a layer of marshmallow, and the rich cookie. She closed her eyes and gave a soft sigh.

Lance watched her reaction and chuckled. She reached out the bag to him.

"Would you like one?" He shook his head. "How could you possibly know how much I love these?"

"I'm an agent with CID. What do you think I do all day, government business? No, I find out things about you." They both chuckled. She took another bite. She wrapped the cookie back in the wax paper holder and slipped it back in the bag.

"I'll save the rest for later," she said after wiping her mouth with a napkin.

"Pam, Major Scott, and a few of his friends have a BBQ every Sunday after church. Would you like to go with me next time?"

"I can't just crash someone's BBQ."

"You won't be, I have an open invitation."

"Lance, I don't date men who already have girlfriends. I know you and Sally have been dating. It's office gossip."

"I appreciate that Pam, but Sally and I are no longer dating."

Before Pam could respond. The Turkish equivalent to SWAT pulled up. Captain Demir and the lead sergeant for the CAT team stepped out of the command vehicle. The sergeant quietly ordered his men to surround the place. Captain Demir stepped over to Lance's SUV.

"Do you know how many men are inside?"

"The few times we staked the place out, there were two bodyguards, Mateo and Dupuis. But I didn't see them enter, so there could be more."

"Thank you, Agent Marquez?"

Captain Demir went over to the sergeant. They made their decision to breach; they did not knock or identify themselves. They just rammed the back door and started yelling orders in Turkish. Orders every law enforcement officer understood in any language.

Lance and Pam watched as the action unfurled. Twenty minutes later, the Polis walked out with four handcuffed men and led them to a waiting prisoner transport van.

Captain Demir came out behind them and ordered one of the CAT officers to stand by the door to record everyone who entered. Then he walked to another Van and spoke with the driver. Five men wearing what looked like Dupont Disposable Bunny Suits followed him back. They carried boxes to haul out the shop's content. They stopped at the door and put on booties and gloves.

Lance stepped out of the vehicle to get Demir's attention. Demir met him halfway.

"Sir, when will you release Emir Rossi?"

"Agent Marquez, it will take a day or two to sort this out with a new prosecutor. I will push for him to be released as soon as an indictment comes down for Judge Borg. We can't arrest Judge Borg without it. I believe Judge Bulut will be convinced by that point that it was a wrongful prosecution."

"You can't let Rossi stay in custody. He is in the most danger now. Mateo and the judge will think by killing him, it will be a signal to the others to keep their mouths shut and your case will fall apart."

"I understand. I will house Rossi with me; he won't be without protection. But you can go pick up Haleh Ersoy now if you like. I will call the men I have protecting her and have them meet you outside the Sallyport." Captain Demir extended his hand to Lance. "Thank you for this. I have seen the corruption in our ranks for years, but I have never had an opportunity to do anything about it. Thanks to you and the others, I hope this will be a good start to cleaning it up."

"You took all the risks, Captain. Thank you."

After maneuvering around the Polis vehicles, Lance called Luke.

"Lance?"

"Yeah, Luke. Captain Demir and his men raided the Print Shop. I'm on my way to pick up Haleh."

"What about Emir?"

"Demir said it could take days for his release. They are still waiting for an indictment to pick up Judge Borg. I'll tell you all about it when I get there."

"Great."

At Luke's, David, Anna, and Jonathan had come to adjust their original plans. Sophie and Jael came out to talk to Luke.

"Daddy, what's going to happen to Jael and her aunt."

"Lance is on his way to pick up Haleh, now. They will be here soon."

"My aunt's coming here?" Jael asked, excited.

"Yes, Jael, she should be here shortly," Luke answered.

"What about her dad?" Sophie asked.

"We are working on that, Sophie. Why don't you and Jael get a snack from the kitchen and go do your homework."

After Luke had made coffee for everyone, they sat in the living room.

"We obviously have to make some adjustments to our plans now. I have no doubt that Judge Borg will do everything he can to eliminate Emir and his family. If he gets rid of the witnesses, anyone with knowledge of his criminal activities will know to keep their mouths shut." David said.

"What about the prosecutor, Yükse?" Jonathan asked.

"He won't be back until Saturday. He hasn't been arrested yet. The judge may try to contact him; threaten him to keep his mouth shut," Luke answered.

"That's going to be a problem. Judge Bulut wants his statement to support his motion to reverse Rossi's conviction," Jonathan said. Luke stood up and looked through the window when he heard a car door slam outside. It was Lance; he went to open the door.

Pam stepped out of the passenger side and opened the back door for Haleh. When she recognized Luke, she smiled and rushed to him.

"Mr. Star, my niece, is she here?"

"Jael is with Sophie in her bedroom," Luke called out for them. The bedroom door opened, and Jael saw her aunt. She ran over, wrapped her arms around her, and cried.

The others in the room stood and waited. When Jael let go of Haleh, Anna moved over to her and smiled.

"Mrs. Ersoy, please come and sit down. We have a lot to discuss." Anna directed her to the loveseat. Luke went to the kitchen to get her a cup of tea. Jael sat down next to her aunt. Sophie sat on the floor in front of the loveseat, using it to rest her back.

Luke handed her a cup of hot water and a teabag. Haleh took his hand.

"Mr. Star, thank you for keeping Jael out of the orphanage," her voice broke.

"Your welcome," Luke gave her a minute to compose herself. "Let me introduce the others." After introductions, Anna spoke again.

"Mrs. Ersoy..." Haleh interrupted her.

"Please call me Haleh."

"Haleh, we are going to have to move fast. Now that Mateo Borg is in custody, he and his brother will do everything they can to stop Emir from testifying. You are the leverage they will use."

"I understand; I told Mr. Star that we are willing to leave everything and go to my brothers. Nothing matters but Jael's safety." Jael scooted closer to her aunt.

David leaned forward on the chair, putting his forearms on his thighs. "Haleh, our plan is to separate you and Jael and get you to Izmir by different routes. When Emir is released, he will meet up with us there. Then we will get you all to Germany together."

"No, I don't want to go without my aunt!" Jael exclaimed.

Anna moved to sit on the arm of the loveseat next to Jael. "Jael, you won't be alone. You, Sophie, Duke, CJ, and I will all take the train. Your aunt will be safe with David and Jonathan. They will drive her to meet us."

"What about my dad?"

"Luke and Lance will transport him to Izmir as soon as he is released." Jael looked at Sophie. Sophie got up and squeezed in next to her.

"Jael, my dad, and Lance won't let anything happen to your dad. I promise," Sophie said. Jael nodded.

"When will we go?" Haleh asked.

"We had reservations on the train for Saturday, but we will change them to tomorrow," David said. "Have you called your brother yet to let him know you are coming?"

"No, when Mr. Star came to tell me what you planned, the Polis showed up before I could." David handed her his cell phone, and she moved to the kitchen to make the call.

When Haleh was done with the call, she came back to the living room.

"I told my brother all that has happened. He wants us to come as soon as possible," Haleh said. Anna went to her.

"You must be exhausted. You can stay at my house tonight. We'll leave in the morning."

"Can Jael stay with me tonight?" Sophie asked Haleh.

"If it is alright with your father."

"Yes, if that's what she wants, she is more than welcome to stay here."

Jael whispered to her aunt, "I have no clothes." Haleh closed her eyes and bowed her head, sorry for all that Jael was losing because of this. Sophie spoke up.

"My clothes will fit you." Sophie smiled and got up to go to her bedroom. Jael hugged her aunt one more time and followed.

"Some of my clothes should fit you, Haleh," Anna offered, moving to the door.

"We will make sure you are taken care of," David moved over to the door to give his wife the keys.

"You take the car, sweetheart. Jonathan and I will walk when we are done here." Anna kissed his cheek and escorted Haleh out. David watched them get in the car and closed the door.

"David. Duke, and CJ are willing to help with this?" Luke asked.

"I promised Duke he would have a say in any future missions that involved our family. We discussed Anna going with Jael; Duke agreed but insisted he go with her. I think he feels if anything happens, at least they would be together. And CJ won't let Duke go without him."

"Zoey is a little upset she can't help, but with Ruby gone, there is no one to watch Liam," Jonathan said.

"So we're set for tomorrow, right? Luke and I will take those going to the train in the morning. Then Jonathan and I will head out with Haleh." David said.

"I'll map out a route tonight. We'll stay off the main roads as much as we can," Jonathan said.

"My dad is arranging a safe house for us in Izmir. He has a contact in Cesme that will take the family across the Aegean Sea to Rafina, Greece. Once there, he will have a contact pick them up and put them on a plane to Germany." David turned to Lance. "How long do you think we will have to wait for Emir?"

"It depends on if Yükse is more afraid of Judge Borg or Captain Demir. Judge Bulut said he needed the prosecutor's confession. Otherwise, he wouldn't be comfortable overturning Judge Borg's findings on Rossi's case. Without the prosecutor's confession, Judge Borg will never be convicted. Which means his conviction against Rossi will stand," Luke explained.

"We need to pray God intervenes," Pam said.

"Ok, we'll wait as long as we can. There are no trials until Wednesday next week. I'll contact Colonel Zimmerman, let him know we will need off tomorrow and Monday. I don't think he will have any reason to object.

### Friday

Luke was up and dressed by 7:30 am; he wanted to make sure the girls could have breakfast before leaving. He knocked on Sophie's door and opened it. The girls were up, a stack of clothes piled on the bed. Sophie turned to him when he opened the door.

"Daddy, we can't get everything in Jael's backpack."

"I see that." Luke knew when Sophie offered Jael her clothes that she wouldn't give her last year's clothes. She had some of her favorites from this year's school clothes her mom sent on the bed for Jael. "I have a small duffle. I'll get it, and we can let Jael's aunt take it in the SUV with her."

"That's a great idea. But I have that cute pink duffle; Jael can have it." Sophie ran to her closet to get it. She handed it to Jael. Jael stopped and looked at all the things Sophie was giving away.

"Sophie, I can't take all this. Some of it has never been worn. It's not right."

"It will hurt my feelings if you don't take it. I will think you don't like my clothes," Sophie said. Jael bowed her head and cried. Sophie put her arm around her.

"Thank you, Sophie. You are such a good friend, and now I will never see you again."

"We can always call and Skype," Sophie said.

"Sophie, I want you two to hurry so you can have breakfast. We have to be at the train station at 9:45. I'll fix pancakes." Luke started to leave.

"Daddy, you have to fix mine and Jael's hair in a French braid, so we can look the same." She took the little stool from her vanity and moved it to the edge of the bed.

"Alright, I'll do yours first." He sat on the bed and spoke to Jael. "Jael, only take the things you need for a couple of days in your backpack. Put the rest in the duffle. And I want you guys to take some things to keep you busy on the train." They both nodded, and Sophie sat on the stool.

After fixing both girls' hair, making sure they had matching barrettes, Luke headed to the door to make pancakes.

"Mr. Luke. Are you going to get my dad out of prison?"

Luke walked back to her and knelt in front of her.

"Jael, I am going to do my best. But I know one thing, he would want you to be safe at your uncle's house in Germany." Jael nodded her head.

# CHAPTER TEN

**Friday 9:30 am**

The group met at the Migros Supermarket's parking lot a block away from the train station. They didn't want to draw any attention to themselves. It was likely Borg would have men watching. Their expectation was they would overlook an American mother with a group of kids. Sophie and Jael wore similar ball caps and clothes to give the illusion of twins or at least sisters.

When Luke pulled into the lot, David's SUV was already there. Luke stepped out and opened the back door for the kids to get out and grabbed the pink duffle out of the back. David and the others stepped out of the other SUV. Jael went to her aunt and spoke in Turkish.

"Tyze, can you come with us?"

"No, tatlim, we must travel separately, so they do not find us." Haleh bent down to be face to face with Jael. "I love you so much. There is no reason to be afraid. I would not let you go with Miss Anna if I did not trust her. She will take good care of you. I will meet you in Izmir." Haleh hugged her tight.

Luke, David, and Jonathan formed a small circle. "I have to go back to Base and get some money from the bank," David said.

"I gave Jael and Sophie all the lira and dollars I had on me," Luke said, then handed David the pink duffle Sophie gave Jael.

"Luke, Mateo's men are going to be hunting Emir once they find out he is released. Will you need more help? Do you want me to go with you? David said he will be alright on his own," Jonathan asked.

"No, Lance is mapping out a route off the main highways as much as possible; I think we can handle it."

"We did the same. I know you don't have any idea how long it will be until Emir is released." David handed Luke a cell phone. "This is a secure line. Anna and I have one too. We will be able to communicate without worrying about it being tracked."

Luke went to Haleh and handed her the passport he took from her nightstand. He gave Jael's passport to Anna to carry for her.

After goodbyes, Anna and the kids grabbed their backpacks and headed to the station.

Lance was in the viewing room at the Downtown District watching the interview of Mateo Borg. They spoke in Turkish, so he was missing a lot with his limited understanding of the language. One thing, however, was universal, and that was body language.

"How did you come in possession of these Bearer Bonds?" Demir asked while placing one in front of Mateo.

"They were in the shop when I bought the confiscated property.

"So, you are saying that Mr. Rossi is a forger?" Mateo shrugged.

"How would I know."

"Do not be ridiculous, Mr. Borg. The other man we arrested with you is the most infamous forger in the world. So you are saying that it is a coincidence he is working for you?"

"He is an old friend. He came to see the new business I started."

"Exactly what business is that Mr. Borg?" Mateo didn't answer. "Listen, you can play games, or you can try to shave some time off your sentence. It's up to you. Only your brother is going to believe that lame story. And since he was just indicted and arrested, he won't be able to be the judge for your trial. And Yükse will not be the prosecutor. We will be arresting him too."

"Look, I bought that business fair and square. The State arrested Mr. Rossi for printing seditious materials and confiscated his property. I paid the State a fair price for the business. If you want to illude something about that was fishy, you need to talk to the State. Now, I want my lawyer," Mateo said with a smirk. Captain Demir told the officer guarding him to bring Mateo a phone.

Captain Demir walked into the viewing room. "Prosecutor Emine Özkan has to get Mateo and Dupuis before a Judge shortly. I'm not sure he can convince a Judge that Mateo should be held in custody until the trial. The same with Judge Borg. Dupuis, however, we will be able to hold. I do not know how long. Venezuela is the only one with a warrant out for Dupuis. They are going to want us to extradite him unless we make a deal with another country."

"If they release Mateo and his men, they will leave the country. And what about Prosecutor Yükse? You don't even have him in protective custody. They will kill him before you can even get his statement," Lance said.

"I know, Agent Marquez. I have my men trying to locate Yükse now. One of his friends must know where he went. His office said they were told he was going to his sister's wedding, but our records indicate he has no sister."

"Can you convince Judge Bulut to release Emir now so we can get a head start?"

"No. Not without a statement from Yükse corroborating our theory. He needs to say he was paid off or threatened in some way to prosecute Rossi."

"When will you interrogate Dupuis?"

"Now."

Lance saw Dupuis enter the same interrogation room Mateo was just escorted out of after his call. A Polis officer stood inside the door.

Lance watched as Demir entered the room with a thick file, slapped it onto the table, and then sat down.

"Mr. Dupuis, you are 'a person of interest' in forgery cases in many countries."

"Being 'a person of interest' is not a crime," Dupuis sat back in his chair, relaxed. They were speaking English since Dupuis did not speak Turkish. Demir opened the file.

"Well, I have been informed Venezuela has a warrant out for your arrest. Apparently, you forged a quitclaim deed for a corrupt general a few years ago. The general has been arrested and offered you up for a lighter sentence." Lance saw Dupuis squirm at the new information.

"You are going to do time somewhere. There is nothing I can do about that. BUT! I can decide who to extradite you to for trial. I can also negotiate what prison you go to."

Dupuis lifted his head, "what would you want from me in exchange."

"I need to know if you were complicit in the false arrest of Mr. Rossi. And I want to hear what you know about Judge Borg's part in it. Then you can tell me why Mateo hired you."

"I will cooperate. But for my cooperation, I want to be extradited to the United States. I also want a promise I will do my time at the Oxford Federal Correctional Institution in Wisconsin. I like the programs they have there. Also, they will have to convince Venezuela to let me do my time for that crime in the US. Now, I want an attorney to make sure you keep your word." Dupuis knew there was no way out of this. He'd known for a long time this could happen, and it would be over for him. His client list would be his ticket to the concessions he wanted in the US.

"You will have to admit to a crime in the United States, then I believe I can get you what you want." With that promise, Demir ordered the officer to give Dupuis a phone and left the room.

Lance stepped out of the viewing room to meet him. "Captain, if he has firsthand knowledge, will Judge Bulut accept that?"

"I'm not sure. Judge Bulut might require Yükse to corroborate any statement Dupuis makes. As soon as Dupuis's attorney gets here, I will bring the prosecutor down to negotiate a deal. He will have to stay with us until he testifies in the Borg trials. Then we will turn him over to your JAG office with the stipulation that your country meets his demand after the trial."

"I have no doubt my country will be happy to do so. But Demir, we need Mateo and the judge held for a few days so we can get Emir and his family out of the country."

"I'll talk to the prosecutor," Demir said.

Anna had everyone settled in their compartment. It was larger than she imagined and had a picture window next to a cafeteria-style booth that converts into a bed. Over the top was another pulldown bed. Off to one side was a table that came down from the wall and two comfortable chairs, one of them reclined slightly. She chose that one to sit in.

The kids were playing the travel-size Chinese Checkers game Anna stuffed in her backpack. She made sure they were the last ones to get on the train, watching for anyone suspicious. There were men on the platform that resembled the ones David told her to look out for, but they didn't get on the train.

Anna and the kids had been on the train for two hours. Their first stop was at Konya, which was still two hours away. The boys won the first few games of Chinese checkers. They started a new game, Duke was lined up against Sophie, and CJ was lined up against Jael. Anna enjoyed listening to the kid's loud banter. She watched as Duke set up his marbles across the board. Anna saw him making it easy for Sophie to get her first marble in his triangle by lining up his marbles. When Sophie saw her opportunity to jump all his marbles, she laughed with glee. Duke smiled. Anna kept Duke's little kindness a secret.

"Mom, we're hungry," Duke said.

"Alright," she opened her wallet and pulled out a stack of lira. "Go to the restaurant car and buy sandwiches and pop for everyone."

"Can we get chips too?" CJ asked.

"Sure. On the way, notice the people you go by. Do you remember dad's description of the men to look for?"

"Yes." Duke and CJ headed to the door when Sophie piped up.

"I want to go." Anna moved over to her.

"I'm sorry, Sophie. You and Jael need to stay hidden. No one is looking for two boys." Sophie sat back down.

"I'm sorry you have to stay here with me, Sophie," Jael said, her head bowed.

"I'm not. I'd rather be with you than Duke and CJ." Sophie laughed.

**11:30 am**

Lance had taken a break but was back at the Downtown District at 11:30 am; Luke stayed away. They agreed one of them needed to remain unseen. Captain Demir's men found District attorney Yükse at his mistress's house one town over. He didn't like being summoned back to the district. The officers put him in an interrogation room, which was the first time he knew of a problem. Captain Demir walked in a few minutes later. Bassavci Emine Özkan stepped in behind him. They sat across from Yükse.

"Savci Yükse, do you recognize the name, Emir Rossi? Demir spoke in Turkish.

"Evet, I..." The Bassavci broke in.

"What you did, Savci Yükse is wait until I was out of town for a few days. Then you colluded with Judge Borg to prosecute Emir Rossi and confiscate his shop. You knew there was no way I would approve a sedition charge using the Bible as the basis for it. It was nonsense, and you know it." Bassavci Özkan stood up and slammed his hands down on the table in front of Yükse. Yükse's arrogant demeanor changed. His shoulders slumped, and his face turned ashen.

"But Bassavci, I was threatened..." Captain Demir kept quiet and let the Bassavci do his work for him.

"Don't give me that. This is not the first time I have questioned your actions. Now I am warning you. If you do not cooperate with Captain Demir, I will make sure you will spend the rest of your life in prison. Do you understand me?"

"But if I confess to collusion, I will lose my right to practice law."

"Oh, Savci Yükse, I promise you this. You will never practice again in Turkey whether I charge you or not."

Savci Yükse slouched in his chair, weighing up his options. "Alright. What do you want me to do?"

David and Jonathan were on the road with Haleh. After stopping on Base to go to the bank, David drove in circles for ten minutes to make sure no one followed them. They had at least a

12-hour drive ahead of them, and that was not including stops to eat and gas up.

"Mr. Scott, have you heard when they will release Emir?" Haleh asked.

"No, but maybe it's time to call Lance. Jonathan, can you make the call?" Jonathan dialed.

Lance saw Jonathan's name on the caller ID. "Jonathan, I can't talk right now. Let me call you back."

Lance brought his attention back to the interrogation room. Captain Demir and Bassavci Özkan left Yükse with an officer and went into the hall. Lance met them there. When he stepped up, Özkan stopped talking.

"Bassavci Özkan this is Agent Lance Marquez from CID at Incirlik Air Base. He is the one who brought this travesty to my attention." Özkan nodded and switched from Turkish to English.

"Captain, please call Judge Bulut. I will recommend Rossi's conviction be overturned. With Dupuis and Yükse confessions of collusion, I don't see how he will have a choice. Can we meet again in the morning?"

Lance spoke up. "Sir, I apologize for interrupting, but we need to get Mr. Rossi out of Turkey as soon as possible. Mateo Borg is in custody now, but he will likely be released until his trial. And I have no doubt he has his men out looking to kidnap his family so Emir will not testify against him."

"That is true, Bassavci. And Judge Borg has Polis on his payroll along with unscrupulous criminals. His reach goes further than his brothers. They will go all out hunting Rossi's daughter. Once they have her, they can control the aunt and Emir," Captain Demir added.

Özkan shook his head. "I had no idea we had such corruption right under our nose." He looked at Demir, "how quickly can you get Judge Bulut here, Captain?"

"I'll call him right now."

Luke pulled into an Orhan Pharmacy parking lot two blocks south of the Downtown District, waiting for instructions from Lance. His phone rang.

"Hello."

"Hey Luke, where are you?"

"I'm two blocks down from the precinct."

"Good. Bassavci Özkan interrogated Yükse himself. Yükse confessed to everything. Captain Demir is calling Judge Bulut to come right away. Once he hears Yükse and Dupuis's confessions, Ozkan will recommend Emir be released.

"So it was the Chief Prosecutor who the captain brought in? That's great. How long do you think it will be before we can get Emir out of here?"

"Maybe two hours. I have the clothes you gave me for him. I'll ask the captain if Emir can use the Polis officer's locker room to clean up and change."

"See if he will let you take him out the back through the Sallyport. I'll find a spot not covered by cameras and wait for you there."

"Sounds like a plan. Will you call David. I promised him I'd call back."

"Sure."

Lance hung up, and Luke called David, filling him in on everything Lance told him.

**1:15 pm**

Luke's phone rang, but before he could say hello, Lance spoke.

"Luke, where are you?"

"Did you come out the back?"

"Yes."

"Go east one and a half blocks. I'm parked on the street across from a store with T-shirts hanging outside. There is a Souvlaki cart on the street next to it. The men are fighting because the smell of the Souvlaki is infusing his shirts."

"We see you." The two men hurried into the SUV. Luke turned to Emir and spoke first.

"Mr. Rossi, I'm happy to finally meet you. My name is Luke Star." Emir shook Luke's extended hand.

"Thank you, but who are you people, and where are you taking me?"

"We'll tell you all about it once we get out of town. I need you to lay down on the back seat, so the cameras don't pick you up in this vehicle." Luke started the SUV and headed out of town.

Emir laid down in the back seat as instructed. He had no idea how he was out of prison or where he was going. Finally, he spoke again.

"Please, tell me what is going on."

"Didn't Captain Demir explain everything to you?" Lance asked.

"No. Yesterday before breakfast, the captain of the guard placed me in solitary confinement. I had no idea what I had done to deserve it. I did my best to stay out of trouble. I asked, but he wouldn't answer. Then hours later, another guard brought me up to the entrance and handed me over to Captain Demir. I've been with him since. A few minutes ago, they handed me over to you, and I walked out of the precinct."

"I'm sorry, Emir, I had no idea Captain Demir didn't explain things to you," Lance said, asking Luke to explain.

"Monday was the first day of the American-Turkish Sister School week. My daughter Sophie and your daughter became partners.

Sophie came home upset because the boys at school were picking on Jael. My daughter told me it was because her dad was in prison for printing Bibles. She wanted me to help her.

"I told her I would look into it. When I did, I found that there was some corruption going on. My friends and I went to Captain Demir and Judge Bulut. Together we set out to make things right."

"Haleh told me someone was trying to help, but I told her Judge Borg would take Jael from us. I only wanted to get her to safety," Emir stated.

"Well, God had other plans. Without His intervention, none of this would have happened." Luke looked at the rearview mirrors making sure no one was following them. He heard Emir behind him praying and thanking God in his native language.

"Luke, I need to call Jonathan and tell him we are on the road."

"But what about my family. Mateo will come after them?" Emir suddenly sat up, afraid.

"Lay down, Emir. Your family is safe for now. Haleh is on the road already heading for Izmir," Lance said. Luke lifted the center console to take out the secure cell for Lance to use.

"What about my daughter?"

"She is on the train with another group. We are all going to meet in Izmir."

"Hello?"

"Jonathan, I'm putting you on speaker."

"Same here, Lance, go ahead."

"We have Emir, and we are trying to get out of town."

Lance could hear the voices on the phone break out in thanks to God. He couldn't help but be touched by it.

"That's great news. Tell us what happened today," David asked. Lance gave a play-by-play account. He told about the interrogation by the Bassavci of Yükse and recapped what Dupuis gave up to Demir.

"You should have heard the Chief Prosecutor tear into Yükse. Captain Demir called in Judge Bulut to hear the confessions firsthand. After hearing them, Bulut signed an order to overturn the findings and released Emir."

Haleh's voice in the background could barely be heard. "May I speak to my brother?" Lance took it off speaker and handed the secure line to Emir. Haleh and Emir cried and prayed and thanked God for a long time before Emir finally handed back the phone to Lance.

"Jonathan, are you still on the line?" Putting the cell back on speaker.

"Yeah, I'm here, Lance."

"Where are you?"

"We've been on the road for almost two hours now. We're on E90; we were slowed down by construction. Are you going that route?"

"I don't see any way around it. Do you?"

"No."

"Ok, we'll keep in touch—one more thing. Captain Demir warned me before we left that Judge Borg has a long reach, not just criminals; he has Polis on his payroll too. He knows if he has Jael, Haleh and Emir will not testify against him and his brother." Emir shot up when he heard that.

"Is my Jael in danger?"

"We accounted for that, and we have backup plans if something goes wrong. Emir, I know this has to be hard, but you'll have to trust us. My daughter, David's wife and son, and Jonathan's son are all on the same train with your daughter. We all have a lot at stake here." Luke said while switching from lane to lane, trying to get through the construction on E90.

Emir laid on his side on the back seat, bending his left arm and putting it under his head. The stress of the last six months had taken a toll on him. He constantly fought to overcome the anger of being unjustly prosecuted. At night in prison, he slept in short burst in case a cellmate came too close. A maximum-security prison is a nightmare. Emir took a deep breath and slid into the first sound sleep he'd gotten in months.

# THE PROMISE

# CHAPTER ELEVEN

**2:30 pm**

Anna sat in the recliner and kept an eye on her watch. The train would be making its first stop shortly. She checked her secure cell to see if she had any bars; none. She could probably get a few bars if she went to one of the other train cars, but she didn't want to leave the kids. David and Jonathon worked missions without Anna at times. But Anna had not worked a mission alone except for Syria, and now. She knew David was anxious about it, but this time they were in the same country. She rechecked her watch.

The kids played all the travel games she brought and even the ones Sophie had stuck in her backpack.

"Duke, I need you to close the curtain. The train will be stopping soon at Konya," Anna instructed.

"But Aunt Annie, I want to watch the people on the platform," Sophie said, the others agreed.

"Sophie, if you can see them, they can see you. We need to keep Jael hidden." Anna stepped over to the window and helped Duke close the curtain. Sophie nodded her understanding.

"Duke, when the train stops, I want you to watch for the porter to step out of the caboose to help the passengers. Once he's off, you and CJ go to the back platform and watch everyone who gets on this train. You know who to look for. Come back when the train starts moving again. Understand?"

"Yeah, mom, we get it."

The train stopped on time, and the boys rushed to the caboose. They watched until everyone had boarded the train and went back to their compartment.

"What did you see?" Anna asked.

"No one that looked like enforcers," CJ said.

"There was a Polis officer by the ticket office door. He was taking notes; it looked like a woman may have had something stolen." Duke added while heading back to the door.

"Where are you going?" Anna asked.

"I need to go to the bathroom." The others said they need to go too.

"Ok. I'll stand by the bathroom. You go one at a time." Anna opened the door and looked both ways. The bathroom was on the opposite side of the aisle at the end of the train car. Duke walked out, and Anna followed, keeping an eye out for anyone coming through.

Finally, everyone had a turn, including her. "Alright, I think it would be a good idea for you all to take a nap."

"Mom. A nap? What are we two years old." Duke complained, standing up raising his arms over his head to stretch out his muscles.

"I want you guys rested and alert." She pulled down the top bunk and grabbed some pillows and blankets from the small closet in the room.

The boys figured out how to put down the table and moved the cushions to form the bed. Anna handed them some pillows and blankets too. The girls used a step built into the side of the booth to get to the top bunk.

It only took a few minutes for the kids to all be sound asleep. Anna closed her eyes.

Luke had been driving now for a few hours. Everyone had put to memory the route the train was taking. All of them had a stake in the safe arrival of the precious cargo on board. The train would have stopped at Konya and gone on its way by now.

"I think I will call Captain Demir. I know Borg and his men, including the judge, have to be arraigned sometime today. I want to know if they are going to be released," Lance said. He pulled out his private cell, made the call, and put it on speaker.

"Hello?"

"Captain Demir, Agent Marquez here. Luke and Emir are in the car with me, and you are on speaker. We wanted to know what happens once you bring the men before a judge."

"In a few hours Pierre Dupuis, Mateo Borg, and Judge Borg will be arraigned in the same session. Judge Bulut will be the presiding Judge. Normally an arrestee will be released until trial on a non-violent crime. However, the judge does have another option on cases involving more than one perpetrator. He can order them held for five days, allowing the prosecutor to have more time to collect evidence. That is what I hope will happen here. Bassavci Özkan said he plans on requesting the judge order the men to hand over their passports. And he wants them to wear a monitor when they are released. Dupuis will stay in custody until he testifies at the trials unless they take a plea deal. Then he will be handed over to the US via JAG. The US must first put in writing that they will honor their word to keep our deal made for his testimony."

"That sounds like you have this under control."

"Agent Marquez, my country takes corruption as seriously as yours does."

"I meant no disrespect, Captain. I just meant it was a bold and aggressive move on your and Bassavci's end."

"Indeed it is. I hope that gives you enough time to get Rossi and his family to safety. Unfortunately, I have no way of helping you once you are out of my district."

"I understand. You have stuck your neck out on this far enough, Captain. I hope it helps rather than hurts your career."

"Either way, it was the right thing to do. Let me know when you are back in town."

"I will. Good day, Captain."

"Be safe, Agent Marquez."

**4:45 pm**

It was quiet in the room when Sophie opened her eyes, with the curtain still drawn over the window. It threw a slightly grayish hue that made everything eerie looking. She turned to see that Jael was awake too. Sophie whispered to her.

"Are you sad that you have to leave your friends and your home in Adana, Jael?" Jael looked up at the ceiling, thinking about it.

"Not really. Without my dad, the house we lived in was not the same. And my friends all deserted me when they put my dad in prison." She turned to face Sophie, touching her hand. "All but you, Sophie," Jael smiled.

"I wish you could have met my best friend, Lizzy. She would have been your friend too."

"Where is she?"

"Her grandmother was sick; her family went to see her in Montana. She will be home soon, I hope."

"Is her grandmother better?"

"No. She died."

"I am sorry."

"Me too."

"I know your dad and his friends are trying to get my dad released. That is all I care about. I do not care where we have to live as long as we are together. But I will miss you." Jael sat up. Her head almost touched the ceiling on the compartment.

The girls heard movement underneath them. They looked over the side of the bed at the boys to see if they were awake. Then hopped off the bed when they saw Anna open her eyes.

"Auntie, can we go to the restaurant car to eat?" Sophie asked.

"We should be stopping at Eskisehir in about ten minutes. Once we are sure no suspicious men get on, we can all go eat in the restaurant car," Anna agreed. The kids all whooped their approval.

"I need to use the bathroom, mom," Duke said.

"Me too," CJ said.

"Me three," Sophie laughed.

"Me four," Jael giggled.

"Alright, you two boys can go. Girls, your hair is a mess. I will redo it; then I'll take you. Deal?" The girls looked at each other's hair.

"Deal."

The train stopped at Eskisehir. The boys watched from the caboose platform again. No suspicious persons boarded, so the small group went to eat in the restaurant car. The next stop was Usak. They would only be 138 miles from their destination at that point.

It was quiet in the SUV David was driving. Lance had reclined his seat and fallen asleep, and Haleh had laid down on the back seat and was sleeping too. David used the time to consider different scenarios of how this could end. He had a lot to lose. David's whole family was on that train, along with others he loved like his own.

David knew that all three routes taken would coalesce in Usak, taking them to Izmir. Maybe it would be wiser to get the kids and Anna off the train and travel together from there. At least they would be together if something went wrong. There was no indication that any of the Borg's men figured out where or by what route they were going,

On the other hand, being together meant that no one would be available to rescue the others if there was real trouble. David lifted his voice to God and prayed quietly, "Lord, only you know the right move. I cannot trust my own wisdom in this. Please direct us."

David decided to call Luke to find out their location. He used the secure line.

"Hello?" Luke and Lance switched seats at the last gas station.

"Hey Luke, I was checking to see where you are."

"The sign we passed a few minutes ago said we were about 50 miles from Eskisehir."

"That makes you about three and a half hours from Usak."

"That sounds about right," Luke said.

"You must have made good time."

"Yeah, we had to slow for construction, but we never had to stop."

"That's why you almost caught up to us. We got stopped by construction twice; one time we had to take a detour," David said.

"Where are you?"

"We're about thirty minutes ahead of you. Both our routes pass through Usak. Luke, I think we should travel together once we get to Usak."

"You sound concerned, David."

"I am. I've had a bad feeling the last couple of hours. I just can't put a name to it."

"Ok. We'll meet up in Usak."

**6 pm**

Anna enjoyed being with the kids eating in the dining car. When they got back to the sleeper car, Anna's watch showed they were only twenty minutes from Usak. She had a strange sense of urgency to be vigilant and prepared.

"Hey kids, why don't we get all our things back in our backpacks and clean up the room."

"Do we get off at the next stop, Auntie?" Sophie asked.

"No, but let's get it together anyway, alright?" The kids shrugged but did what she asked.

Twenty minutes later, the train slowed for the next stop. Duke closed the curtain.

"Ok. Duke, CJ, you know what to do."

"Yeah, mom. We'll watch the platform." Duke was young when Anna disappeared into Syria. When she returned, he found himself watching her to reacquaint himself with her non-verbal cues. He recognized her furrowed brows; she was worried.

"Mom, what's wrong?" She almost said 'nothing', but he would know she was lying, and it would hurt him.

"I don't know, sweetheart. I have a bad feeling. I know better than to ignore it."

"Don't worry, Mom. CJ and I are here to help you protect Jael." Anna wrapped her arms around him.

"I know, sweetheart."

Duke and CJ headed for the caboose's platform like before. There were lots of people waiting to get on the train. It was hard to see through the crowd. As the passengers got on, CJ saw two large men getting on the train. He poked Duke and pointed, "Luke, look." The men were dressed in dark dress slacks, collared polo shirts, and black leather jackets. The boys rushed back to the sleeper compartment.

"Mom, two men are getting on the train. We think they could be the men dad was talking about." Anna took a minute to decide what to do.

Lance was driving when his private cell rang.

"Hello?"

"Lance, I have some information you need to hear."

"Captain, I appreciate anything you can tell me. I'm putting you on speaker now. Luke and Emir are with me."

"By the time the Bassavci finished with Savci Yükse, he spilled everything he knew. He was still giving us information when you left. He gave me a list of officers on the take."

"That's bad news. But you expected that."

"Yes, but in the viewing room before Rossi was released, you mentioned you were heading to Izmir."

"I remember."

"When we opened the door, do you remember an officer was standing there?"

"Please don't tell me he was one of Mateo's men."

"He is, and he has access to Mateo's holding cell. When I saw him on the list, I got my hands on him. I threatened him with everything I could think of. He broke down and told me he took Mateo a burner cell earlier in the day. When he heard you say Izmir through the door, he told Mateo. Mateo ordered his men to take a helicopter to Usak; then, he hired some locals to get on the train and hunt for the girl. Everyone knows to get to Izmir from Adana; all roads go through Usak."

"Thank you, Captain. We will warn the others right away." When Lance hung up, Luke took the secure cell out to call Anna. When she didn't answer, he called David.

"David?"

"No, Luke. It's Jonathan; I'm going to put you on speaker." Luke did the same.

"What's up?" Lance told him everything the captain had said. David broke in.

"Luke, we'll call you back after we get ahold of Anna."

"Alright, we need to get off the train. Let's get to the caboose's platform. We'll get off on the opposite side of the train station, then hide in the bushes until the train is out of sight. Grab your stuff." Anna heard her cell ring, but there was no time to answer it.

Anna jumped off the platform first, then CJ. Jael sat on the edge, a little frightened.

"Jump, Jael. CJ and I will catch you," Anna said.

Sophie stepped over to the edge. Her eyes got big, and she got dizzy. She turned to Duke. "I can't do it, Duke." He understood.

"Come on, Sophie, we'll catch you," Anna said again.

"Mom, she can't. Sophie is afraid of heights; she won't even jump off the low board at the pool." Duke took her backpack and tossed it to CJ.

"Sophie, sit down and close your eyes. I'll put my arms under yours, and I will lower you down to Mom and CJ. They will grab your legs and take you to the ground." Sophie did as Duke said. She whispered to him.

"Thank you, Duke." They heard the conductor yell "gemideki herkes".

"Hurry," Anna stage whispered. "The train is getting ready to move. As Sophie's feet hit the dirt beneath her, the train jerked. CJ started running next to the train. Duke tossed his backpack off.

"Jump, Duke. Land on me." Duke jumped, landing on top of CJ. Both boys ended up rolling on the ground, laughing. Anna had moved the girls behind some bushes. As the boys headed back to meet up with them, they heard some men yell at them on the platform. It was the men who got on the train. The train was going too fast now for them to jump off. When they got to the bushes where the others were hiding, he told his mom.

"I need to call David." Anna led the kids across the tracks and up a steep incline. Duke grabbed Sophie's hand to help her up, and CJ held Jael's to help her. There was a small copse of trees next to the platform. "You stay here. I'm going to check out the surroundings. Don't move. Do you understand?"

"Yes Mom, we get it. But there is no way those men could know Jael is with us."

"Maybe not, but I can't take that chance. I have no doubt Judge Borg, if not Mateo, can find someone in town to look for us if they think she is." Anna took out the secure cell then handed her backpack to Duke. She moved to the road crossing the street to stand in front of a store, pretending to look in the display window. She used the window as a mirror to see behind her. Anna dialed David.

"Anna?"

"David, we have a problem. We think two of Mateo's men got on the train. We got off, but Duke says the men saw him and CJ."

"We know, Captain Demir called Lance and told him Mateo found out we were heading to Izmir. He sent men to intercept us in Usak. Where are you and the kids now?"

"The kids are hiding in some trees. I'm on the street across from the station."

"You need to get off the street." He lowered the phone and spoke to Jonathan, "Jonathan, get the map of Usak. We need to find somewhere they can hide." He lifted the phone to his ear again. "Hang on, Anna." Haleh scooted up between the front seats hearing there was a problem.

"Are they safe?"

"Anna had to get the kids off the train in Usak. We are going to pick them up," David responded.

David put Anna on speaker so that Jonathan could speak to her. "Anna, the station is on the Afyon circle. That must be where you are standing."

"Yes, it's a one-way street."

"Ok, walk against the traffic and turn on Istasyon Cd. About three-fourths of a mile down that road on the right is a church. You should be safe in there until we come," Jonathan finished the directions.

"Anna, we are about an hour and a half from where you are. Call me back when you are safely in the church."

"I will, David." Anna crossed the street and back to where the others were waiting.

"We are going to walk to a church about a mile down the road. David and Jonathan are coming for us."

Jonathan called Luke back and put him on speaker.

"Anna called; they had to get off the train. I sent them to a church in Usak to get them off the street. We need to pick them up."

"Ok, how do you want to do this?"

"We need to meet on the access road leading into town. I would guess we are still about a half-hour ahead of you. We will transfer Haleh to your vehicle and then go pick up Anna and the kids.

We'll want to find a spot on the way out of town to meet. We need to get out of town as soon as possible," Jonathan said.

"Alright, I see a spot on the map just off the freeway where we can meet to transfer Haleh." There was silence for a moment, then Luke spoke again. "It's an Opet gas station at the first exit into Usak, right off the freeway off-ramp."

"Have Mateo's men found my daughter?" Emir was frightened for his daughter. Luke could hear it in his voice.

Luke turned to him from the front passenger seat.

"No. Anna got them off the train. We are going to pick them up." Luke's attention went back to Jonathan on the phone.

"Ok, Luke, we will wait for you at the Opet."

They had been walking for ten minutes. Anna led the way. CJ held Jael's hand, and they were walking ahead of Duke, who was holding Sophie's hand. CJ saw a tear slide down Jael's cheek.

"What's the matter, Jael?" CJ asked.

"I'm scared." She looked up at him, "are those men going to take me away?"

"No, Jael. My dad and Uncle David are on their way to get us. We will keep you safe. Don't worry." Jael tried to smile confidently at him, but he could see she was frightened.

Anna saw Istasyon Cd. up ahead. She turned and made sure the kids were right behind her. They crossed the street at the corner light and turned left on Istasyon Cd.

They walked fifteen minutes before the large Catholic Church came into view. It took up a large portion of a long block. Birds were resting on the high steeple that once held a bell. They headed up the dozen wide steps and stopped at a huge double door made of old wood, arched at the top.

The well-kept church seemed out of place among the many shops lining the streets on both sides.

# CHAPTER TWELVE

**6:45 pm**

Anna stepped up to the door and held it opened for the kids to enter. It was as heavy as it looked. Her eyes scanned the street at the passing cars, looking for anyone suspicious.

The large foyer had no chairs. There was a small room to the right with a window and a speaker for mothers to take their fussy little ones. On the other side was a gift shop. It was closed, but a window displayed rosaries and books about saints. Sophie saw a rosary so tiny it fit in a little plastic egg.

Sophie and Jael walked into the sanctuary. Duke and CJ waited for Anna, who was still holding the door, watching the street. Sophie watched as Jael put her fingers in some water on a marble stand. She genuflected while crossing herself.

The ceiling in the sanctuary went up forever. Sophie looked at the stained-glass windows that lined the walls on both sides. They each had a story to tell. "I wonder who those men are?" She said mainly to herself, but Jael answered.

"Those are some of Jesus's disciples," Jael explained.

A door closed off to the side; the girls turned to look. A woman walked out of a big box and went to the front of the church. She knelt on a padded kneeler in front of a table full of candles. The lady put money in a metal box, took a long match standing in some sand, lit it with the flame from another candle, and used it to light one for herself. There was a similar setup on the other side of the church.

"Where did that woman come from?" Sophie asked.

"That is a confessional. It is where Catholics ask the priest for forgiveness for their sins," Jael said.

"How do you know so much about the Catholic Church? I thought your family went to an Evangelical Church?"

"We do now, but my mom was a Catholic. I went to church with her until she died." Jael's eyes saddened at the memory of her mom.

Sophie walked closer to the front of the church; looking up, she saw a dome high above the raised platform. It had a beautiful painting of angels and clouds surrounding the painting of the Virgin Mary holding baby Jesus. It matched a statue on the left above the candles. Then Sophie's eyes landed on a huge cross with the form of Jesus on it.

"Why is Jesus on the cross?" Sophie asked.

"He died for our sins," Jael answered.

"I know that, but he is not still on the cross. He's in heaven. He rose from the dead."

"Yes, on Easter."

"Then why do they still have Him on the cross?" Sophie asked again, but Jael had no answer. For some reason, the idea of Jesus being depicted on the cross really bothered Sophie.

There were only a few people in the vast sanctuary; Sophie noticed Anna walking in. The girls went to her.

"What do we do now?" Sophie asked.

"We need to find a safe place to hide." Anna looked around. She pointed to a confessional on the right. "I want you to go into that confessional and wait until I come to get you," Anna instructed.

"Mrs. Scott, we can't hide in there; there is a priest in that one. See the little light above the middle door," Jael pointed to it.

"I see. Ok, go into the one over there." She directed them to the other side. "There is no light on there." The kids followed her instructions. The two girls went into the door on the right and the boys in the door to the left. No one entered the one in the middle that was for the priest.

Anna stood there for a moment, weighing up what to do. She finally walked over to the confessional. A priest was in there; maybe she could get help from him. Anna walked in and knelt on the padded kneeler.

The priest opened the small sliding window between them but said nothing.

"Do you speak English, Father?"

"Yes, you may confess in English," the priest said.

"Father, I do not wish to offend you in any way. But I did not come in here to confess; I am not a Catholic. I came in to ask for your help."

"You do not offend me, miss. How can I help."

"I am traveling with four children. One of them is being hunted by criminals. I am trying to get her to safety. We were on the train at the Usak station when the men looking for her got on the train. I knew they were there to take her, so we got off. I called someone to come for us, but they are still an hour away. I was hoping you could find a place to hide us until then."

"Yes, of course, let's step out of the confessional." Outside the confessional, Anna extended her hand to him and introduced herself. He introduced himself as Father Kurt. Anna walked over to the other confessional and opened the doors to let the kids out.

"Kids, this is Father Kurt. He agreed to find a place for us to wait for our ride." They all smiled at him. He directed them to follow him.

Father Kurt led them to a door off the side of the foyer that opened into a large office; two windows looked out onto the side street. Two large couches and a few chairs, all made from a rich, soft, chocolate brown leather, sat along two walls. A large desk took up a good portion of the room, and behind it a bookcase overburdened with books. The father pointed to a door off to the right.

"That is the rectory, where my fellow priests and I live. They have gone to Rome to visit the Vatican, so I am here alone today. If you need to get out in a hurry, a door opens to the alley through there. Give me a description of the men; I will stay in the sanctuary to keep an eye out for them."

"Thank you for helping us, Father Kurt."

"That is what I am here for." He started to leave, then went into his rectory and returned with a handful of snacks and some water. "Just in case you get hungry." Then he headed out to the sanctuary.

"Ok, you can grab a snack and some water. Then find a place to sit. You will have to talk in whispers. We don't know how close someone might come to the door." Anna instructed them.

When everyone got comfortable, Anna sat in the oversized leather chair and took deep breaths to bring her pulse rate down. She sat for a while watching Duke and CJ play checkers. They got loud a few times, and she had to quiet them. Sophie and Jael were using the couch's arms as a backrest; they took their shoes off and stretched their legs out on the couch. Sophie was reading Nancy Drew; she was almost through the entire series. Jael was reading a Turkish translation of National Velvet.

Fifteen minutes later, Anna reached into her backpack and pulled out the secure cell.

"Hello Anna," David answered

"Hello, love," she responded.

"Are you safe?"

"Yes. We are in the Catholic Church. The Father allowed us to hide in his office. The rectory is attached to it, and he said there is a door to the alley through there. How close are you?"

"We will be in Usak in twenty minutes, but we have to wait for Luke. He's a half-hour behind us. We are going to transfer Haleh to his SUV. Then we will pick you up. We will travel together once we meet up again on the way out of town."

"That sounds like a good plan."

"How are the kids doing?"

"Jael is scared, but you would be so proud of the boys. They have taken such good care of Jael and Sophie. Did you know Sophie is afraid of heights?"

"No."

"Yes, when we were jumping off the train, she couldn't do it. Duke knew why. He had her close her eyes, and he lifted her off the platform and down to us."

"I've noticed he is protective of her," David said.

"I also noticed he lets her win games they play together," Anna said. David laughed.

"I've seen that too. I've seen CJ do the same for Lizzy."

They sat in silence on the phone for a while. "I've been worried for you."

"I know, love. We all have so much to lose if this goes wrong."

"Maybe we shouldn't have involved the kids in this mission," David said. Anna was silent on the other end for a moment.

"David, his scars from me being missing are too fresh. I don't know that he would have forgiven me if I left him again."

"That's true, and CJ would never let Duke go without him being there to cover his back. And Jael needed Sophie. That girl is fearless."

"She certainly is, except for being afraid of heights. I have no doubt she will overcome that in time," Anna chuckled.

"We will be there soon, sweetheart," David said.

"I love you."

"I love you too."

**7:30 pm**

David pulled into the Opet Gas Station up to one of the pumps. Jonathan turned to Haleh before getting out of the car.

"Haleh, would you like me to grab you something to drink or a snack?"

"No, thank you," Haleh replied. Jonathan headed around the car and asked David the same thing as David lifted the nozzle to pump the gas.

"Not right now, but maybe we should get some water and juice for the kids...and some snacks."

David waited for Jonathan to pay for the gas, then filled the tank. He pulled the SUV over to a parking spot on the side of the building. Haleh got out to stretch, and David opened the back to lift the third seat. They would need it once they picked up Anna and the kids.

Jonathan put the snacks in the back seat; then moved to the front of the car. David was leaning against the front end, looking at the street map of Usak.

**7:55 pm**

By the time Lance pulled up by a pump, they had found a route out of town and a spot to meet back up with Luke.

Emir stepped out of the SUV and spotted his sister; he ran over to her and gave her a big hug. After Lance and Luke moved closer to David's SUV, Lance introduced the others; Haleh and Emir moved aside to talk privately.

The men were happy to see each other. Lance went in to pay while Luke pumped the gas and spoke with David and Jonathan.

"We found a spot we can meet after we pick up the kids," Jonathan said.

"Good, how long will it take you to meet us there?"

"Probably twenty minutes to a half-hour, depending on traffic in the city. Text me when you find a safe place to park," David said.

"Lance and I will head straight there. Call us if there is any trouble," Luke said. David waved Haleh over; her brother came with her.

Emir spoke to the men, "I cannot tell you how grateful I am to all of you."

"It was the right thing to do," David responded.

"Jael is my daughter's friend. Sophie would have never forgiven me if I hadn't tried to help," Luke said with a smile. Emir smiled too.

"My daughter would have done the same," Emir said.

David directed them to Luke's SUV. "You and Haleh will ride with Luke now. Jonathan and I are going to pick up Anna and the kids at the Catholic Church in town."

"I would like to go with you," Emir said.

"I don't think that's a good idea. The men after them know your face. It could be a hindrance." Emir bowed his head but nodded his agreement. David and Jonathan hurried to their SUV and left. Jonathan was in the driver's seat; David called Anna.

"Hello, David,"

"Anna, we are on the way; we will pull up in the alley in about twenty minutes."

"Alright, we will wait outside by the door to the alley."

"No, wait inside. You will be too exposed in the alley."

"Alright, knock on the door, and we'll come out."

"Stay safe, honey."

"I'll be glad when this is over, love."

"Me too."

Ten minutes after Anna spoke to David, she told the kids to get their things together. She led them to the door to the alley through the rectory. Anna wanted to let Father Kurt know they were leaving and thank him again, so she told the kids to stay there.

Anna went back through the rectory and out the office to the foyer. She noticed Father Kurt standing a few feet inside the sanctuary. He was watching someone.

"Father Kurt," Anna said. He turned to see Anna walking toward him. He shook his head at her, but it was too late. One of the men searching the sanctuary looked up after hearing her voice, just as she turned to see who Father Kurt was staring at.

"Run," Father Kurt said as he moved to the center of the foyer entrance. He stretched his arms out, trying to delay the men. Anna ran into the office and locked the door behind her. Then she ran through the rectory door and locked it. She hollered to the kids to run. CJ was nearest the door, he opened it, and the kids stepped out; it had turned dark fast. They waited for Anna, then they all ran down the alley. She whispered loud enough for Duke to hear. He was in front, pulling Jael along with him.

"Turn right on the main road and duck into the first shop you can."

**8:05 pm**

Father Kurt had tried to slow down the men, but they bowled right over him, knocking him to the ground. The sturdy locked doors stalled the men; it took them some time to breach. They got to the alley in time to see Anna turn the corner toward the main road.

Duke turned into a small clothing store.

"Jael, ask the clerk if there is a back door," Anna said as she directed the kids to hide behind some clothes racks. Jael spoke to the clerk; by the length of the conversation, she did more than ask about a back door. The clerk finally pointed to the back room. Jael thanked her, and the group ran out the back door.

They landed in another alley. Anna wasn't sure what to do. She stood there for a moment. Then it came to her.

"We need to go back to the alley behind the church. They won't expect that, and your dad could already be there." Anna spoke directly to Duke. The group started to move forward. When Anna didn't move, Duke went back.

"Come on, Mom, we need to get out of here."

"No, I'm going to misdirect them." Duke took her hand.

"No, Mom, you need to come with us." Anna looked into his eyes, then nodded.

"Ok, let's go." The moment they turned into the alley behind the church, they saw the SUV. David was knocking on the door.

Duke rushed ahead and spoke loud enough to make sure his father heard him.

"Dad, they found us. We need to get out of here." David turned and opened the back doors, making sure the kids and Anna were all in safe. Then he got in the front passenger seat. As Jonathan was driving down the alley, the two men appeared. Jonathan slammed the gas pedal to the floor. If they didn't get out of the way, that was their choice. The men moved when they realized the SUV had no intention of stopping.

**8:15 pm**

"David call Luke on the secure line," Jonathan said, watching the road, so he didn't hit anyone.

"Luke, Mateo's men caught up with Anna and the kids. They've seen our SUV, and no doubt they have our license number."

"We expected them to have someone watching the freeway ramps. But now that they know what vehicle you're driving in will make it impossible to sneak by."

"Yes, that's what I'm thinking."

"When we studied the map of Usak, it showed an access road running parallel to the freeway. It looked like it was the main highway to Izmir before they built the freeway bypassing the city." Jonathan told him.

"That's where we'll go," David said.

"I'm in a dentist's parking lot.

. I'll move to park on the street, honk when you pass by, and I'll follow." Luke said.

"Alright, we are probably five minutes out," David responded.

"We'll be ready."

Jonathan watched for Luke's SUV on the street. He honked as he drove by and headed to the access road.

It was dark, which helped, but it also made it difficult to know if they were followed. The two SUVs made it to the access road. Cars were few and far between. It appeared few used it anymore since it added twenty miles to the trip. David kept his eyes on the highway shoulder to see if a car was lying in wait.

"Slow down, Jonathan," David said, grabbing the binoculars out of the glove box. He flipped on the night vision. "There is a car on the shoulder up there. We need to get off the freeway." David scanned the landscape, looking for someplace to pull in.

Anna called Lance to let him know what was happening. An angry driver whizzed by them.

"Jonathan, there is a trail to the left about forty feet ahead. Don't put on your blinker; just turn." David hoped Luke would be quick on his response.

Both vehicles made the sharp turn onto what couldn't even be called a trail. Instead, it looked like cars had trampled the wild grass enough times it laid on the ground. They followed it to the end. Jonathan and Luke parked off the side of the trail as far as they could to not be seen by the road. The surrounding trees made for good cover.

It appeared this was a teenage hang-out. Someone had dragged fallen logs to form a semi-circle around a large bonfire pit. There were a few beer cans in a pile, but overall it was clean.

Emir was the first to get out of the SUV. He headed to his daughter in the other vehicle. Jael saw her dad, got out, and ran into his arms crying, speaking to him in Turkish.

"Daddy, you got out!"

"Yes, Jael. God has answered our prayers." Haleh moved up behind them and wrapped them both up in her arms.

Sophie saw her dad get out of his SUV and went to him.

"Daddy, Mateo's men almost caught us. But we got away."

"I know, princess."

"We took care of each other, just like you told us," Sophie said. He lifted her.

"Yes, you did. You were all so brave." Luke set her back down.

"What are we doing here?"

"We are deciding what to do next." Sophie nodded and went back to her friends.

The men gathered as the kids went over to the unlit bonfire.

Before the men had a chance to talk, Lance heard cars coming up the path.

# THE PROMISE

# CHAPTER THIRTEEN

**8:40 pm**

"Everyone get in the cars and stay out of sight." David hollered. Lance, Luke, David, and Jonathan stood behind the SUVs waiting to see who they would be dealing with. Emir refused to hide; this was his fight.

Four cars came bouncing along the trail, music playing loud spilling out the open windows. The vehicles pulled around the pit and parked. Ten teenagers hopped out. They looked at the men leaning against their cars but went on about their business. The four girls went to look for fallen limbs and sticks for the fire, and the boys unloaded the cars. They hauled snacks, beverages, and sleeping bags out and laid them by the logs. It was apparent they planned on staying late.

Two teenage boys finally walked to where the men were standing. They spoke Turkish. Emir responded. By the length of it, he must have told them the whole story. Soon all the others came to listen. Finally, the two young men introduced themselves as Mirac and Baki. Emir introduced his friends, and they all exchanged handshakes.

Emir called out to the others, saying it was safe to come out. Anna, Haleh, and the kids came out and stood next to the others. Luke asked Emir to explain.

"These young people are members of the upcoming senior class student body council. Every year before school begins, they come out here to decide what to focus on to benefit the students."

"That is very impressive. Please tell them we are sorry for crashing their summit. We will be out of their way soon," David said.

Emir translated Mirac's response. "He said we are welcome to stay as long as we need."

The teenage girls introduced themselves to Jael and Sophie. Duke and CJ were at the pit watching another teenager lighting the fire.

Jael translated what the teenage girls said. "They want to know if we would like to eat with them." Sophie ran over to her dad.

"Daddy, can we eat with them?"

"Were you invited?"

"Yes, Jael said they invited us."

"Alright, as long as you were invited." The girls ran over to the pit and started assembling sucuk beef sausage on sticks to put over the fire.

While the teens entertained the kids, the others worked on a plan to get past the sentinel on the highway.

The young people sat around the fire cooking their dinner and talking. Haleh and Anna joined them. Baki asked Jael why they were at the pit. Jael told them about the car parked on the side of the road ahead. They were afraid some bad men who were after them were waiting to take her and her father. Baki went to talk to his friends. A few minutes later, the teenage boys went to speak with Emir.

"Sir, is it true you believe there are men in a car down the road who wish to do you harm?"

"Yes. We believe the men were sent by Mateo Borg, the criminal I told you about."

"We have a plan," Baki explained. Emir translated everything said.

"No, Emir. I won't put them in harm's way to help us," David said. Emir translated Baki's response.

"He says if they feel they are in danger, they will leave immediately." Everyone talked it over and decided there was little risk for the teens. The boys asked the girls to stay behind, but they refused.

**9:30 pm**

Ten minutes later, the plan was in play. "Stay close behind us," Mirac told Emir. The teens squeezed into two cars and led the way.

The caravan pulled back onto the highway. Luke and Jonathan were driving. They turned off their headlights and stayed close behind the two cars full of teens. The teens approached the sedan on the side of the road. One of the cars pulled at an angle in front of it, and the other pulled alongside. They jumped out and blocked the view of the other cars driving by. The teens engaged the two men inside.

"Are you broken down?"

"Do you need help?"

"We will be glad to take you to a gas station or take you to a phone to call for help." Every teen had something to say, causing chaos to distract the men inside.

When the men got angry and told them to buzz off, the teens immediately left. They promised not to push it. By then, their new friends were long gone, undetected.

The men kept their car beams off for two miles using the light of the moon and the white lines on the highway to navigate.

**Izmir, Saturday 1 am**

The safe house was housed in one of the commercial businesses in the industrial area on the outskirts of Izmir. The other industry buildings were locked up tight for the night. Emmett called ahead to passed on the expected time of arrival of the new guests. The kids traveled with Luke and were asleep in the back seats.

They found the address Emmett gave them and pulled in front of a large, two-story, concrete brick building. They honked, and a large garage door immediately started rolling up. Both SUVs were able to park side by side on this end of the warehouse. In front of them were two utility vans also side by side facing the matching rolling door on the other end. The left side of the building had crates two deep and five high, stacked from front to back.

On the right side was an office and storage area that ran the length of the warehouse. It took up about a quarter of the width. A set of wooden stairs started about the middle of the building and accessed the rooms upstairs that ran the length and width of the office and storage downstairs.

The doors of the SUVs opened as the passengers were anxious to get out and stretch. The kids woke up when they heard the door roll-up. They were tired and groggy.

David went directly to the man who let them in and gave him a man hug. They spoke quietly for a moment, then David brought him over to introduce the others to him.

"Neval, these are my friends. You know Anna and Duke, Jonathan and CJ," he moved closer to the others. "This is Luke Star and his daughter Sophie, and this is Lance Marquez." He turned to Emir, "and this is the family who needs our help. Emir Rossi, his daughter Jael Rossi, and his sister Haleh Ersoy. Emir, this is Neval Yavuz, a dear friend to Mission of Peace and our contact in Turkey." Jonathan and Anna hugged him, everyone else acknowledged and thanked him.

"It is a pleasure to meet you all. Let's go upstairs and get these kids in bed. Then we can discuss what happens next." Neval spoke English like a man who grew up in England.

Neval led them to their rooms. Sophie and Jael were escorted into a room with two double beds. Duke and CJ had the room next to them with two bunk beds and a couch that folded out to make another bed. When they were settled, the others went into a common area. This room had a small kitchen along the wall to the left. The center of the room held a kitchen table and two couches, and on the opposite wall was a television.

Neval had put on a pot of decaf coffee and a kettle for tea. Emir, Haleh, and Anna chose tea; the others had decaf. The men sat at the kitchen table. Anna and Haleh took their tea and sat on the couch.

"Our contact in Cesme is expecting you at dawn," Neval said to Emir. "We will have to leave here at 5 am to get there in time."

"What will happen then," Emir asked.

"Emmett's contact there will take you and your family across the Aegean Sea to Rafina, Greece. It is a small coastal town. Another friend will take you to the airport to catch the last daily flight leaving for Germany. I will give you a burner phone, so you can call your brother to meet you in Frankfurt." Neval took a sip of his coffee. "That is where your brother lives, right?" Emir nodded. "I was told you did not need passports?"

"That is right," Haleh said. "Luke took our passports out of the house when the Polis arrested me." She turned to Anna, "Anna, you have Jael's, right?"

Anna reached for her purse sitting next to her. She opened it and pulled out Jael's passport handing it to Haleh.

"Good, that is one less thing to worry about. I suggest you all get some sleep. I will check the warehouse, make sure it is secure; then I will wake you at 4:30 am so you can be ready to go at 5 am." Neval stood and headed out of the room. David stopped him.

"I'll go with you." Neval smiled and nodded. The others headed to their rooms.

David and Neval walked the perimeter of the warehouse, checking all the entry points.

"Neval, how are Lena and the twins? They are 12 now, right?"

"Yes, everyone is healthy. Thank you for asking." Neval reached up to make sure he had locked a window. "David, Lena wants to go back to Ely, Cambridgeshire."

"She wants to go back to England?"

"Yes. Lena's parents are getting older, and her father is sick. She wants our children to know their grandparents before it is too late. And Lena wants to help take care of her father."

"How do you feel about it?"

"I want to make her happy."

"So, will you sell the business?"

"Not right away, there is a young couple in our church; the husband is out of work. I could afford to give him a good salary to work the warehouse. I want to approach them about being part of Mission of Peace and taking over the safe house. But that will have to be your father's decision."

"So you would still run the business?"

"I can run the business online from anywhere. In time though, I hope this couple will want to buy it. It has allowed my family to have a comfortable life. I believe it would do the same for them, even after paying me for the business."

"Have you talked to my dad yet?"

"Yes, he and Jarod are coming to talk to them in two weeks."

"Dad's coming to Turkey?"

"Yes, he said it would be a good excuse to see you."

"That's great." The men finished the rounds, and Neval turned on the security system.

Neval knocked softly on Haleh's door to wake her at 4:30 am.

"Mrs. Ersoy, it's time to get up." Haleh sat up, crept to the door, and responded.

"Thank you; we will be ready," she whispered. When Neval moved to wake up Emir, Haleh stepped to the girl's bed, shook Jael, and said. "Jael, we have to get up."

Jael sat up and rubbed her eyes. The movement woke Sophie.

"Jael, I'm going to hop in the shower. When I finish, I need you to hurry to take yours."

"Alright, Tyze." Jael picked up the pink duffle Duke brought up from the car for her, and Sophie helped her pick out an outfit. Sophie picked up the zip lock bag filled with hair clips, looking for the perfect barrettes.

"Jael, use these today; they will match your top." She handed them to her.

"Thank you, Sophie." Jael sat on the edge of the bed and lowered her head; tears filled her eyes. Sophie sat next to her, putting an arm around her.

"I'm sorry you have to leave your home and all your friends, Jael." Jael lifted her head.

"I am not crying because I have to leave. I have my dad back; that is all that matters to me. I am upset I have to leave you. You are the best friend I ever had. Once dad went to prison, only two of my old friends would even talk to me."

"I'll miss you too, Jael. I wish you could have met Lizzy; you would have loved her. I gave you my online contact info. Will you promise to stay in touch?"

"Yes, of course. I will never forget you. You saved my dad, Sophie."

"All I did was ask my dad to help."

"If you had not done that, my dad would still be in prison. I will never forget it." She wrapped her arms around Sophie and cried.

Haleh stepped out of the bathroom and saw how hard this was for her niece. Leaving was going to be the hardest on her.

"Jael, we cannot be late; it is time for you to take your shower." Jael took her things and went into the bathroom. Haleh squatted down in front of Sophie.

"Sophie, you are a special young lady. I will forever thank the Lord for you. Thank you for being Jael's friend."

"It was easy to be her friend," Sophie said, wiping away a tear. Haleh hugged her and then got up to put the clothes Anna gave her back in the small suitcase.

Twenty minutes later, they were all in the kitchen having koulouri with jam and juice. Haleh was surprised to see the others had gotten up to say goodbye. David, Jonathan, and Luke walked downstairs with Neval. He opened the Van doors so his passengers could get in. Jael grabbed her pink duffle and backpack and walked to the top of the stairs. She turned to hug Sophie again.

Sophie moved over to the wood railing that looked over the warehouse. She stepped on the lowest horizontal plank and leaned her waist over the top handrail, waving goodbye. Jael turned one last time and threw Sophie a kiss before she stepped into the van. Sophie threw a kiss back, tears running down her cheeks.

"Neval, how long will it take you to get to Cesme?"

"Less than an hour, David."

"We will still be here. There is no reason for us to rush off. Maybe we'll have more time to catch up."

"I'll call Lena. She can bring some lunch over, and you can see the boys again."

"I would love that."

David waited until they were all in the van and Neval was in the driver's seat. Then he walked to the roll-up garage door and pushed the button. As soon as the van was through the door, he closed it. The men decided there was no rush to get home, so they suggested everyone go back to bed and wake up at their leisure.

Sophie walked back to her room and sat on the bed.

Luke knew Sophie was in her room alone, so he went in to make sure she was alright. When he walked in, she was sitting on the edge of the bed, still crying. He knelt in front of her and wrapped his arms around her.

"Sophie, don't cry. You know Jael would have loved to stay here and be your friend. But you brought her father back to her; she will never forget you."

"I know, Daddy; I wish she didn't have to lose so much. It wasn't right what those men did to her dad."

"Life isn't always fair, princess. I'm sure if you ask Jael, she will say she was glad to give up everything to have her dad back." Sophie moved back and looked at him.

"She did say that. It's not just Jael. I miss Lizzy so much. I don't even know when she is coming home."

"I'll call Manny and find out for you when we wake up. Now get some sleep."

"Will you stay in here with me?"

"Of course, princess." Luke pulled the bedspread over the other bed and laid on top of it.

They had been on the road for four hours; it was 2 pm when they left. Lena had brought the twins and lunch over to the safe house. After lunch, the twins asked their dad if they could open the rear roll-up so they could play soccer outback. Duke, CJ, and Sophie went with the twins and spent their time playing.

Anna and Lena spent their time cleaning the rooms and changing the bedding. They wanted to get the rooms ready for whoever Mission of Peace sent them next.

The boys were supposed to ride with David, but Sophie didn't want to ride alone. Luke asked if Duke and CJ could ride with him and Lance. He lifted the third-row seat and made room for them.

Duke and CJ laid down the passenger side of the middle row to make a flat surface. They were able to use it to play games while they traveled.

"Daddy, did you call Uncle Manny?" Sophie asked. Luke caught her eyes in the rearview mirror.

"Yes. Manny said Lizzy wants you to call her."

"Is it too early to call there?"

"A little. Let's wait till we stop for dinner. Then you can use my phone."

"Thanks, Daddy."

After dinner, when they were back on the road, Sophie asked, "Daddy, can I call Lizzy now?"

"Sure." Luke was in the passenger seat; Lance was driving. He dialed the number for her then handed it back.

"Hello?" Manny answered.

"Uncle Manny, can I speak to Lizzy?"

"Sure." Manny went to find her and handed her the phone.

"Hello?" Lizzy said.

"Lizzy! It's me, Sophie."

"Sophie! I'm so happy you called. I tried to Skype with you yesterday, but you didn't log on."

"I know, I was out of town. I'll tell you all about it when you get home. When are you coming home, Lizzy?"

"Saturday."

"You're coming home Saturday?"

"Yes."

"Yay! I can't wait."

Sophie leaned against the door and put her legs over the flattened part of the seat. They spoke on the phone for the next hour while Duke and CJ played the 'War' card game in the third row. The boys got loud, and Sophie shushed them so she could hear her best friend.

When Sophie hung up, she said, "Lizzy is coming home Saturday! Daddy, we have to have a big party." She turned to the boys in the back seat. "Duke, will you and CJ help me make a big sign?"

"Sure, we can go to the Rec Center; they have all the art supplies."

"Daddy, can we have the party at our house?"

"Of course."

"Uncle Lance, you'll come, right?" Lance smiled; he liked being included among the 'uncles'.

"If you are inviting me."

"Of course, you are invited; you're part of the family. Will you bring Pam too?

"Yes."

"Daddy, can I use your phone to call Aunt Anna. She will make a beautiful cake."

"Sure, honey."

Sophie spent the next fifty miles planning for a 'Welcome Home' party.

Sophie kept everyone busy with party arrangements all week. Luke had just left to pick up the Diaz family at the airport. Sophie planted herself at the front picture window of her home to watch for them. When the SUV pulled in, she ran to the door, yelling at everyone.

"They're here." As she ran out the door to greet her friend, Lizzy jumped out of the car before Luke had a chance to put on the emergency brake.

"Sophie," she screamed as she ran to her and hugged her best friend. The girls were jumping and giggling as the others spilled out of the house to greet their friends.

After everyone said their hello's, they headed for the backyard for the BBQ. And the world was back on its axis: Lizzy was home.

# CHAPTER FOURTEEN

Two weeks later, after church, the BBQ was at David's house. He introduced Emmett and Jarod to everyone. Sophie ran up to Emmett and wrapped her arms around him. Surprised, Emmett squatted down in front of her.

"Hello, angelface," Emmett said. Sophie put her hand to her mouth and giggled.

"No, my name is Sophie."

"That can't be right. You look like an angel," he said.

Lizzy stepped up to him and hugged him. Emmett turned to her.

"I know who you are. Anna told me your name is sweetie." Lizzy and Sophie both giggled.

"No, I'm Lizzy."

"I don't think so. I'm sure Anna said, sweetie."

Luke stepped over with Manny and Ruby; Ricky was holding Manny's hand. Luke extended his hand to Emmett.

"I'm Luke Star." Emmett stood up and shook Luke's hand. Then moved to Manny and Ruby, shook their hands, and patted Ricky on the head.

"This is David's younger brother, Jarod." They all shook hands.

Lance and Pam came through the backyard gate carrying a pie. Anna and Zoey stepped out onto the porch with big bowls of side dishes and welcomed them. Ruby had already placed her pie on the table.

"David, are you done with the meat yet?" Anna asked.

"Yes, sweetheart."

Anna called the boys over from the hoop. They were playing 21.

"Mom, we're at nineteen. Can we finish?"

Anna responded, "you will still be at nineteen after lunch." The boys reluctantly put down the ball.

A long lunch full of catching up and laughter followed. When it was over, Lance and Pam excused themselves, saying they wanted to make the early show on Base.

"You guys want to play soccer?" CJ asked the other kids. They all headed to the yard. The BBQ was the first opportunity the group had to talk about the transition from the Army to civilian life.

"Austin is a wonderful place to live. There are great public and private schools. We have two homes on the cul-de-sac where David and Jonathan live that will be available this summer. You can move into those, then decide if you want to buy them. If not, there will be others available soon, or you may choose a different part of town," Jarod said.

"We will furnish it until your belongings catch up with you. We have a warehouse full. We use it to stage homes when we put them on the market." Emmett added. David spoke up.

"The offer Jonathan and I made you last month is still on the table. We want you to be partners with us. I realize that it might take some time," David turned to Manny, "until you make that decision. The firm will pay you a salary double what you are making now until you decide. And if Ruby still wants to work, we would like to offer her the office manager position. We don't need to have an answer yet. But the offer is open."

"David, how will you be able to pay me so much. A new firm won't have that kind of money?" Manny asked.

"We have savings, and we talked it over with our wives," waving his hand to include them. "Having an experienced investigator is crucial to a successful law firm. I will front the money and will recoup the funds when we start being profitable," David responded.

"You are worth the investment, Manny. As we grow, we will naturally increase your salary. Hopefully, you will decide to become a partner at some point," Jonathan added. David turned his attention to Luke.

"We will set the buy-in for you and Manny when we all are finally in Austin. That way, the success of the business won't cause your buy-in to change."

"David, I appreciate the offer, but I don't know how long it will take me to come up with the money to be a partner. And you already promised me a generous guaranteed salary until then."

"We are willing to wait, Luke. If we don't sign you up, some other firm will.," Jonathon said. Before they could say anything else, Duke hollered.

"Dad, you guys want to play soccer with us." The men figured they could finish this talk another time. The men, including Emmett and Jarod, joined the kids.

Emmett cheated to let the girls get some goals. He grabbed Duke by the waist so he couldn't chase after the ball. The others started cheating too. They spent more time laughing than playing.

When Luke and Sophie got home, Luke notice Sophie had gotten quiet. She had gone to her room to change. He walked in to see her sitting on the edge of the bed.

"What's wrong, princess?"

"Daddy, I wish I had a grandpa."

"Sophie, you did. Your grandfather and grandmother loved you very much." Luke moved to the bed and sat next to her.

"I don't remember them."

"You were a toddler when they died."

"How did they die?"

"My dad died from a massive heart attack. He was young, only fifty. My mom died from complications from diabetes," he lowered his head. "I always thought she died from a broken heart. My folks loved each other so much."

"Daddy, promise me you will never die." Sophie turned to him and looked in his eyes.

"Oh, Sophie," Luke wrapped her in his arms. "You know we never die; we just change addresses."

"You mean heaven."

"Yes, we move on to heaven. I will see my parents again. As long as I keep Jesus as my Lord and savior."

"I know that Daddy. But I want you to stay here on earth where I can hug you and talk to you. So promise me you will never leave me." Luke knew it was wrong to promise such a thing, but she needed to hear it.

"I promise, princess. I will never leave you."

"Do you think Mr. Emmett could be my grandpa, too?"

"I don't think you have a choice. It seems Emmett already decided you are part of his family." Sophie smiled.

"You think so?"

"I do. He and Jarod are going to be here a while. Why don't you ask him?"

"Can I do that?"

"Of course, Sophie." Sophie stood up and hugged her dad again.

"Can I have some ice cream?"

"Sure, we'll share."

Emmett and Jarod spent a lot of time with the kids over the next two weeks. They picked them up after school, took them to the park or for ice cream. On Saturday, they took them ice skating, and on Wednesday, they took them to an early movie on Base.

Emmett and Jarod decided to extend their stay. At the park that Saturday, Sophie took a break from soccer and sat at a picnic table. Emmett came over to sit with her.

"You ok, angel?"

"Yeah." Sophie lowered her head. "You are going to leave us soon, aren't you?"

"Jarod and I do have to go back to Austin. But you will be coming too, soon."

"I don't have a grandpa."

"Yes, you do." Sophie lifted her head to look at him. "You are part of my family. That makes me your grandpa."

"Really!" Sophie jumped up and clapped her hands.

"Yes, of course," Emmett said. Sophie hugged him.

"Grandpa," Sophie repeated. "I like saying that." Emmett laughed.

"Come on, angelface. Let's see if the others want ice cream."

The time of Luke's transition out of the Army was fast approaching. The group spent all their off-duty time planning the transition. The only days they took off were Thanksgiving and Christmas Eve.

Christmas Day Clair came down to see Sophie; she knocked on the door at 10 am. Sophie answered.

"Mommy," Sophie gave her a big hug.

"Hello, sweetheart," Clair said. Luke walked over to the door to greet her.

"Hello Clair, come on in. Do you have a few minutes? I need to schedule something with you." Luke led her to the kitchen and put a pod of vanilla, medium roast in the Keurig for her.

"Sure, I have a hotel this time. I plan on staying a few days. I was hoping you would let Sophie stay with me."

"I'm sure she will love that," he turned to Sophie.

"Do you want to stay in a hotel with your mother?"

"Yes, Daddy," Sophie readily agreed.

"Then you need to go pack for a few days. Mom will come to help you in a minute. I need to discuss something with her."

"Ok, Daddy." Sophie went off to her room. Luke brought over coffee for Clair. He popped a pod in for himself, waited for the coffee to brew, and then took it to the kitchen table.

"How are you, Clair?"

"I'm good, Luke. You look well." Clair took a sip of coffee. Luke could see she was a little nervous. They had not spent much time talking since the divorce, even when she came to pick up Sophie.

"I want to coordinate Sophie's summer visit with you. I plan on taking Sophie to Disneyland Paris before we go back to the States. I can't get leave until my replacement comes, the second week of July. I want to propose that Sophie visit you the last week of June and the first week of July. Then I will pick her up, and we will spend the week with some of our friends at Disneyland Paris."

"I have no objection to that. But I would like to spend a day or two with her at Disney. I would love to do some rides with her."

"She would love that. Thanks, Clair." Luke watched Clair take the last sip of her coffee and stand up.

"I better censor Sophie's packing. She will pack her whole closet if I don't," she laughed. Luke laughed with her.

Sophie came around the corner. Clair expected her to use the new duffle she sent to replace the one Sophie gave away. Instead, she was pulling a suitcase. Luke and Clair exchanged a look and smiled.

"Sophie, your mother and I were discussing the date you will go visit her this year. Would it be alright if you went the last week of June for two weeks?"

"I guess." Sophie said and hesitated before asking, "mommy, can Lizzy come. PLEASE, PLEASE, PLEASE! We will be extra good. I promise." Sophie waited for an answer, her eyes wide, staring at her mother as she thought about it.

"I think that would be fun," Clair said. Sophie ran to her, throwing her arms around her waist.

"Thank you. Thank you."

"Don't thank me yet. Lizzy's parents have to approve. I don't want you saying anything to her until your father gets approval from her parents."

"I won't, I promise." Sophie turned to her dad. "You'll call today, won't you, Daddy?"

"I will." Luke walked them to the town car and waved goodbye as it drove off.

The last day of schools 'Field Day', took Luke by surprise. He scrambled to move an appointment so he could spend an hour watching the kids run the obstacle courses.

Jarod had sent pictures and the floor plans of the two homes available for them to choose from. Luke, Manny, and Ruby spent hours looking over the floor plans at Manny's kitchen table. Luke liked the smaller ranch-style home. But he didn't want to choose until he knew what Manny wanted.

Neither of the homes was small. The 'smaller' one was 2400 square feet on one level. The other was 2800 square feet over one and a half stories.

Luke insisted Manny choose first.

"Luke, Ruby and I would like the bigger house. We have been talking about having another child. But we do not want to take it away from you."

"No. That's perfect. Sophie and I love the ranch, but it's less expensive. I didn't want you to have to buy something that would put you in a financial bind."

"We decided to use part of Ruby's inheritance for a down payment. With that, it will make the home affordable for us."

"Then it's agreed. Great. I'll send Jarod a text. I know he said we could lease it first, but I like the idea of having Sophie close to her friends. And it would mean they would all go to the same school. I'm going to go to the Government Credit Union to get a loan using my GI bill benefits."

"I'm doing the same." Manny got up from the table to grab a couple of Pepsi bottles for him and Luke; Ruby had gone to check on Ricky. "I have to say; I'm excited about the move and our new jobs."

"Me too. I'm more convinced every day that keeping the group together is the right thing to do. And I have no doubt that David and Jonathan will put together a top-notch firm."

"Ruby wants to take the office manager's job for a while. If we do decide to have another child, she wants us to have plenty in the savings account so she can stay home with the kids."

Manny and Luke were allowed to walk the girls to the gate at the airport because they were minors. Since Clair invited Lizzy to come, she felt there was no need to pick Sophie up in Adana and fly back with them. She paid for first-class tickets, nonstop to Paris, and paid extra for supervision. Since Sophie was older and not alone, Luke felt it was a reasonable request.

Lizzy was nervous about going on a plane without her dad. "Daddy, I wish you were coming with me." Manny bent down in front of her.

"Lizzy, sweetheart, I don't want you to be afraid. You and Sophie will have so much fun. But if you decide you don't want to go, it's not too late."

"No, I want to go."

"All of us will be there in two weeks. If you want to come home before that, call me," Manny hugged her tight. Once she got there, he knew it would be harder on him than her, having her gone for two weeks.

Sophie saw how nervous Lizzy was. She went up to her and put her arm around her. "Lizzy, don't be scared I will be with you the whole time. I promise I will take care of you." Sophie kept her arm around her, and they sat down to wait for the boarding call.

The airline announced boarding would start in ten minutes. A stewardess came out looking for her wards for the flight. Luke recognized her, and a huge smile crossed his face. The stewardess caught his eye at the same time.

"Luke?"

"Marci," he reached for her and gave her a casual hug. Sophie looked up when her dad said her name.

"Marci," Sophie ran to hug her. "I'm so glad to see you," Sophie pulled on her hand and led her to where Lizzy was sitting. "Lizzy, this is Marci. She is my friend. She will take extra special care of us."

Marci squatted down in front of Lizzy. "Yes, I will, Lizzy. You don't have anything to worry about. Let's get your things together so I can get you comfortable before the other passenger's board. Luke introduced Manny to her and they both thanked her. They gave their girls one final hug and watched as they walked toward the jetway.

Lizzy and Sophie both stopped before they stepped onto the jetway and turned. They threw their dad's a kiss and waved goodbye. Luke and Manny waited until the plane was in the air before they left, feeling a little lonely.

"Luke, do you mind if we stop at the Personal Services Division on the way home. Ruby wants me to pick up more boxes and bubble wrap."

"I wanted to go by there too. I plan on wrapping up the memory wall this weekend. I'm sending it home via UPS. You've heard all the horror stories of missing or damaged property in transit. I didn't bring much, other than Sophie's bedroom, but I could replace any of that. But Sophie would be devastated if we lost the memory wall."

**Monday**

Luke headed into work a couple of hours early Monday morning. His replacement was coming either Monday or Tuesday next week. He had to go through all the files to ensure they weren't missing anything. He also wanted to have a good handle on the open cases to bring the new Lieutenant up to speed.

The offices were dark except for the two dim security lights they keep on over the bullpen. Luke headed to his office, unlocked it, and turned on the lights. Everything was as he left it Friday. He had three stacks of files on his small conference table. One stack was case files he hadn't gone through yet to make sure they were complete. One stack was folders he had gone through and completed, and the third was open files.

Luke had gone through ten files noting what was missing before he could store them away. He heard Ruby's phone ring. He was still the only one in the office, so he answered it.

"Captain Star."

"Captain Star, this is Private Sorensen from the MP station."

"Sure, Private Sorensen, I remember you. What can I do for you?"

"Master Sergeant Diaz asked me to request a Jag officer come to the station."

"I'm the only one here." Luke wondered if he should be involved with any new cases, but he couldn't ignore a request. "I'll be there shortly."

Ruby was walking out of the elevator when Luke locked his office door.

"Ruby, I received a call from the MP station. Manny requested a Jag officer. I'll be back soon. I hope." Luke traded places with her on the elevator, Ruby was holding the door, so it wouldn't close. He pushed the button for the ground floor.

Luke walked into the MP Station 10 minutes later. Private Sorensen stood to greet him. Luke removed his cap and put it under the arm that was holding his briefcase — allowing his right hand free to shake hands.

"Captain Star, I will let Master Sergeant Diaz know you're here."

"Thank you, Private Sorensen." Luke stood in the waiting area. He was watching rain start to drizzle outside the window when Manny stepped up to him wearing his black beret to indicate he was 'under arms'.

"Good morning Luke. I didn't think they were giving you new cases." Manny extended his hand to Luke.

"I was the only one in the office when the call came in. What's the situation?" Manny led Luke to his office before speaking. He directed Luke to take a seat.

"That's the problem, Luke. I'm not sure what I have." Manny played with the letter opener on his desk, turning it end over end on his desk.

"Well, tell me what you do know."

"This morning at 6 am, Private Sorensen got an anonymous call, saying there was a dead man in Major Casale's house."

"The caller called the station, not the emergency line?"

175

"Yes. The caller blocked his number too."

"How on earth could he have known that unless he was inside?" Luke asked.

"He didn't say. But when we got there, there was a dead man, but it wasn't Major Casale. It was a Private Connelly. I had Private Sorensen unscramble the number so we could locate the caller. There was no way he could have seen the body from outside."

"Which begs the question, what was he doing there?"

"Exactly. We tracked the GPS on his phone and picked him up. His name is Corporal Sig Hofmann; he is in an interrogation room."

"So, how did he explain it?"

"He won't talk. He asked for a lawyer," Manny said.

Luke sat there for a moment staring out the window behind Manny; the rain was coming down faster now. He wondered if he should wait for Captain Patel to take this over. Then he realized she would probably be the prosecutor on this case. Luke slapped his hands on the arms of the wooden chair and lifted himself.

"Can you have him taken to the conference room for me?"

"You're welcome to use the interrogation room he's in."

"No. I'll have a better chance of him telling me the truth if he doesn't feel like he's under arrest." Luke stopped at the door and turned. "He's not under arrest, is he?"

"Not yet, but if he didn't kill the guy, he was in there to steal something. We have had a few break-ins this month."

"Let's not jump to conclusions." Luke smiled and walked out the door.

# CHAPTER FIFTEEN

Captain Star stood when Master Sergeant Diaz escorted Corporal Hofmann into the conference room. He shook his uncuffed hand, introducing himself; Manny left. Luke pulled his yellow pad and pen from his briefcase, setting his cap on the table.

"Are you my attorney?"

"I will be one of them. My discharge date is in six weeks. My replacement, when he comes, will be co-counsel until I'm gone. If we don't get your case settled by then, my replacement will take over. But if what you are asking me is if this is a privileged communication? It is." Luke leaned forward and folded his hands on the table. "Why don't you tell me what this is all about."

Corporal Hofmann squirmed in his seat. It appeared he wanted to weigh up how much to tell.

"Captain, I've gotten myself in some trouble with a nearby Turkish gambling house. I owe them $30,000. When I told them I couldn't pay it, they gave me a way to clear my debt."

"By stealing?"

"Yes. Somehow these guys know what's in the homes they send me to. They would tell me exactly what to take and where it was."

"How could they possibly know?"

"I have no idea. But they were right. At least the two times I worked for them."

"How did you get in?"

"They gave me a bump key. I used it on the back door."

"Do you have it on you?"

"No, I got rid of it. I was afraid the MPs might figure out I was the one who called."

"Alright, Corporal, your creditors told you to go into Major Casale's home to steal what?"

"A Kinkade original."

"What did you steal from the other homes?"

"A three-carat diamond ring."

"The three-carat diamond ring alone would have paid off a good portion of your debt even if they took it to a fence."

"I know. After I handed over the ring, I asked how much they were taking off my debt. I know they make a hefty profit because they have a black-market website." The Corporal looked at his hands, "they said one thousand dollars. I knew that meant they were never going to clear my debt. The other item was a jade statue. They credited me $100."

"Ok, so you went into the Major's house to steal the Kinkade. What happened when you walked in?"

"I went to the living room where the painting was supposed to be. It wasn't on the wall, and a man was lying on the floor. I checked his pulse, but he was dead, and there was blood pooled around his head. I got out of there. Then I felt bad just leaving him there, so I called the station."

"You're telling me you didn't kill him." Luke leaned closer to his client.

"I'm telling you; I did not kill that man." He mimicked Luke's posture.

"Alright, Corporal Hofmann, they don't have anything to hold you on. I will inform Master Sergeant Diaz that you will be leaving unless he plans on arresting you. Wait here." Luke walked out of the room.

Luke knocked on Manny's door. "Enter," came the response from inside. Luke walked in; Manny stood at ease until Luke took his seat.

"Manny, are you planning to hold Corporal Hofmann?"

"If you're asking if I'm arresting him, the answer is no. Not yet, but I need to get some information from him, Luke."

"What time did the ME say Private Connelly died?"

"He wasn't sure. The air conditioning was on the highest setting, and that will make it difficult to pin down," Manny answered.

"Where were Major Casale and his family when all this happened?"

"They went on vacation Sunday morning."

"Was it a planned vacation?" Luke asked.

"I'll ask Lance to check that out. He's at the scene investigating," Manny said. Luke decided he needed to ask the Corporal a few more questions.

"I'll be right back, Manny." Luke hurried back to the conference room. When he opened the door, he saw Sig had folded his arms on the table and laid his head on them. His head sprung up when he heard the door open.

"Are they letting me go?" He asked.

"Yes, but I need you to answer a few more questions and wait until I come back."

"Sure, what do you want to know?"

"Was the air conditioning on when you entered the house?" Luke asked. Sig looked up and to the left, trying to remember.

"Yes, I remember even with gloves and my balaclava mask on, I could feel a chill."

"When you got close to the body, did it stink? Was it stiff?"

"I don't remember any smell. I took my glove off to check his pulse. The body was cold, but I didn't touch his arm or any other part of his body to see if he was stiff."

"Ok, wait here, I'll be right back." Luke walked back to Manny's office and walked in after knocking.

"Manny, I can't let you talk to my client. There could be an assortment of ways he could have known there was a body in there."

"Like what?"

"Someone could have told him."

"Is that what he told you?" Manny laughed. "Give me a break."

"My client could put himself in an incriminating situation if I let him answer your questions. I'm sorry."

"Luke, he is the only witness we have to what may have gone down there. I need him to talk to me." Manny stood up, placing his hands on his desk.

"I'm sorry, Manny, really. But I can tell you; I believe he had nothing to do with the murder of Private Connelly," Luke stood.

"So you are saying he was just a concerned citizen with x-ray vision passing by the Major's house?" Manny snarked. Luke laughed.

"You could say that." Luke walked toward the door, "I'm going to inform my client he is free to go."

Manny was not happy, but he had no evidence linking Luke's client to the dead body. "Alright, Luke, but your client is guilty of something, and I will find out what that is. When I do, you might want to encourage him to be cooperative," Manny responded. Luke stopped at the door.

"Am I still invited to dinner tonight?" Luke asked with a smile.

"Of course, Luke," Manny tried not to smile.

Luke went back to his client to give him some instructions; he sat across from him.

"Corporal, you are free to go. But they are going to figure out that you are the one who has been breaking into these homes." Luke waited for a response. Sig lowered his head.

"I don't know what to do. How do I get out of the mess I'm in without being court-martialed and ending up in jail?"

"There might be away. Our MPs and CID have worked on joint task forces with the Turkish Polis before. The Army and the Turkish Polis are aware of the traps some of these underground gambling joints set for unwitting enlisted men. Maybe I could get you immunity if you help to bring down one of the organizations in cooperation with the Turks."

"What would I have to do?"

"You would have to explain exactly how you ended up in this situation and what they wanted you to do to pay off your debt. CID may want you to wear a wire, to capture the boss telling you to rob a home."

"If I go back there without that painting, they will be furious."

"That will make them more likely to say too much. Along with the Turkish Polis Counter Attack Team, SRT will be close if things go awry."

"They gave me until Thursday to bring the painting to them."

"That doesn't give us much time. I need to talk to the Judge Advocate General about getting you immunity. Then we need to talk to Master Sergeant Diaz and CID."

"What should I do now?"

"Are you scheduled to work today?"

"Yes."

"Then go to work and talk to no one about any of this."

"Ok." They both got up, walked out of the room, and left the station. The rain had soaked Luke's uniform jacket by the time he made it into his car. The sky had turned dark.

Luke was driving back to the office. But his mind wasn't on the Corporal. He was wondering how the girls were doing in Paris with Clair when his cell rang.

"Hello?"

"Daddy, hi. I miss you," Sophie said bubbly.

"Hello, princess. Is everything alright?"

"Yes, we are having so much fun. I showed mommy the pictures of our new house. She wants to decorate my new room but needs the size or something. Hold on; she wants to talk to you." Sophie lowered the phone. Luke heard her holler, "Daddy's on the phone, Mom." It took a moment for her to get to the phone.

"Luke?"

"Yes. Sophie says they are having a good time."

"I had no idea how much fun a couple of girls could be," she laughed. "Sophie showed me your new home in Texas. It's very nice. I would like to decorate Sophie's room and replace her furniture. I see you are giving her the master bedroom."

"Yes, I figure she needs the privacy of the ensuite bathroom. As for the walk-in closet, she has ten times the clothes I do. Thanks to you."

"You always have been selfless when it came to your daughter...and me." Clair swallowed and continued. "I'll need the dimensions of the room and the window. I'll also need a contact for someone who can let in the workers to set up her room before you get there."

"I can get that for you."

"I'm calling Ruby tonight to get permission to buy some new furniture for Lizzy too."

"Clair, that is extremely generous of you."

"I had no idea how close these two were. Lizzy is such a gift to Sophie. I can afford to do it."

"I agree; Lizzy is a gift. Thank you, Clair. I will get you the information as soon as I can. Can I say goodbye to Sophie?" Clair handed Sophie back the phone.

"Daddy, are you coming soon?"

"Yes princess, we will all be there in less than two weeks."

"I love you, Daddy."

"I love you too, sweetheart."

Luke could hear the buzz from the active Jag unit before the elevator doors opened. He liked the noise better than the quiet darkness he walked into early this morning. Ruby was at her desk when he stepped off the elevator.

"Good morning, Captain Star."

"Good morning, Ruby. Is Colonel Zimmermann in his office?"

It took the Army almost two years to send an appointed Judge Advocate General, Colonel Reginald Zimmermann. He replaced Major Scott, the acting Judge Advocate General. The colonel's experience in fragile diplomatic foreign relations made him perfect for Incirlik Air Base. It took longer than expected to get the right fit for the position, leaving Major Scott to fill in.

"Yes," Ruby answered. Luke leaned on the counter and whispered.

"Have you heard from Lizzy?"

"Yes. She is having a wonderful time."

"I'm glad she was able to go." Luke walked back to Colonel Zimmermann's office and knocked on the door.

"Enter," Colonel Zimmermann responded. Luke walked in, held his salute, and waited.

The colonel returned the salute. "Please sit, Captain. I hear you caught a case this morning."

"Yes, sir. That's what I wanted to talk to you about. Corporal Hofmann called in what he thought was an anonymous tip to the MP Station. He informed them there was a dead body in Major Casale's home..."

"Major Casale is dead?!"

"No sir. Major Casale and his family left on vacation Sunday morning. CID is investigating the death now. They took my client in because they knew there was no way he could have known about the body unless he was in the house." Luke went on to explain everything that happened.

"So you want to see about immunity in exchange for information. Does the corporal know enough to take down this gambling ring targeting enlisted men?" Colonel Zimmermann questioned.

"Yes sir. Our men are targeted around the world by criminal organizations like this. These gambling houses set out to get enlisted men in debt way over their heads. That way, they can use the debt to blackmail them into doing what they want. We can use this opportunity to take down one of these blackmail rings."

"I tend to agree, Captain. Talk to CID and work something out. Is he going to be arrested for murder?" Colonel Zimmermann asked.

"There is a good chance. But I don't think he had anything to do with it. The ME hasn't pinned down the time of death because the air conditioner was on full blast. Other than the obvious trauma to his head, the ME hasn't explained how he died yet." Luke answered.

"Alright, Captain, keep me informed."

"Yes sir." Luke stood up to leave.

Before Luke went to his office, he knocked on David's door.

"Come in, Luke. I heard you caught a case today," David said as he directed Luke to have a seat.

"I did. It's a strange one." He proceeded to tell David all about it. They continued to speak of other cases. Luke was getting ready to go when David asked.

"Before you go Luke. Has Lance decided if he wants to come with us to Paris?"

"He put in for the time off. He is trying to convince Pam to go with him. He offered to pay for her flight and her room, but she hasn't made up her mind yet."

"I noticed Lance has been sitting with you at church the last few weeks."

"He has, and he asks a lot of questions, but as far as I know, he has not committed his life to Christ yet," Luke responded.

"Ann told me Pam was concerned she was getting too serious about him. She doesn't want to get too invested and get hurt or end up hurting Lance. She will never marry a man who is not a committed Christian."

"That must be why she's hesitating. I believe Lance reserved a room for her, just in case. I don't know if he paid for her ticket. He knows he can't get a refund," Luke said.

"I would say they are suited for each other, but that's contingent on Lance giving his life over to Christ. The Word says in 2 Corinthians 6:14, 'Be ye not unequally yoked together with unbelievers... ' I know you see the wisdom in that." The Major picked up a cup of coffee that was sitting on his desk.

"I do, David. I learned the hard way," Luke said as he stood to leave. "I'm going to call Lance now. I'll get back to you."

The medical examiner had informed Agent Marques he would have to get back to him on the time of death. The ME wanted to check the stomach contents and corneal cloudiness to get an accurate time. The air conditioner delayed rigor; it also made the temperature of the body and liver an unreliable estimator.

They were able to get prints in the room that likely belonged to the family. They would run them all through AFIS.

Lance was walking through the house to see if anything else was disturbed. He checked up on the Major before he came. He and his wife have one daughter; by the looks of the pictures displayed, she graduated this year. Her room was messy, indicating they left in a hurry or she was a typical teenager. Lance looked around for pictures of her girlfriends or a boyfriend.

Above the dresser was a padded board with crisscross elastic to hold pictures. There were so many pictures the girl layered them on top of each other. Lance took photos of the girls that appeared in more than one picture. He planned on locating her yearbook and seeing if Pam could match up a name with a face. He searched the board for a photo of a boy. There were two hidden behind other pictures. In one, they were hugging; his back was to the camera. In the other, they were walking in the Adana Merkez Park holding hands. They were too far away to make out the faces. Lance snapped a shot of that one too.

Lance had tried to inform Major Casale of the break-in, but he didn't answer his phone. He was ready to leave when his cell rang.

"Hello?"

"Lance, it's me, Luke."

"Hi Luke, how are you?"

"I'm good, but I need some information from you."

"Sure, what do you need to know?"

"I understand you caught the case of Private Connelly's death at Major Casale's house."

"That's right."

"Can we meet somewhere?"

"I'm on my way to lunch; why don't you meet me at the PX food court. I'll order us some fish and chips."

"Sounds good. I'll be there in fifteen."

Lance waved as Luke walked into the food court. He was seated at one of the sets of red two tops that pushed together. The tables had a single heavy round stand, and the chairs were a brushed black cross back with a red padded seat. The seating was more comfortable than it looked. He stood to greet him and extended his hand.

"Hi Luke."

"Hey Lance. Good to see you." They both sat down.

"I ordered for us already." Lance heard their number called over the speakers and headed to pick up their food. They sat quietly for a while, eating their lunch while it was hot.

"Lance, I'm defending the person who called in the tip about the dead soldier in Major Casale's home."

"Is he accused of the murder?"

"No. Corporal Hofmann was brought in because the MPs knew there was no way he could have known there was a dead body unless he was in the house. It's obvious that if he killed the guy, he wouldn't have called in the body. But on the other hand, he was in the house for some reason. Logic dictates it was to steal something." Luke dipped his heavily battered fried fish in the homemade tartar sauce and took a bite. The food court had the best fish and chips in town.

"What can I do to help you, Luke?" Luke told him about the situation the young, enlisted man had gotten himself into.

"You want us to work with the Turkish Polis to take down the theft ring."

"Yes, I was authorized to give Corporal Hofmann immunity if he cooperates."

"So they blackmailed him into stealing from his brothers in arms to get out from under his debt?"

"Yes. I know the man has no integrity, but you know how many criminal organizations target our enlisted men. Gambling houses and bars allow them to rack up bills far beyond what they know they can afford." Luke finished the last bite of his lunch and pushed the basket away.

"Luke, I can appreciate that. It's just that these guys are adults; they know what they are doing." Lance shook his head as he picked up a French fry and stuffed it in his mouth. "Regardless, we do need to do something about it. I assume the Corporal was in the Major's house to steal something. Did he get it?"

"No, but he said the Kinkade he was supposed to steal was already gone." Luke gathered the empty baskets and got up to toss them in the garbage. When he sat back down, Lance replied.

"What was Private Connelly doing in the Major's house?"

"Hofmann has no idea. After he checked his pulse, he got out of there." Luke drank the last of his soda and wiped his mouth with his napkin.

"Ok, Luke. After I get approval from my SAC. I'll get ahold of Manny, and we will approach Captain Demir about it." Lance stood. They both dropped their drinks and napkins in the garbage as they walked out.

"I'll bring Agent Hill up to speed on Private Connelly and let her take the lead until this sting is over." They walked out together and said goodbye.

# CHAPTER SIXTEEN

**Tuesday**

Lance and Manny were on their way to meet with Captain Demir at his office. Lance had gotten word from his SAC that the Commanding General gave his go-ahead for the sting.

Captain Demir greeted them as they walked into his office. "Good morning Agent Marquez and Master Sergeant Diaz. Please have a seat." Demir sat behind his desk. Lance and Manny sat across from him in metal chairs after saying hello.

"I hope you are not bringing me more work. You have managed to keep me quite busy the last few years." Demir laughed. When Lance and Manny looked at each other, Demir quit laughing. "What can I do for you, gentlemen."

"Captain, we have an enlisted man who has gotten in trouble with one of your local gambling houses," Lance started.

"These bars and gambling houses set up just blocks away from the Base to draw our men in," Manny added. The captain was familiar with the problem.

"This gambling house is a theft ring. They give credit to a low-paid enlisted man who they know can't pay it back, then offer them a way to work it off," Lance said.

"Turkish policymakers passed legislation, making Casino's illegal. But it seems all it has accomplished is to take the gambling underground. We are aware many bars are fronts for gambling houses." Demir pushed his chair back and crossed his ankle onto his other knee. He was tapping his pen, knowing where this was going. "Which bar is fronting this one?"

"Eğlenceli Ev Barı," Manny answered.

"Is that located across from the Base?"

"Yes."

"I am aware of their underhanded practices. But what you are saying is they are using the debt to force these men to steal for them."

"Yes, to steal from homes on Base. And the strange thing is they know what valuables are in the house and which room," Manny said.

"Well, it is possible that the occupant hired some 'day workers' to do lawn maintenance or something. Someone on the crew might case the place," Captain Demir said. Lance and Manny agreed.

"We want to shut them down by doing a sting. Corporal Hofmann is willing to wear a wire. He was supposed to steal an original Kinkade from a Major's home. When he broke in, it was already gone, and a dead man was on the floor." Lance explained. Demir's eyebrows went up.

"A dead man? Did this Corporal kill him? Was it the resident?"

"No, the Corporal says the man was dead when he went into the room to steal the Kinkade. I believe him. We're investigating the death," Lance said.

"If the Corporal didn't get the Kinkade, then how do we go forward?"

"I went into the evidence lockup and found a pair of diamond pear-shaped earrings, total weight 2 carats. They were recovered from the thief. The owner never reclaimed them," Manny answered.

"Why would the owner not reclaim them?"

"Most likely, they received an insurance check for more than they were worth and didn't want to return it," Manny answered Demir, who nodded and said.

"Those earrings do not come close to the value of that Kinkade."

"I know, but it will get him back in the door. That's all we need. The man who gives the orders will likely get angry and order him to steal something else right away. That's what we need to get on tape. Then you can bust him, Captain."

"The man who runs that place is Nijaz Gul; I have had a few run-ins with him. He was a small-time crook until he came up with this new scheme. Gul has amassed a large amount of money in a short time. He has managed to stay out of jail so far," Demir explained.

"Interesting. Are you willing to work with us on this, Captain?" Lance asked.

"Yes. When is your man supposed to report back to Gul?" Demir asked.

"His name is Sig Hofmann. He reports back on Thursday," Lance answered.

"I can work with that. I'll talk to our Counter Attack Team (CAT) and work out a plan. I will let CAT know that your SRT will want to be involved."

"Thank you, Captain Demir," Lance and Manny stood and shook the captain's hand, then left.

Agent Pamela Hill was working the crime scene at Major Casale's home, looking for anything out of place. She was sitting at the Major's desk in his office, scanning the papers. A copy of the trip's itinerary to Sicily was lying on top of the desk. She placed it in a plastic evidence bag to take with her.

Pam pulled out her cell and called the airlines.

"Alo, Türk Hava Yolu. Size nasıl yardımcı olabilirim?" The airline receptionist answered.

"Do you speak English?" Pam asked.

"Yes ma'am. How can I help you?"

"My name is Agent Hill from CID at the Incirlik Air Base. I need to verify that a family got on a plane to Sicily. I have the time and flight number."

"What is the information?" The woman asked. Pam gave her the itinerary information. She listened to the keys click on a keyboard while she searched. A few seconds later, she responded.

"Those boarding passes were used. However, they switched to an earlier flight, Agent Hill."

"How much earlier?"

"They were scheduled to leave early Monday morning with no layover. Instead, they left early Sunday with a stop in Rome."

"Ma'am, I need to see the surveillance for the time they were in your airport."

"I'm not authorized to do that. I'm sorry."

Incirlik and the Adana Sakirpasa Airport have a long-standing agreement. It states the airport will supply surveillance upon request. I need the video for the terminal and the gate they left from."

"I will need to get permission from our Airport Security to do that."

"I understand. When you have it, will you send it to CID in care of Agent Hill?"

"Yes Agent Hill. I would not expect it before tomorrow morning."

"Thank you, ma'am. What is your name for my notes?"

"My name is Ayleen Ates."

"Thank you for your help." Pam hung up and looked through some of the other papers on the desk. She noticed a bill for a Turkish storage building. Pam didn't have the authority to open it, but she opened the desk drawers to see if there was a file for paid bills. In the bottom drawer on the left, she found what she was looking for.

A bill from the Adana self Servis Depolama showed he paid for a unit in their facility, number 205. That was her next stop after she finished looking around.

Pam moved into the daughter's room. Her name was spelled out in large wooden letters, painted in pastel colors on the wall. Mia's room was cluttered. Pam doubted it was ransacked; more likely, it was how she kept it.

The board with pictures Lance told her about was still in place on the wall. She removed some of the photos looking for Mia's friends to talk to. She found a picture of Mia, a petite blond, pretty, wearing a big smile with her arms wrapped around two girlfriends.

Lance had taken shots of some of these, so there was no need for her to do it again. She found Mia's senior yearbook on the vanity table. Lance said he put it there for her when he discovered it in the bookshelf. Pam sat on the vanity stool and searched for the girls in the pictures. She needed their names. Pam found them and wrote the names down in her notebook. She moved on to the master bedroom; if anyone took anything, it wasn't obvious to her.

**Paris**

Clair couldn't believe the girls had been with her almost a week already. Being with two girls laughing and giggling was a new experience for her. One she wished she had been exposed to years ago. This was the fourth furniture store today; they decided on all but the beds.

"Lizzy, come look at this bed; it is so you." Sophie hollered to Lizzy. Lizzy was standing with Clair looking at comforters.

"Ms. Clair, please, you don't have to buy me anything. I promise I won't get jealous of Sophie. She is my best friend; I want her to have nice things. And she is so giving; she shares everything," Lizzy pleaded.

Claire placed her hands on the outside of Lizzy's shoulders and turned her so she could see her face.

"Lizzy, you are more than her best friend; you are her sister. The one her father and I never gave her. There will be times she will feel she can't confide in her father or me, but she will confide in you. That makes you an incredibly important person in her life, and it makes you incredibly important in mine too. Having you in her life allows me to love two beautiful girls instead of one.

"I did wrong by Sophie, the way I left her; I can never make that right. What I can do is make sure she has everything she needs materially and emotionally now. I want to do this; please let me. Your mother said it was alright." When Clair finished speaking, she noticed Lizzy's eyes were watering.

"Thank you, Ms. Clair," Lizzy said and hugged her.

"Lizzy, where are you? Come see this." Sophie hollered again.

**Adana**

Agent Hill decided to see the two friends in the picture with Mia before she went to the storage facility. They were sisters and lived two blocks over.

Pam pulled her car to the curb a few houses down and walked to the property. One of the girls was outside on her phone.

"Carrie?" The girl looked up.

"No. I'm Liv."

"Hello Liv, I'm Agent Pamela Hill from CID." Pam showed Liv her badge.

"You must be paternal twins. You are both juniors in high school."

"No. Carrie is a year older, but she has dyslexia. They didn't detect it right away, so they held her back. She needed time to learn how to manage it."

"You are both friends with Mia Casale?"

"Yes. Carrie should have been a senior with Mia."

"I'm looking for Mia. I wonder if I might be able to ask you a few questions?"

"Is she missing? I thought she was on vacation," Liv said as she headed to the front door. Pam followed.

"I don't think she is missing. It is more that I can't get ahold of anyone in her family."

"Oh, that's because they are in Sicily. Apparently, they left Sunday morning."

"Why do you say apparently?"

"Because we had plans to go to a movie Sunday night. Sort of a bon voyage type of thing. But she never showed."

"So they were supposed to leave on Monday?"

"That's what we thought." Liv opened the door and invited the Agent inside. "Mom, there is an Agent lady here to talk to us." Mrs. Johnson hurried to the entry.

"An Agent?" She asked. Pam extended her hand.

"Hello Mrs. Johnson, I'm Agent Pamela Hill from CID." Mrs. Johnson shook her hand and led her into the formal living room, directing her to have a seat.

"May I get you something to drink?" Mrs. Johnson offered.

"It is kind of you to ask, but no, thank you. I need some information from your girls."

"What about?"

"I'm looking for the Casale's. Their home was broken into, and we haven't been able to notify them."

"I see. I know Rita, I mean Mrs. Casale. Was anything stolen?"

"We're not sure. That's one of the reasons we want to talk to them."

"They are on vacation in Sicily, but I have her cell number; I'll get it."

Mrs. Johnson stood to retrieve the number as Carrie walked into the room and sat by her sister across from Pam.

"Carrie, have you talked with Mia since they left?" Pam asked.

"No. We were supposed to meet Sunday night, but they left early. I haven't heard from her," Carrie replied.

"Does she have any other friends that she may have contacted?"

"I don't think so. I'm Mia's best friend." Carrie said as her mother came back with a piece of fancy notepaper with Rita's phone number on it.

"Does Mia have a boyfriend?" Pam directed the question to the girls.

"She had a few boyfriends in high school, but nothing serious. She didn't take anyone to the graduation party," Carrie answered. Something in the way Carrie answered struck Pam odd.

"So she hasn't been seeing anyone?" Pam repeated the question.

"Maybe, I'm not sure," Carrie said, looking away.

Mrs. Johnson broke in, "Mia was allowed to date, but her father was strict about who she could hang out with."

"He didn't trust her?"

"No, it wasn't that. It was all the enlisted men. He was worried she would get involved with someone more experienced," she hesitated, "more worldly than Mia. He was afraid she might get talked into something." Mrs. Johnson answered.

"I see." Pam stood to leave. "Thank you for your time. If you hear from any of the Casale's, will you let me know?" She handed them a card. "Or have them call me."

"Yes, of course." Mrs. Johnson stood and walked Pam to the door. Liv and Carrie watched her walk away. When Carrie's mother left the room, she ran out to catch Agent Hill.

She whispered, "Agent Hill." Pam turned around.

"Yes."

"I think Mia was seeing a soldier."

"Why do you think so?" Pam asked.

"Mia told me she was seeing someone but wouldn't tell me who. The only reason she would be so cloak and dagger was if he is a soldier. She knows how her father feels about that."

"Isn't she 18 now?"

"Yes, but she doesn't want to fight with her father. She really loves her dad," Carrie said.

"How long do you think she's been seeing him?"

"About three weeks. Saturday, she called to let me know she was telling her parents she was meeting me. She would only do that if she were going out with him."

"You have no idea who it could be?" Pam asked.

"No. Please don't tell Mia's father. I don't want to get her in trouble." Carrie was wringing her hands.

"Thank you for being honest, Carrie." Pam gently laid her hand on Carrie's. "I'm just trying to make sure the family is alright."

Carrie headed back into the house, and Pam got in her car and grabbed her notebook, writing down what she learned.

A theory started formulating in Pam's mind. It seemed farfetched even to her. She had no intention of sharing it with anyone yet.

It was after 5 pm; Pam decided the storage facility could wait until tomorrow. She wanted to look through Private Connelly's things. She called Lance.

"Hello?"

"Lance, it's Pam. Connelly lived at the barracks, right?"

"Right. He was on a waiting list for an apartment."

"Did the Crime Scene Lab collect his things?"

"Yes, they have them downstairs."

"Thanks." Pam started to hang up.

"Wait. Do you have a theory?"

"Maybe." Pam hedged.

"Will you share it?"

"Not yet. It's pretty out there."

"How about dinner tonight?" Lance offered.

"If you don't mind eating late. I want to go through Connelly's things."

"I'm ok with eating late. Why don't I help you?"

"Alright. I'm on my way now. Thanks, Lance."

Twenty minutes later, Lance was holding the door for Pam to step into the Crime Scene Lab.

"Thanks," she said. Lance went to check the board to see which bin Connelly's possessions were in. He led the way to the storage area. Pam found the bin and Lance opened it.

They sorted through his belongings. Pam felt terrible that this bin could contain his life. Lance noticed her demeanor.

"What's wrong? You don't see what you're looking for?"

"It's not that. It's just...sad. A few days ago, this young man had no idea that his choices in life would dictate eternity for him. I'm sure he never even thought about it. Although, there is no doubt he had the opportunity."

"What do you mean he had the opportunity?"

"The Bible says in Timothy 2:4 that 'God desires all men to be saved and to come to the knowledge of the truth.' Somewhere along the path of his life, Private Connelly heard the Gospel of Salvation."

"Are you saying he didn't make heaven?"

"I have no way of knowing whether he was born again," Pam explained. Lance turned to her.

"I believe there is a God, Pam."

"I know you do, Lance. But are you ready to turn your life over to Him, ask forgiveness and become a new creation?" Pam was still sorting through things. Lance never had a chance to answer her question before she blurted out.

"Here it is. What I was looking for." She held up the item and showed it to Lance.

"Is this part of your theory?"

"Yes."

**Wednesday 10 am.**

Luke, Manny, and Lance were with Corporal Hofmann at the SRT unit office in the morning. Demir and his CAT unit leader were on the phone with them, finalizing details for Thursday's sting.

Captain Demir had worked with both Sergeant Ty Solomon, the SRT leader, and Başçavuş Simsek, the Turkish CAT team leader. They all worked well together.

"Sergeant Solomon, have you gone over the plan we agreed on with your men?" Başçavuş Simsek asked Sergeant Solomon.

"Yes sir. And as you requested, our Mobile Command Vehicle will be out of sight. You can run your operation from there. We will make sure we record a copy of everything that happens for you."

"Sergeant, can we meet at the location at 1900 hours tomorrow night?" Başçavuş Simsek asked.

"Yes, that will give us an hour to be up and running."

"Agent Marquez, is Corporal Hofmann up to speed on exactly what we expect him to do?" Captain Demir asked.

"Yes Captain."

"Are there any other questions?" No one responded. "Then we will meet at 1900 hours." Captain Demir signed off, and the meeting was over. Lance turned to the Corporal.

"Corporal Hofmann, are you sure you can pull this off?"

"Yes sir. But what's going to happen to me afterward. I know I have immunity, but will I be dishonorably discharged?" Hofmann turned to Luke for the answer.

"Sig, you broke a myriad of regulations. Gambling, stealing, breaking and entering, are only a few of the crimes. The fact you have immunity is a gift. I don't see the Army overlooking those moral lapses and allowing you to remain enlisted. Maybe I can get you a general discharge; your immunity will leave you without a criminal record. A general discharge will reflect that there was bad behavior and you will lose some of your GI Bill benefits. But it's viewed better than a dishonorable discharge. I'm sorry, Sig, but that is likely what will happen," Luke said. Sig lowered his head almost to his chest. It was obvious it wasn't what he wanted.

"I know better than this; my Christian parents raised me to know right from wrong. I walked away from my faith in High School when I chose my friends. Then I compounded that by joining the Army, thinking I could run away from God."

"Don't let this define you, Sig. Recommit your life to Christ. He is faithful to forgive our sins. Go home and be the man God intended you to be when He formed you in your mother's womb." Manny tried to encourage him.

"Thank you for that, Master Sergeant Diaz," Hofmann looked up.

"We'll meet back here at 08:30 pm tomorrow and travel with the SRT. Corporal, I'll need you to stay in holding until this is over." Manny directed.

Lance asked Pam to wait for him until he finished his meeting with Demir. He wanted to go with her to the storage facility.

"Hello?"

"Pam, it's me. Where can I meet up with you?"

"Right now, I'm at CID headquarters. I've been interviewing some of Connelly's friends. I wanted to find out what kind of a man he was, so I can see if my theory holds up."

"Good. I'm on my way. I'd like to sit in on one of the interviews. Then we can go to the storage unit."

"Sounds like a plan."

# THE PROMISE

# CHAPTER SEVENTEEN

**Paris**

It was lunchtime. The girls had been trying on school clothes for the last few hours while Clair helped them pick out the newest fashions.

Wesley was home; he had a surprise planned for them. He had managed to get tickets to a live performance of 'Beauty and the Beast'. They had one performance in English at 8 pm. Clair was surprised at how engaging he was with Sophie and Lizzy during this visit. She wondered if he realized how empty life could be without a family.

"Mom, can we eat at the French Bakery across the street from your condo?" Sophie asked.

"Are you girls tired of shopping already?" Sophie and Lizzy nodded. "Alright then, let's go." On the way out, they passed by a bookstore.

"Can we look in here?" They headed into the store. Clair was looking at some new fashion magazines while the girls looked around. Sophie spotted something. She grabbed Lizzy's hand and tugged her over to see.

"Look, Lizzy, they have Bibles. Mom doesn't have one. I want to buy it for her."

"My mom always talks about the King James Bible. Make sure we get that one."

"Yeah." The girls found a pretty burgundy leather-covered Bible. The small sign on the shelf said they could engrave it. Sophie and Lizzy made sure Clair wasn't watching them and then took it to the cashier.

"We would like to buy this. How much is it?" Sophie asked, putting it on the counter. The cashier lifted the box it was in and scanned the barcode.

"This one is €75," the cashier said. Sophie and Lizzy's eyes got wide.

"Do we have that much?" Sophie asked, digging in her purse. Lizzy dug too.

"I have €40," Lizzy said, putting it on the counter. Sophie took everything out of her wallet, €35. She handed it to the lady.

"We would like to get it engraved," Sophie smiled, excited.

"That will be an additional €5." The girls' faces fell. They had cleaned out their wallets already. The cashier saw their disappointment, hesitated for a moment, then smiled.

"Oh, I forgot. We are having a special today. Engraving is free." The girls got so excited they were afraid Clair would hear them.

"What do you want engraved on the Bible?"

"Mom." Sophie smiled a big smile.

"Do you want it in gold or silver?" The cashier asked. Sophie looked at Lizzy.

They both said, "silver."

"Alright, I will have it ready in ten minutes." The girls went back to the books to look around. They managed to stall Clair long enough to get the Bible from the cashier.

**Adana**

Lance and Pam had Private Clayton Colagnee sitting across from them in the CID conference room. Lance had Pam take the lead.

"Private Colagnee, I understand Private Connelly was a friend of yours."

"Yes, is he in some sort of trouble. I know he didn't show up for work the last few days."

"We are trying to determine that. Were you friends?" Pam asked again.

"Yeah, I guess."

"What does that mean?" Lance asked.

"Pete...I mean, Private Connelly kept to himself. He mingled but never told anyone much about his life."

"So he would go out to the bars with his buddies?" Lance asked.

"Um...I wouldn't say, buddies. He did go out with us, though. He never drank alcohol; he volunteered to be the designated driver."

"Did he have a girlfriend?" Pam asked. Private Colagnee rolled his shoulders and leaned his head back, trying to think.

"Maybe. Recently. I remember the guys asked him if he wanted to go to play cards off base. He was usually up for that. He generally won. But that night, he said he had other plans, and I remember when I walked past him, he had aftershave on."

"He never said who she was or gave a hint?" Lance asked.

"No."

"Is there anyone else he might have confided in? Someone he was close to?"

"I don't know. I never saw Pete with anyone other than our small group," he hesitated. "I do remember once we were all talking about why we enlisted. He said something about not having a choice," Colagnee said.

"No choice, like a judge gave him the option to join or go to jail?"

"I have no idea." Pam put down her pen and stood. Lance and Private Colagnee stood too. "Thank you for coming in. If you think of anything else, will you please get in contact with me." She handed him one of her cards.

When the Private left, Lance said, "if he was in trouble in the States, maybe that trouble followed him here. We need to check court records. Where was he from?"

"Colorado, I believe. I'll check on that when we get back from the storage unit," Pam said.

"Sounds good to me," Lance agreed.

**Paris**

Clair was walking the girls across the street. They just finished their lunch at the French Bakery across from her penthouse.

Wesley was waiting for them. He opened the door and said, "did you all have a nice day?"

"Yes. It was fun, Mr. Wes," Sophie smiled at him.

"I have a surprise for you. I would like to take you girls to see the live performance of 'Beauty and the Beast'."

"What?" The girls squealed in unison. The exact response Wesley was hoping for. Sophie and Lizzy threw their arms around him in a big hug.

"Really, Mr. Wes. 'Beauty and the Beast'?" Lizzy repeated. Clair stepped up, happy the girls responded to Wes's surprise. She knew he wanted to connect with them.

"Well, if we want to go to 'Beauty and the Beast' we will be out late. You girls better take a nap. I'll see that your dresses get steamed."

"Ok, Mom." The girls squealed again and ran off to their room. Clair wrapped her arms around Wes's neck and kissed him.

"Thank you for making an effort to be a part of Sophie's life. It means a lot to me."

"Clair, I don't know why I resisted for so long. I've centered my life on making money. I've missed out on so much." He shook his head, thinking of all the wasted time.

A few hours later Wes hollered, "girls, hurry, we can't be late." Clair and the girls rushed to the door. "You all look so beautiful," he smiled. Sophie ran up and hugged him.

"Thank you, Wes. This is the best surprise." It was the first time Sophie spoke to him without the honorific of Mister in front of his name. Wes passed a look to Clair. She understood what it meant to him.

Wes got them to the Palais Garnier an hour early. He wanted the girls to look through the vendor's offerings of mementos, and they all enjoyed people watching.

**Adana**

Agent Hill and Agent Marquez drove to the Adana Self Servis Depolama. The young man in the office didn't speak English. They managed to let him know that they wanted to get into unit number 205. He kept shaking his head. Pam decided to ask if his boss was in the building. The young man shrugged.

Lance and Pam walked to the second floor to see the unit anyway. They were surprised to find these storage spaces were not solid units but cages.

"Look at this, Lance. We can see right into his unit."

"I see that." Lance stepped close to the cage and visually examined the contents. Pam did the same. Most of the items were in crates or bins. The one large crate looked like it could contain a couch—hard telling what was in the bins.

"We'll have to come back with an interpreter," Lance relented.

"Yeah, but that doesn't mean he will let us in the unit without a warrant," Pam said. She went to look inside again.

"Lance, come here. Is that a Transon Art Tube?" Lance moved to look over her shoulder.

"It looks like it."

"Do you suppose the missing Kinkade is in there?" Pam asked.

"I would bet the bank on it. Do you think SAC will let us seek a warrant to get into his storage unit?"

"Not a chance. Major Casale is the victim here," Pam answered.

"Let's go back to the office. I'm still curious about Colagnee's statement that Connelly had to join the Army. If you search the records in Colorado Springs, I'll call his parents. His unit commander contacted Connelly's parents about his passing. I know my call will be difficult for them," Lance said.

**Paris**

Wes slipped off to the vendors during intermission while the girls took a bathroom break. He saw how the girl's ooh and aah over an Ivory China Mrs. Potts and chip. Wes rushed over, purchased two sets, and asked the cloakroom to hold them under the same claim ticket.

Wes waited in line for beverages for everyone. He couldn't help but think how much fun he was having; he loved watching the girls. They bounced on their seats with excitement and sang along with the characters. It was a good call on his part to get a private box. Other patrons may not have enjoyed the girls' enthusiasm. Wes saw them approaching and waved them over.

"Tell me what you would like to drink, and I'll bring it up to the box," Wes offered.

"Lemonade," Sophie requested.

"Soda," Lizzy said.

"I'll take a cappuccino," Clair said and leaned over to kiss Wes on his cheek. She then took the girls' hands and went back to the box.

On the way home, Sophie and Lizzy were singing 'Be Our Guest' and 'Something There'; Wes and Clair joined in.

When Sophie and Lizzy got in bed, Clair went to check on them. She kissed each one on the forehead and was leaving when Sophie stopped her.

"Mom, you need to brush our hair." Clair walked over to grab a brush off the vanity and sat on the bed.

"Turn on your tummy, Sophie." She brushed Sophie's hair exactly fifty times and then went to Lizzy's side of the bed and did the same for her. By the time she finished, they were both sound asleep.

### Thursday Adana

Pam had already left when Lance got ahold of Connelly's parents Wednesday night. She hadn't found anything new in her search for any police record other than a sealed juvenile record.

"Good morning Agent Marquez," Pam said with a smile as she headed for her desk. "Did you get ahold of Connelly's parents?"

"Yes."

"Tell me."

"It was a tough call. Pete's mom was broken up; his father tried to be a rock for her, but he barely held it together. He had a lot of questions I couldn't answer."

"Did you ask them about why he joined the Army?"

"Yes. The dad said that Pete was a shy kid. He didn't have many friends until new neighbors showed up with a teen Pete's age. They became fast friends. In the summer before their senior year, they were dirt biking in the hills behind their house. Pete's friend took a nasty fall without a helmet; he died. Pete took it hard; he started drinking and causing trouble. If he hadn't already taken most of his required courses to graduate, he would have never gotten his diploma.

"So, how does that get him an ultimatum to join the military?" Pam asked.

"That summer, Pete started drinking and drove home drunk several times. He was caught once by police; instead of a ticket for DUI, they gave him a reckless driving ticket."

"That's still an expensive ticket," Pam acknowledged.

"Yes, it took every cent Pete had saved for his senior trip. He stopped drinking after that," Lance said.

"Or so they thought," Pam guessed, finishing his sentence.

"Exactly. A week before graduation, Pete was involved with a hit and run."

"He killed someone?"

"No. Just property damage. The judge gave him a chance to have that conviction and the reckless driving expunged. But he had to do four things."

"Join the military was one of them." Pam nodded her head, knowing what was coming.

"Yes, he had to get his diploma, go into rehab, pay for the damages out of his pocket, and join the military."

"There is nothing in his history to indicate he was in the Casale's home to steal."

"I agree; Connelly had no priors for stealing. Why would he start now? It makes your theory more plausible," Lance said.

"I'm going to talk to a few more of his co-workers. He must have told someone something," Pam said.

"Ok. I have to get ready for the bust tonight. Let me know what you find out," Lance said, getting up from his desk. "How about dinner tomorrow night, Pam?"

"I'll have to get back to you on that. I want to keep working this while the trails hot." Pam could see Lance was disappointed.

"Sure, let me know." Lance headed to meet up with Manny.

**Paris**

Clair was in the kitchen making waffles. Usually, she would leave that to Ava, the housekeeper, but she wanted to do it herself. Beau abandoned the girls when he smelled food. He was sitting by the stove next to Clair, waiting for some scraps, when Sophie and Lizzy walked in. Sophie's hair was a mess, most of it out of the ribbon. Lizzy's hair was still holding her blond locks nicely.

"Hey mom, Lizzy, and I bought something for you." Clair stopped what she was doing.

"You did?" Sophie handed her the box that contained the Bible. Clair sat down and opened it. She took the leather-bound Bible from the box and ran her hand over the smooth surface. Stopping at the silver engraved name 'MOM'. She caught her breath.

"Sophie, Lizzy, this is beautiful. Thank you." Clair clutched it to her chest, then set it down and stepped over to hug the girls. "Thank you."

"Now you can go to church, Mom," Sophie said. Clair looked at her quizzically. "You didn't go to church with daddy and me. It was because you didn't have a Bible, right? Now you can go." She had a huge smile on her face, confident that had to be the reason.

"Thank you so much. I love it." Clair said, not responding to the rest of the comment.

"You'll read it, won't you, Mom?" Sophie asked.

"Of course, darling. I'll read it." She put it back in the box. "Now, you two need to eat breakfast, then take a bath and get dressed. Wes is taking us on a ride in the country." Clair said, trying to hide the catch in her throat.

**Adana**

Manny and Corporal Hofmann were waiting for Lance in Manny's office at the MP station. They wanted to drive over to the meet location to familiarize themselves with the area.

"I don't know about this, Master Sergeant Diaz. If I show up with a pair of earrings worth so much less than the Kinkade, he is not going to be happy," Hofmann said.

"We are hoping he'll be mad enough to order you to steal something else. Once we get that on record, we can arrest him." Manny hesitated, "do you have any idea where Gul stores all his stolen merchandise before he sells it?"

"Well, I met him at a warehouse once. There were crates of merchandise stacked up. But I have no idea if it is the stolen items," Hofmann responded. Manny turned to Lance.

"Corporal, do you have an address or directions to this warehouse?" Lance asked.

"I remember where it is."

"Let's take a drive over there. We have time. If we can confirm that it is stolen goods, we can have that raided tonight, too," Lance said.

The men climbed into Lance's SUV. Ten minutes later, they parked a block away, watching the warehouse for any movement. When they felt confident there was no one there, they walked to the backside of the building to look in the windows. It was like Hofmann said, crates stacked up all around. Darkness edged in around what little daylight they had left.

"We need to see what's in those crates," Manny said. He checked the back door, but it was locked with a deadbolt. Lance tried some of the windows, but they wouldn't move. The men moved to the other side of the building. There were wooden stairs that led to what looked like an office. Lance ran up the stairs and checked the door. It was unlocked; he looked down at Manny and opened the door.

Manny looked around; he saw no one watching. The three men ran through the office and down the stairs that took them to the warehouse inside. Manny pried one of the crates open. Lance pulled out his penlight to shine inside the crate. The crate had random merchandise in it wrapped in bubble wrap and packing straw.

"There is no way to know by looking at this stuff if it is stolen," Manny said.

"You're right. We'll contact Captain Demir and see if he wants to coordinate a raid on this property. He can check the ownership of the warehouse and determine if this property is stolen," Lance said.

As Lance drove back to Base, Manny called Captain Demir.

"Captain, can you look up an address for us? We need to know the property owner." Manny rattled off the property's address. They waited as they heard a keyboard working.

"It looks like it belongs to a Mirya Avci," the captain relayed.

"Not Nijaz Gul?" Manny asked.

"No, but just a minute." Demir tapped on the keys again. "Mirya Avci married Nijaz Gul two years ago," Demir said with a chipper tone.

"Captain, we think that property is the holding area for the stolen goods. Would you be interested in raiding it once Gul is arrested?"

"Yes, that is an excellent idea." The captain thanked Manny for the information and told him he would see him in a few hours."

Agent Hill called the motor pool where Private Connelly worked; he repaired the big rigs. She asked for a mechanic; the office transferred her to the shop.

"Corporal Hinsen."

"Corporal Hinsen, this is Agent Pamela Hill."

"Yes, ma'am, what can I do for you?"

"Can I have you meet me at CID headquarters?"

"I'm sorry, ma'am, we are shorthanded since..."

"I can come to you. When do you get a break?"

"I get a break in twenty minutes," Hinsen said.

"I'll meet you outside your shop. I'll bring you a cup of coffee," Pam offered.

"Alright...sure," came the reply.

Agent Hill was sitting outside the auto shop when Corporal Hinsen stepped out of the bay area. She looked around and noticed Pam as she got out of her car.

"Agent Hill?"

"Yes Corporal." Pam handed her one of the hot cups of coffee she was holding.

"Thank you, ma'am." Hinsen stood in front of Pam, who was leaning against her car. "What is it I can do for you?"

"You worked with Private Connelly?'

"Yes ma'am."

"Were you friends?"

"We were, we dated a few times, but we decided we were better at being friends than a couple." She laughed at the memory, "I will miss him."

"Did you keep up with his life after you dated?"

"Yes, we work side by side here."

"Was he in debt to gamblers or loan sharks?"

"NO! Why would you ask that?" The Corporal snapped back.

"You are aware he was found dead in Major Casale's home, right?"

"Yes, but how do you leap from that to he's in debt with gamblers?"

"I'm trying to determine what he was doing there. The only reason we can come up with is that he was there to steal something," Pam explained her reasoning.

"No, he wasn't like that. He had plans for the future."

"What kind of plans."

"Our tours are almost up. I told him I was going to re-up. He said he was transitioning out at the end of the year; he wanted to get married. With the mechanics training he learned here on big rigs, he would be able to support a wife in civilian life."

"He was planning on getting married? Do you know who he was dating?"

"He wouldn't say who he was dating, but I know he was dating someone."

"Is there anything you can tell me that will help me find out what happened to him?" Pam asked, sipping her coffee allowing the Corporal to think.

"I really can't, ma'am. He was a nice guy, quiet; he kept to himself most of the time."

"Thanks for your time." Pam extended her hand to her. They shook and Corporal Hinsen went back to work.

# CHAPTER EIGHTEEN

Manny, Lance, and Sig ate dinner at the Base mess hall before Sig changed into civilian clothes. They picked up Luke at his office then headed to the SRT staging area early.

Sergeant Ty Solomon came over to speak with Lance. "You are sure Corporal Hofmann can pull this off?" Lance moved Ty further away from Hofmann before he answered.

"He is nervous, Ty, but he knows he has to do this to stay out of jail. He will get what you need on record." Ty nodded his head and went back to the command vehicle.

One hour later, they were out of sight at the agreed location behind an abandoned gas station. Captain Demir stepped into the command vehicle and said his CAT team was in place and ready. The team was holding two blocks on the other side of the target location: Eğlenceli Ev Barı.

Sergeant Solomon got on the comm and gave the first instruction to his team.

"Team two, this is team leader. From this point, you will take your orders from Başçavuş Simsek, CAT's team one leader." Solomon signed off and said to Captain Demir, "the command is yours, sir." The captain, in turn, nodded to his CAT leader.

Başçavuş Simsek addressed the teams in Turkish and English, giving final instructions. He then turned to Hofmann and asked if he was ready. Luke moved Hofmann a few feet away and explained what he needed Gul to say on record before they breached. Hofmann nodded his head, and Luke gave him the box holding the two-carat earrings.

Sig Hofmann stepped out of the command vehicle and walked the two blocks to Eğlenceli Ev Barı, the bar and gambling joint. He stepped in the front door and saw the bouncer. He nodded to Sig and told him to go back to the office; Mr. Gul was expecting him. Sig took a deep breath that carried over the comm.

Sig knocked on the office door, one of Gul's enforcers opened it and gestured for him to come in.

"Sig Hofmann," Nijaz said like they were friends and moved around his desk. His smile formed into a scowl. "I do not see the gift you promised me."

"Gift? You mean the 'gift'," Sig used air quotes, "like the other 'gifts' you force me to steal?"

"Potāto, Potato, tomāto, tomato," Gul snickered.

"You watch too many old American movies," Sig said, trying to seem at ease.

"Yes, that is true, and in the old movies, the man who disappoints his boss gets whacked." Nijaz laughed at his own joke, but Sig knew he wasn't joking.

"Now tell me where my painting is?" It appeared Gul's lighthearted banter was over. He was staring Sig in the eyes; Sig looked away and told him what happened.

"I entered the Major's house on Monday. I went directly to the room you told me to, and there was no painting. What I did find was a dead body."

"A dead body?"

"Yes. So I grabbed what I could find quickly and took off," Sig said.

"You will learn, I do not accept excuses." Gul nodded to his enforcer, who grabbed Sig's shoulder and turned him around. He punched him once in the face, then pressed his forearm against Sig's windpipe and pushed him against the wall, pinning him.

When Başçavuş Simsek heard the enforcer roughing up Sig, he moved his team closer to intervene if necessary but kept them out of sight. Manny and Lance exchanged glances; they were concerned about Sig's welfare. They trusted the captain's men and had been in enough police actions to know better than to try to step in during an active one. Saying anything would only create chaos and lead to mistakes.

Sig reached his hand out that held the earrings.

"What is this?" Gul opened the small package. He looked at the earrings and tossed them on his desk after saying.

"This is nothing. I wanted that Kinkade."

"I know," Sig tried to speak, but the enforcer was pressing on his windpipe. Nijaz nodded to the man to let him go. Sig coughed in spasms and slipped down to the ground. "I told you it wasn't there," Sig whispered still trying to get his breath.

"Well, this will go in the negative column in the books," Gul said, walking back to his desk and sitting in his chair. The enforcer grabbed Sig's arm and dragged him to a chair across from his boss. Nijaz sat there thinking for a while.

"I will allow you to make it up to me," he paused. "I do have an item I would like from General Hughes's home," he smiled, "and I think you are just the man to get it for me."

"You want me to break into General Hughes's home?"

"Yes, I understand he has a gun collection that includes a colt .45 revolver owned by Wyatt Earp. I want it."

"You will never be able to sell it," Sig said.

"I do not wish to sell it. If you get me that revolver, I will clear your debt."

Captain Demir broke in, "we have enough Başçavuş Simsek, take him down."

"Teams one and two breach, breach." Team one breached the back door, and team two went through the front. They restrained the bouncer and the two bartenders, confiscating their guns. The others cleared out the bar.

Team one made it to the office door first and entered. Nijaz and his enforcer heard the commotion outside the office. Nijaz came around the desk and grabbed Sig around the neck, using him for cover. He put his gun to Sig's head.

A CAT officer broke down the door. The enforcer shot the man hitting his vest knocking him down and out of commission. One of the SRT members returned fire, not killing him but taking him down. Five officers were now in the room, three CAT and two SRT. Everyone focused on the hostage situation.

"Get out of my way, or I will shoot this man in the head," Nijaz threatened, speaking in Turkish. A CAT member responded in kind.

"Nijaz Gul, put your weapon down and let him go, or I will shoot you." Nijaz waved his weapon at the men directing them to move from the door, the only escape route.

The officers moved, keeping their weapons trained on Nijaz, waiting for an opportunity to shoot.

As soon as Nijaz backed out the door, two officers grabbed him and slammed him to the ground. A third officer snatched Sig away from him.

"We need medics," one of Solomon's men shouted into the comm. Nijaz Gul was in custody.

Each team had a medic; the SRT medic tended to Sig. The CAT medic tended to the enforcer and sent him to the hospital. Luke rode with Sig to the Incirlik hospital. Manny and Lance stayed at the scene with the captain.

Once the standoff ended, Captain Demir told Başçavuş Simsek he wanted his men to hit the warehouse.

"I want everything in the warehouse confiscate. The SRT was to clean up the scene here, with strict orders to return with the earrings.

**Paris**

Everyone was asleep, exhausted. Another day in the country, flying kites and having a picnic, was their new favorite thing to do. Clair couldn't sleep. She went to the French balcony, sat on the padded rod iron chair, and held Sophie's gift to her chest. Clair stayed up late reading it the night before. She had heard Luke tell new believers to start reading the Bible in the New Testament, so that's what she did. Clair opened to the spot she marked the night before.

Sophie woke late in the night, thirsty. She walked into the kitchen to get some water; Beau padded his feet behind her. Beau loved having two little girls to sleep with every night. He spent his whole day following them around, getting petted and played with. Beau would sit at the door when they were out of the apartment and wait for them to come back.

When Sophie finished drinking her water, she noticed the French doors were open. Sophie went to shut them when she saw her mother sitting outside.

"Mom?" Clair turned to see her daughter.

"Sophie. What are you doing up?"

"I needed some water." Sophie sat in the other chair. "Mommy, why didn't you come to church with daddy and me? It wasn't because you didn't have a Bible, was it? Don't you believe in God?"

"Oh sweetheart, I don't know. I do believe there is a God. I guess I just didn't believe there was any necessity to get to know Him. I've always felt if I'm a good person, I would go to heaven. I am a good person, aren't I, Sophie?"

"Of course, Mommy." Sophie got up and hugged her. "Mom, it isn't about being good. There is only one way into heaven, and that is through Jesus. All you have to do is repent of your sins. The Bible says, 'That if you confess with your mouth the Lord Jesus and believe in your heart that God has raised Him from the dead, you will be saved,' that's in Romans 10:9."

"You memorized that scripture."

"Summer Bible Camp. You win stuff if you memorize the most scripture. I won two times." Sophie said with pride, then sat back down in her chair.

"I know I did wrong by you and Luke, Sophie. Can you ever forgive me?"

"Mommy, I don't know that I will ever understand why you left us. But I'm a big girl now and know some moms and dads get divorced. Daddy's happy now, and so are you; that's all I care about," Sophie saw the tears running down her mother's beautiful face.

"What about you Sophie, are you happy?" Clair took Sophie's hand. Sophie thought about it for a moment.

"Yes Mom, I am, and I do forgive you."

"I'm afraid I won't get to see you very often when you go back to the States." Clair looked out on the lights of the Eiffel Tower.

"You can come to see me," Sophie said.

"I will, darling."

"You promise?" Sophie asked.

"I promise. And will you come to see me?" Clair asked.

"I will, I promise."

"I love you, Sophie."

"I love you too, Mom."

"You better get back to bed. Wes has planned on shopping with us tomorrow. He took the whole week off."

"Really?"

"Yes," Clair turned to her and leaned forward. "He regrets not spending time with you. You have to understand; he spent most of his life alone. His parents sent him to boarding schools. He only saw them a few times a year."

"How sad," Sophie responded.

"It is sad. Now Wes is hoping it's not too late to be a part of your life. Can you forgive him, too?"

"Of course, Mommy. But he will never be my dad."

"I know that. He just wants to be a part of your life." Sophie nodded her head. She stood and leaned over her mom to kiss her. Clair placed her hand on both of Sophie's cheeks and kissed both sides.

"Goodnight, Mom."

"Goodnight, darling. And I'm so glad you brought Lizzy along this time. She is a wonderful friend."

"Lizzy's my best friend."

It was almost 10 pm, and Agent Hill was still at the CID office. She was hoping to hear what happened with the bust of Nijaz Gul. So far, no news.

Pam had been trying to get a hold of Major Casale since Monday. It was 9 pm in Sicily; she was a little concerned about trying to call again so late. She did it anyway. Pam tried to hide her surprise when he answered his phone.

"Hello?"

"Major Casale?"

"Yes. To whom am I speaking?" The Major questioned.

"Sir, this is Agent Hill from Incirlik Air Base. I have been trying to contact you since Monday."

"I see. What can I do for you?"

"Someone broke into your home Monday, and we would like to speak with you about it," Pam said.

"Was anything taken?"

"We are not sure; that is one of the things we need to find out. There is a possibility a Kinkade was stolen."

"You don't know?" He asked.

"Sir, we need you to come back to base."

"I am on vacation. If anything is missing, coming home early isn't going to change that fact. I'll deal with the insurance when I get home," the Major insisted.

"Sir, there is more to it than that. I need you to come back to Base, sir." Pam was more resolute. Major Casale was quiet on the other end.

"What is really going on, Agent Hill." Pam was hesitant to spill the beans about the dead body, but she needed him to get on a plane and come back to Base.

"Major Casale, there was a dead soldier found in your home."

"What? Who?"

"His name is Private Connelly; he worked in the motor pool," Pam explained. She heard a big sigh on the other end of the line.

"Alright. I will get a flight back tomorrow."

"I would like to speak with your wife and daughter too, sir."

"Absolutely not; I am not changing their plans for this."

"Sir, I need to talk to your daughter," Pam said again.

"My wife and daughter are back in the States, Agent. They will not be coming back." Pam was shocked at this revelation.

"In the States, sir?"

"Yes, Mia decided she wanted to spend her summer before college at home, so Rita flew back with her." The Major explained. Pam didn't believe it for a second; more convinced than ever, he knew something about this.

"Alright, sir, I will expect you at CID tomorrow." Pam finally said. He hung up with no response.

Pam hung up and leaned back in her office chair, livid; he knew sending his family out of reach would hinder her investigation.

Pam was still chewing on the situation when she heard the door open. Manny and Lance walked in.

"Hi Pam, what are you still doing here?" Lance asked with a smile.

"I'll tell you in a minute; first, I want to know how the bust went." They came and sat across from her.

"Well, Corporal Hofmann is in the hospital," Manny said. Pam sat up in her seat.

"What?"

"Gul's enforcer choked him. He will be alright; they're keeping him overnight for observation," Manny continued.

"So you shut down his operation?" Pam asked.

"Yes, and confiscated all the stolen goods in his warehouse," Lance said.

"Hofmann told us he knew where the warehouse was, so we checked it out before the bust. It was full of crates. We told Captain Demir and he raided it after we had Gul in custody," Manny said.

"The captain called and verified it was stolen property," Lance added.

"That's great. Congratulations," Pam relayed. Lance shifted in his seat.

"So, what kept you here late?" Lance asked.

"I finally managed to get ahold of Major Casale. He is coming back tomorrow. But he sent his wife and daughter to the States," she said with a scowl.

"Major Casale sent them to the States. Why?" Manny questioned.

"Casale said his daughter wanted to spend her summer at home. I don't believe it." Both men nodded in agreement. "I had to tell him there was a dead body found in his home to get him to come back. I didn't want to do that," Pam recounted.

"That's a shame; it would have been nice to see his reaction," Lance said.

"I didn't ask him if he knew the dead soldier," she said with a small smile. "I still have that."

"Well, it's time to go home." Lance turned to Manny, "how about we do those After-Action Reports tomorrow?" Manny put his hands on the arms of the chair and lifted his tired body.

"Sounds good to me."

"Come on, Pam; I'll walk you out," Lance said. Pam nodded.

**Friday**

Major Casale's flight from Sicily landed at the Adana airport just before noon. On the flight, he played the situation over and over in his mind. He needed to talk to someone. As soon as he cleared the jetway, he pulled out his cell and dialed.

"Hello?"

"Major Scott, this is Major Casale. Can you meet me somewhere?"

"Sure. Tell me where and when."

"Now, not on Base," Casale insisted.

"What about the Çalıkuşu Restaurant across the street from the front gate."

"Alright, give me forty minutes; I'm at the airport."

Major Scott hung up. David and Major Casale were well acquainted. They had lunch together at the Officer's Club on occasion and played a few rounds of golf together, but this did not feel like a social call. He knew Major Casale's house was a crime scene, but he had not heard that the Major was a person of interest.

Major Scott made it to the restaurant early and grabbed a table for them. Major Casale walked in ten minutes later. He looked around and spotted David. Walking up to the table, he spoke first.

"Hello, David." David stood to shake his hand.

"Hello, Oscar. Why all the cloak and dagger?" They both sat. The waiter came over and took their drink order.

226

"I need legal help, David. I'm supposed to meet with Agent Hill today concerning the break-in at my house."

"Ok. I don't see any problem with that," David said, confused.

"David, can you be my lawyer?"

"Yes, Jag lawyers are available to all enlisted men and officers."

"I'm asking if you will be my lawyer?"

"What's going on, Oscar?"

"I will tell you everything, but I need an answer."

"Yes, everything you say from this point on is privileged," David confirmed. The waiter brought their coffee and took their order.

Oscar told David everything that happened. David asked questions, and they took a break while they ate their food.

"Let's get this over with. Just answer Agent Hill's questions. I'll stop you if you shouldn't answer." David was unhappy with the situation. "I wish you would tell her what happened. I can handle the situation better if you tell them everything."

"No, I will not allow my family to be involved in this situation." Oscar was adamant about the course he was taking.

"Alright, but when you do answer a question, make sure it's the truth or don't answer."

"I understand."

"We need to go by your house to see if anything is missing," David suggested.

"Alright."

Major Scott and Major Casale were escorted to the CID offices by a guard from security downstairs. When they walked into the office at CID headquarters, they looked around for Agent Hill. She noticed them and walked over to greet them.

"Major Scott, Major Casale, please follow me." The men followed her to a conference room; she opted not to use the interrogation room. Lance was going to join them as soon as he filled in the brass about last night's operation.

Agent Hill shook their hands and asked them to be seated. She sat across from them at the small conference table.

"Major Casale, I apologize for cutting your vacation short. But we can't account for the dead soldier found in your home."

"I understand. Let's get to it. What is it you need to know?" Pam showed the Major's a recorder and said.

"Sir, you don't mind if I record this, do you?" Both men nodded in acceptance. "You are aware there was a break-in at your home on Monday?" Agent Hill asked.

"Yes, I was informed by you yesterday when you called me."

"Have you had time to go home and see if anything is missing?"

"I have. The only thing that is not in its place is the Kinkade."

"Do you believe someone stole it?"

"I can't say," Oscar hedged his answer. Pam looked at him quizzically.

"That is a strange response, Major. Do you believe it was stolen?" She persisted.

"Move on, Agent Hill," David interrupted. She sat for a moment looking at Major Casale. Lance stepped in and acknowledged the Majors and Agent Hill. He sat down next to Pam.

"Major Casale, do you hire locals to do your lawn work?"

"Yes, one local company. I checked their references and found they had a good reputation."

"Do you know if they ever entered your home for any reason?"

"I'm not usually there when they are working. My wife would know that."

"Yes, but your wife is not available is she, Major?" Pam goaded.

"No, my wife and daughter went back to the States, as I explained before," Oscar said.

"Was that a planned decision or spur of the moment?"

"I don't see how that is relevant to a break-in at my house," Oscar said, agitated. Agent Hill didn't want to push him so far that he'd walk out, so she let it go.

"Major Casale, did you know there was a dead soldier in your home before you flew to Sicily?" Agent Hill asked. The Major didn't answer.

"Move on, Agent Hill," David instructed. Lance stepped in.

"Not so fast, Major Scott. We need to have an answer to that question."

"Not at this point. Do you have any other questions?" David shut him down. Pam pulled out the photo she had of a deceased Private Connelly from the folder. She placed it in front of him.

"Do you know this man, Major?" Agent Hill watched his face closely.

"No."

"Are you sure?" Pam asked.

"He's not your daughter's boyfriend?" Pam pushed on. Major Casale squirmed in his seat.

"I wasn't aware my daughter had a boyfriend."

"So she was seeing him without your permission?"

"I didn't say that. I'm saying I disagree with your statement that he was my daughter's boyfriend," Oscar repeated.

"So it would be a surprise to find out she was dating?"

"Mia has dated boys from her school. So no."

"What about enlisted men?"

"Mia understood I was not comfortable with her dating enlisted men."

"Why is that?" Lance asked.

"They are more experienced and usually have one thing on their mind. I didn't think my daughter would be able to handle herself." Oscar said truthfully.

"I see, so you would have been upset if you found out she dated an enlisted man behind your back," Lance pressed.

"I wouldn't have been happy, no."

"What day were you scheduled to leave?" Pam switched subjects to keep Major Casale off-kilter.

"We left on Sunday morning."

"I'm aware that is when you left. What I am asking is, when were you originally scheduled to leave?" Pam asked again. Major Casale knew he couldn't keep skirting these questions. He turned to Major Scott.

"Agent Hill, Agent Marquez, I need a moment with my client," Major Scott insisted. The two agents left the room.

"David, they think I killed him."

"It appears that way, Oscar. You need to tell them the truth."

"I won't do it. I'll just confess."

"No. Let's get a Jag prosecutor in here and see if we can work something out. We can tell a hypothetical story about how it may have happened. That way, if they don't believe you, they can't use your testimony against you," David suggested.

"We can do that?"

"If they agree." David stood and stepped out of the conference room to find Lance and Pam. They noticed him and stepped over.

"Can you get a Jag prosecutor over here? We need to make some stipulations before my client speaks to you again," Major Scott explained.

"Alright, I'll make the call," Lance stepped over to his desk.

# CHAPTER NINETEEN

**D**avid asked Oscar to go over the detail again while waiting for the Jag prosecutor.

"Tell me exactly what happened." Oscar let out a deep breath and complied.

"Every Saturday night, Rita and I have a standing date with two other couples at the Officer's Club. We have dinner and play canasta until after ten."

"Don't get ahead of yourself; start with what time you left the house," David cautioned him.

"Ok. Rita and I headed out the door at about 5:45 pm."

"What does Mia do during this time?"

"She usually goes out with her friends," Oscar replied.

"Was that her plan last Saturday?"

"She dressed up, so I asked her. She said she wasn't sure yet. I kissed her cheek and asked her to leave me a note and be home by 11 pm, then Rita and I went to the club.

"We were waved through the gate because my car has a Base sticker, and the guard recognized me. When I got to the club, I realized I forgot my wallet. We turned around to go back to the house. I asked Rita to wait in the car while I rushed inside to get my wallet.

"When I got inside, a young man was standing in my living room. He was too old to be one of Mia's schoolmates. I was just about to ask who he was when Mia came out of her room and yelped, 'Daddy!'. That's when I realized this man was her date.

"I started yelling at her, 'Mia, what is this man doing here. You know I don't approve of you dating enlisted men. And you are doing it behind my back.' Things like that.

"We yelled back and forth. Mia insisted she was 18 and could date who she wanted. I responded by saying not in my house. Before she could react to that, the young man spoke up.

"He introduced himself and said he had wanted to come and meet me, but Mia was afraid I would order him not to date her, which I would have. I was angry, and my volume was escalating. I was shouting at Private Connelly to get out of my house.

"Private Connelly was facing me, about four feet away. He was my height but smaller in the chest. Connelly was standing in front of our fireplace. It has a heavy granite mantel about five feet from the floor and a three-foot granite base out from the wall. The base is raised about two inches from the floor. Mia stepped between Connelly and me. She was facing me and placed her hand on my chest, asking me to calm down and move back. Then she turned to say something to Private Connelly, just as he moved to get his jacket to leave. When Mia turned, they stumbled over each other and tripped on the two-inch granite lip. Connelly went down with her right on top of him. His head hit the mantel and then hit the base: hard.

"Mia scrambled to get off of him, and I ran over to see if he was alright. I checked his pulse; he was dead. Blood was pooling from behind his head onto the granite. Mia was screaming hysterically; she kept screaming she killed him.

"She didn't kill him; it was an accident. But she was inconsolable. By then, Rita had come in to see what was taking me so long. She gasped and grabbed ahold of Mia."

"Oscar, why didn't you just call the MPs?" David asked.

"My daughter was a mess. She kept saying she killed him. I was afraid they would believe her, and the MPs would arrest her. I had to get her out of there, so I told Rita to take Mia to the car; I had to think.

"I took the suitcases that were already packed for our trip and put them by the front door. Then I looked around; I don't even know what I was looking for. I noticed the Kinkade had blood splatter on it and took it down. That must have been when I turned the air conditioning up, although, I don't remember doing it. I made a few trips to the car, putting everything in the trunk. I went back one more time, turned out the lights, and locked the doors.

"I took Mia and Rita to a hotel near the airport. Rita had some sleeping pills in her purse for the trip; she gets insomnia when she travels. Rita gave one to Mia to calm her down.

"When Mia fell asleep, I told Rita she needed to get some sleep too. I spent the next hours getting our flights changed and upgraded to first class. I knew Mia couldn't take being around strangers in economy seating. Then I took the Kinkade and tried to get the blood off it. I took the painting out of the frame and took them both to my storage shed. I put the frame in a bin and put the canvas in an art tube." Oscar finished and sat with his head lowered.

"Oscar, I believe you. But there are a few issues that can cause some criminal charges to be attached to what you did." David asked Oscar to look at him; he needed to see his reaction. "Some of your actions make his death appear premeditated. Taking the painting, turning up the air conditioner, it looks like you staged the scene. CID could interpret your action as evidence of premeditation. They can say you did those things to protect yourself and set it up to have it look like a burglary. Sending Mia back to the States is also suspect," David said.

"But that's not true. You believe me don't you?" Oscar looked in his friend's face for validation. David put his hand on Oscar's shoulder.

"I do believe you, and I will do my best to make sure they do too. But even if CID believes you, they could determine that you obstructed justice by not immediately calling the MPs. You disturbed the scene," David pause. Oscar's eyebrows furrowed. "Can you give a reasonable explanation for taking the painting, sending your daughter to the States, and turning up the air?

"I don't remember turning up the air conditioning. I sent Mia home because I was afraid this accident would ruin her life once the press finished with her."

"What about taking the painting?"

"I needed to get the blood off of it before it set. Rita loves that painting. I don't understand why one's mind processes things like that in a time of crisis. But I wasn't trying to stage anything." Oscar closed his eyes and tilted back his head for a moment.

"Did you think the body would just disappear while you were gone?" David asked. Oscar jetted up, pushing back his chair, and started pacing.

"I don't know. How many ways can I say it? I don't know what I was thinking. All I wanted to do was get Mia and Rita out of there and away from whatever came next."

"Oscar, sit down and calm yourself. If they think you are hot-headed, it will give credence to their theory that it was murder." David stood to direct him back to his seat.

"I'm sorry, David, I'm so worried about Mia. Rita says she is in bad shape. I want to be with her."

"They are going to want to talk to her to corroborate your story," David could see Oscar panic at the thought.

"David, you can't let them make her come back here. She is a basket case already. I need to protect her."

"You also need to protect yourself. If you go to jail, the guilt Mia feels now will only grow exponentially," David said. Oscar nodded.

A knock came at the door, and Agent Hill stepped in.

"Captain Patel is here from your office, sir."

"Can you give us another minute?" David asked.

"Yes sir." Pam closed the door.

Major Scott turned back to Major Casale. "Listen to me, Oscar, tell them what happened but don't go into all the details. Don't mention anything about the Kinkade."

"What about turning up the air conditioning?" Oscar asked.

"What would your answer be?"

"David, I don't have one. I just did it; I don't know why."

"You were probably in shock," David theorized.

"I guess, maybe."

"Ok, take a few deep breaths. I'm going to let them know we are ready."

After all the greetings were out of the way, and everyone was seated, Captain Patel spoke.

"Well, Major Scott, this seems to be your party; tell me why I am here?"

"Captain Patel, did Agent Hill bring you up to speed on the deceased soldier found in Major Casale's home?"

"Yes."

"Major Casale has a theory about how that may have happened. If we can agree to a course of action after hearing his hypothetical, we can take it from there. If, however, we cannot agree on how to handle it. Anything that is said here today will be inadmissible. Is that agreeable with you?" David asked.

"Has he been read his rights?" Captain Patel asked.

"No ma'am. We brought him in for an interview; we hadn't gotten that far yet," Pam said.

"Well, you better do it now."

"No," David interrupted. "Him not being mirandized is our insurance nothing he says here can be used against him." Captain Patel was not pleased but moved on.

"Alright then, Major Casale, tell us your story."

The Major repeated almost everything he told David earlier, leaving out a few things here and there.

"That's quite a story, Major. If it's true, why didn't you just call the MPs?" Patel asked. David put his hand on Oscar's arm to stop him from answering.

"Captain, my client wasn't thinking right. His daughter was hysterical."

"Major Scott, your client is a Major in the Army; he has seen way worse than this in combat. You can hardly expect me to believe he was in distress." Patel rebuffed David's response.

"Captain, no one can say what they would do in a situation like this. We are talking about his daughter. She was hysterical; she blamed herself. He needed to consider what was best for her."

"Is that why you sent her back to the States, Major?" Lance asked.

"Yes, she had a complete breakdown. I needed to get her home, away from the intense interrogation you would have put her through. Along with all the gossip and the stares she would have undoubtedly faced if she stayed here," Oscar said. His voice weak from the sheer weight of what was happening.

"Tell me why you put the air conditioning on full blast, Major." Pam requested. Oscar's shoulders slumped, and he let out a sigh, then looked up at Agent Hill.

"I honestly don't know. I can't say I even remember doing it. I was on autopilot," Casale answered.

"Major Scott, can I speak with you for a minute, please," Captain Patel requested. David turned to Oscar.

"Stay here and rest. I'll be right back." David turned to Pam, "could you please bring him some water?"

"Yes sir." Pam stepped out.

Agent Marquez seated Major Scott and Captain Patel in an adjacent smaller conference room.

"Major, you don't expect me to believe this at face value. At the very least, he is guilty of failing to report a crime and willful disturbance of a crime scene? And that's being generous. He could be prosecuted for hindering the investigation. Or even accomplice after the fact."

"After the fact of what? It was an accident, not a crime." David replied.

"We need to talk to the ME; I can't assume what Major Casale is saying is what happened." Patel turned to Lance. "Can you see if Lieutenant Colonel Strasburg is available to meet with us? If he is, please tell him we'll be right down."

"Yes ma'am." Lance left the room to make the call. When Lance left, the captain said, "Major Scott, I'm having a hard time reconciling this. The fact he turned on the air conditioning doesn't bode well with it being a freak accident."

"Captain Patel, I can see your point of view. But I also know that when your child is traumatized and having a breakdown, you don't always act rationally." Patel didn't respond right away.

"I need to hear what the ME has to say."

"I agree."

A few minutes later, Lance and Pam stepped in.

"The ME says he is available now. If you would like to come down to his office," Lance reported. Captain Patel and Major Scott stood up and followed the Agents down to the basement. David headed toward the ME's office, but Lance told him he was waiting for them in the autopsy lab with the body.

As they stepped in, the ME had them move around the steel table with the body.

"I know you've been waiting for my report. I have some questions before I assign his death as an accident or murder. I can tell you how he died, though. "

"What can you tell us, sir?" Patel asked. The ME pulled the sheet from Connelly's face. He turned Connelly's head to the left to expose the wound.

"You can see here," the ME pointed with a pen to the left side of his head, "this wound and," he turned his head to the right, "and here. These wounds show his head hit a hard surface. He walked them over to the X-rays on the light board. These cracks are consistent with his skull hitting his head on the mantel of the fireplace and then hitting the granite base." He stepped to a table and picked up a pair of shoes. "These shoes have been spit-shined recently, but if you look at the back of the shoes, you can see new scuff marks. It insinuates he backed up and tripped over the lip of the fireplace."

"Are you saying it was an accident?" Patel asked.

"I would, but I have a question about why he was stepping backward." The ME pulled Connelly's hand from under the sheet. "Neither of his hands has defensive wounds," he exposed Connelly's chest. "But there is slight bruising on his chest and abdomen. It is not consistent with being shoved, but I'm not sure what caused him to go down."

"So you have ruled out being pushed because of the bruises?" Patel asked.

"I can't be one hundred percent certain. But it is unlikely you could move a man his size and strength from his standing position unless someone shoved him pretty hard. Those bruises would be more prominent and the size of a hand. The bruises on his body are light and run down most of his body," the ME speculated.

"Sir, may I run a scenario for you that might explain it?" Major Scott asked.

"Yes, of course."

"Could a woman smaller than him have tripped into him and caused both of them to fall backward?" David suggested. Lieutenant Colonel Strasburg considered it.

"You're suggesting someone fell into him?"

"Yes sir."

"How would you know that?"

"There was a witness," David replied.

"But you said it would take a lot for Connelly to be knocked off his feet," Pam said.

"That's true. But momentum that results from a collision, that's a different story. It could produce enough energy to knock him backward."

"Would that be consistent with the bruising?" Patel asked, confused.

"Yes. Pressure from the one who fell would be distributed throughout Connelly's torso. Brute force would have been concentrated in one area," the ME explained. "So if you have an eyewitness testimony and the source is reliable. I would be comfortable signing off on this death as an accident."

"Thank you, sir; we will get back to you on that as soon as the testimony is corroborated," David said. The others left Lieutenant Colonel Strasburg and went back upstairs. They grabbed some coffee and headed back to the small conference room.

"David, I can't just take Major Casale's word for this. I need to speak to his daughter," Captain Patel insisted.

"He won't bring her back here. She is too fragile; he doesn't want her traumatized more than she already is," David replied.

"Where is she?"

"Spokane, Washington."

"Fairchild Air Force Base is in Spokane, right?"

"Yes," David said.

"We can make arrangements with the MP station on Base to let us do a remote interview. Would Major Casale be agreeable to that?"

"I will make sure he is." David stopped and thought for a moment. "Remember Spokane is 10 hours behind. So it's probably about 5 pm there."

"I better hurry and get a call in to the MP Station while someone on day watch is still there. Should we schedule it for around 8 am, their time?" Pam suggested; Agent Hill agreed. "That would make it about 10 pm here. Is that doable?" Everyone agreed.

"I think their home is about forty-five minutes from the Base." He turned to Pam, "Once you have a time-locked down. I will send Oscar home, and he can call his wife tonight so she can arrange for someone to drive them. I doubt his wife will be in any condition to do it." David said.

Major Casale was emotionally rung out by the time he left CID. David walked him out to the parking lot.

"David, is there any way we can do this without Mia? I'm worried about her?"

"I'm afraid not. The ME is agreeable to ruling it an accident if we have sufficient testimony to back it up."

"I witnessed it; can't that be enough?"

"No, we need someone to corroborate your testimony," David spoke softly, trying to ease Oscar's concerns. Oscar stopped and put his hand on David's shoulder.

"David, you have to promise me if Mia starts to break down, you will stop the interview. You can't let her go over the edge. Promise me."

"I will watch out for your daughter, I promise," David assured him.

"Is it alright for me to call in the hazard material cleaning crew to get rid of the blood?" Oscar asked.

"Agent Hill said they already requisitioned it, but I saw they hadn't gotten to it yet. You can make another request."

**Saturday 9 pm**

Major Scott pulled into the parking lot at CID headquarters. The offices on the second floor were dark except for the conference room. When he stepped off the elevator, he could see Agent Hill setting things up. He walked in and addressed her.

"Good evening, Pam." She turned from what she was doing and laughed, startled.

"Hello, you're early."

"Can I help you?" David asked.

"No, I'm just moving in this television so everyone can see the interview."

"Pam, can I ask you a question?"

"Sure."

"The questions you asked at the first interview with Major Casale. I got the impression you considered him a suspect."

"I was leaning that way. What are the chances that a dead man is going to show up in a total stranger's home? There had to be a connection somewhere. He could have been a thief, but that didn't add up either, based on what I learned about Private Connelly, even if you tried to concoct a story that he had a partner. It just didn't add up. There had to be some other reason for him to be there."

"But what set your sites on the Major?"

"It was after interviewing Mia's and Private Connelly's friends. Both sides agreed they were seeing someone secretly. I found out Major Casale was adamant that his daughter not date enlisted men."

"So you dug deeper. But why suspect Major Casale? At the time, we thought he had already left on vacation."

"Yes, but the air conditioning being on didn't sit right. If someone other than the resident of the property killed him, why would they stop to turn on the air conditioning? What clinched it was when I found this in Connelly's personal items." Agent Hill reached into the file on the table and handed David a strip of photos from a photo booth.

"I see. Private Connelly and Mia were a couple."

"Yes."

"That gave him a connection to the house. But I have to say I did not anticipate the way it happened." Agent Hill hesitated, "I would like to know one thing. Did he tell you why he turned on the air conditioning?"

"I don't think he remembered doing it until we told him. If you want my opinion, I think subconsciously, he knew there was a chance the body could be there until he returned. It was a way to protect his home from the smell."

Agent Hill turned when she heard the others coming. She finished hooking up the laptop to the television that she rolled in. Then she left to grab some bottles of water for everyone.

"Hello, David," Lance said as he walked into the conference room.

"Hi, Lance." David looked to see if Pam was close, "have you gotten an answer from Pam yet about Paris?"

"No, and there is not much time left. I'm going to bring it up again when this interview is over." Lance whispered as Pam came back into the room with her hands full of bottles of water.

"Good evening, everyone," Captain Patel said as she came in behind Pam and sat at the seat where the laptop was.

"Good evening," the others chimed.

"Agent Hill, what arrangement did you make with Fairchild Air Force Base?" Patel asked.

"Staff Sergeant Ferraro will be contacting us at exactly 8 am Spokane time." She checked the clock on the wall, about ten minutes, ma'am," Agent Hill responded.

242

"Captain Patel, I am sure you are aware you are dealing with a young woman in crisis. If I have any concerns that she's unstable, I will let you know," Major Scott said.

"Are you acting as her attorney, Major?" She responded.

"No, but I promised her father I would watch out for her mental state. And we do not interrogate mentally unstable people, Captain. Remember, this is an interview. She is not a criminal." The captain did not reply.

# THE PROMISE

# CHAPTER TWENTY

A few minutes later, the conference video opened up. An Air Force Staff Sergeant's face appeared on the screen.

"Hello. Staff Sergeant Ferraro here. Is this Agent Hill?"

"No, Staff Sergeant, I am Captain Patel from Jag. Has Mia Casale made it to your office?"

"Yes ma'am. Miss Casale and her mother are here. I will turn her over to you." The Staff Sergeant turned the laptop to face Mia.

Major Scott was taken back by her appearance. Her face was pale, her eyes puffy and red. But it was the dark shadows under both eyes that made her look like she was at death's door.

"Miss Mia Casale?" Captain Patel opened.

"Yes ma'am."

"For the record, I want to inform you this interview is being recorded. I will list everyone present at this interview for the record. Here at Incirlik Air Base, present is Captain Patel from Jag and Major Scott from Jag. Also from CID are Agent's Hill, and Marquez the investigators. As I understand it at Fairchild Air Force Base, the following are present, Staff Sergeant Ferraro, Mrs. Rita Casale, and Miss Mia Casale." She heard Staff Sergeant Ferraro say that was correct.

"Miss Casale, may I call you Mia?"

"Yes."

"Can you please tell me how you know Private Pete Connelly?"

"We were dating...sorta."

"What does that mean, 'sorta'?"

"Our first real date was going to be last Saturday. We were going to go out to eat and to the movies. Before that, we just met at the PX food court," Mia explained.

"How did you meet?"

"Last month, a few friends and I were at the PX food court, and Pete and his friends were sitting next to us. My girlfriend thought they were cute, so she started talking to them. Pete didn't say much, but before we left, he asked if I would meet him again the next Saturday." She almost smiled, reliving the moment. "I agreed, we ate lunch and went for a walk. We did the same thing the next Saturday. He was so nice, sweet, shy in an attractive way."

"So why didn't you introduce him to your father?" Mia's demeanor changed, stiffening up.

"Pete felt bad about sneaking around. He wanted to introduce himself to my dad, but I knew my dad didn't want me to date enlisted men. Dad said they had too much experience and would talk me into doing things. He treats me like I'm twelve. I think he will always see me as his little girl." Her lips curved up a little again. "I love my dad; I didn't want to argue with him. I had planned to ask my mom to approach the subject while we were on vacation."

"Did your mom know?"

"I hadn't told her yet; I was waiting until we were in Sicily," Mia said.

"Ok, Mia, can you tell me what happened on Saturday night?" Captain Patel asked. Mia collapsed into herself even more.

Mia told the story up to the point of her stepping in between the two men. Then she broke down sobbing. Her mother's arm appeared on the screen, rubbing Mia's up and down. Captain Patel gave her a moment to collect herself. Mia calmed down enough to go on.

"I told dad to step back and calm down. But he kept asking questions, 'how old is this guy', 'has he touched you', things like that. He started shouting at Pete to get out of his house."

"Captain, she is getting more unstable, I think we should end this interview." David whispered to Captain Patel. Before Patel could respond. Mia sucked in a big breath. She started speaking faster, thinking she could get it out in one breath.

"Pete tried to explain, but dad just kept shouting at him to get out. Finally, I figured it would be best for him to go. I turned to tell him just as he had bent down to get his jacket, and we got tangled up." She gasped for air again. Captain Patel opened her mouth to stop the interview; the girl was falling apart. But Mia kept talking. "I fell against him, and his foot caught on the lip at the base of the fireplace." She started hyperventilating.

"We started falling backward with me on top of him. I heard a big crack. The next thing I knew, we were on the ground; I rolled off of him. I got up to see if he was alright, but there was all this blood…pooling…" Mia lifted her head and let out a wail that startled everyone and the girl shattered right in front of them.

David had never heard such a raw, primitive expression of anguish in his whole life. It was terrifying to look into the fracturing of a mind. Her mother had her wrapped in her arms, and he could hear Staff Sergeant Ferraro call out for an ambulance.

Ferraro turned the laptop to face him. "Captain Patel, this interview is over. You can contact me again if you need to." The screen went black. No one spoke for a moment.

"I should have stopped it sooner," David lamented, shaken up.

"No, Major. I could see she was breaking down; I should have ended it," Captain Patel said, visibly shaken herself.

"Her testimony verifies what Major Casale said. There is no way that girl was lying," David said.

"I agree. I don't doubt that is exactly how it happened. It must have been horrible for her," Pam added.

"I'll inform Lieutenant Colonel Strasburg of our finding and send him a copy of the interview. Agent Hill, do you agree we have determined the death of Private Connelly an accident? Lance asked.

"Yes," she replied. Major Scott addressed Captain Patel.

"Captain, do you plan on charging Major Casale with anything?" The captain was staring at the file; he could see she was distressed over the interview.

"What?"

"Do you plan on charging my client with anything?"

"He failed to report an accident and disturbed the scene...but I think the family has suffered enough. No, I will not be bringing charges. If Strasburg has any other questions, he can call me." Patel stood and gathered her papers, putting them in her leather briefcase. Without speaking another word, she nodded to everyone and headed out of the room. Lance was staying behind to help Pam put things back in order.

David hurried to catch up with her. "May I walk you to your car, Captain Patel."

"Yes, thank you." As they walked out, she said to him. "Major Scott, you have to know I never intended to cause her to break down like that."

"I know, Captain. I should have stopped it."

"Will you let me know how she's doing when you find out?" They reached her car, she opened the door and looked at him.

"I will, Captain. It wasn't your fault, Maya." David could see she felt terrible.

"Thank you, David, but I'm not so sure of that."

David walked to his car and headed home. The weight of what happened still heavy on his mind. He looked at his watch. It was 11:15 pm, he hoped Anna was still awake. He just wanted to wrap his arms around her. Having her close always made him feel better.

Lance called just as he pulled into his driveway.

"Hey, David. Pam asked if the offer to go to Paris was still open. She wants to come. I didn't even have to bring it up."

"That's great, Lance."

"Yeah, I can't wait…That interview was tough, huh?"

"Yes, it was. I'll be praying for the Casale's for a long time."

### Second week in July

Mommy, you have to finish my French braid. Daddy is going to be here soon. Clair had just finished Lizzy's and walked over to Sophie, who was sitting on the vanity chair. Wes walked in.

"Wes, are you and mom going to spend time in Disneyland Paris with us?"

"If it's alright with your father," he replied.

"Will you take Lizzy and me on the 'Tower of Terror'? Please," Sophie asked.

"Sophie, I don't think Disneyland Pairs has the 'Tower of Terror'."

"How about 'Big Thunder Mountain'?" Lizzy asked.

"If it's alright with your fathers, and you meet the height requirement." Wes laughed, excited to be able to be with them at Disneyland. He had wanted to take Sophie before, but Luke had asked Clair not to take her because he had made plans to go with her.

Clair was putting the last barrette in Sophie's hair when the doorbell rang. Sophie and Lizzy ran to the door; Beau struggled to keep up with them. Sophie opened the door before Ms. Ava could get there.

"Daddy." Sophie threw herself in his arms. Lizzy did the same with her dad.

"Sophie, princess, I missed you," Luke said as he lifted her and swung her around.

Wes and Clair came to the door pulling the girls' luggage behind them. Luke put Sophie down.

"Manny Diaz, this is Clair and Wes Cornish. Manny stretched out his hand to them.

"I can't thank you enough for allowing Lizzy to spend this time here with you."

"Don't be silly," Clair said. "She is a dream to have around."

"We enjoyed having her," Wes agreed.

"Please come in for a moment." Clair led them into the living room. "I called your friend Jared in Austin, Texas. I will be sending the girls and Liam's school clothes to him. They will deliver the furniture for their rooms there too.

"Thank you, Clair. That is very thoughtful," Luke said.

"Mrs. Cornish, you and your husband, have been too generous," Manny said.

"It was our pleasure. Please call me Clair."

"Luke, is it still alright if we meet up with you a few days at Disneyland Paris to spend time with the girls?" Wes asked.

"Yes, of course. We are staying at the Disney Hotel. We thought we would take our time in the morning and go down for breakfast at 10 am. You are welcome to have breakfast with us, and we can leave from there," Luke answered.

"Thank you, Luke," Clair said. "We'll be there."

"Well, we need to get settled into the hotel; we'll see you tomorrow," Luke said. Sophie and Lizzy gave Wes and Clair big hugs. The girls put on their backpacks while their dads grabbed a suitcase in each hand.

Clair and Wes were waiting when the group convened downstairs for breakfast. Luke introduced them to everyone.

Breakfast was noisy, the kids were ramped up and excited to get into Disneyland. They were out the door before the rest of them could finish paying the bill.

The group waited for a horse-drawn streetcar and loaded on. They decided the night before that they would go to the furthest part of the park and work their way back.

Everyone started out going on the rides together, but soon the adults were getting worn out. They decided to split up 'rides' detail, allowing other adults to rest or shop. Luke noticed when Pam and Lance weren't on rides, Lance would grab Pam's hand to hold it.

The kids all wanted to go on the Indiana Jones Temple of Peril ride, but only Duke and CJ were tall enough.

"You guys can't go without us, Duke," Sophie pouted.

"Sophie, we really want to go on this ride, but CJ and I promise to ride 'It's a Small World' with you as many times as you want," Duke compromised.

"You promise?"

"Yes," Duke and CJ chimed at the same time.

While the boys waited in line with all the men for the ride, Clair and Pam took the girls on the 'Dumbo Flying Elephant' ride. Ruby and Zoey went the other direction and took Liam and Ricky on the 'Buzz Lightyear Laser Blast.'

It was early afternoon before anyone wanted to break for lunch. They agreed to feed the kids something from the vendors and wait to have an early dinner.

The group walked into Captain Jack's restaurant at 4:45 pm. Wes spoke with the hostess, insisting he wanted to pay the group's bill secretly.

By the time everyone ate and spent another ten minutes insisting on paying Wes back, unsuccessfully, it was 6:30. The group decided to go back to the hotel to let the kid's swim.

The men got in the pool with the kids and tossed them around for a while; then, they played pool volleyball. The ladies took the opportunity to shop on Disney Main Street; taking a break an hour into it, they stopped for coffee and pastries. Clair listened to the conversations. She never had a group of friends that were as close as these women.

"Thank you for letting me crash your shopping adventure," Clair said. Anna reached her hand across the table and covered Clair's.

"You did not crash anything. We wanted you to come. It's a pleasure to meet Sophie's mother and your husband. Sophie is such a wonderful child."

"Yes, she is, but I'm afraid I had little to do with that," Clair's voice reflected her regret.

"Don't underestimate your influence. Sophie is one of the most giving and generous children I have ever met. I'm sure that comes from modeling you," Ruby said.

"Sophie is so lucky to have you all in her life. I understand Luke's choice to leave the Army and join your husbands in a new law office. Austin seems so far away," Clair lamented.

"Planes fly just as often from Austin to Paris as they do from Turkey to Paris," Zoey tried to comfort her.

"True, it just felt like she was closer, being on the same continent."

The following day started the same. It was hot outside, and they had to regulate the activities so that the kids could rehydrate. They insisted the next thing they did be indoors and not physical.

They decided that 'Mickey's PhilharMagic' was a perfect reprieve. Before they entered, Clair asked Luke if she could talk to him. They sat on a bench outside the theater.

"Luke, I wanted a chance to tell you, I know how wrong I was by getting involved with Wes when we were married. And then the way I handled leaving you and Sophie was even worse," she turned her face away from him. "I hope you can forgive me."

"Clair, I would be lying if I said I did everything right. I was so angry at you. I carried it for too long. The Lord delivered me, and I don't feel that way anymore. But to let go, I had to forgive you. And I did, a long time ago," Luke smiled at her.

"You have done such a good job with her, Luke. She is a wonderful person."

"You have your part in that," Luke said. Clair looked at her hands. She wasn't convinced.

"Sophie and Lizzy pooled all their money to buy me a beautiful Bible. They even had engraved 'MOM' on it in silver. Sophie commented that now I could go to church because I have a Bible. I suppose in her young mind, she had convinced herself that was why I didn't go to church with you."

"She asked me all the time why you wouldn't come. I said you had to work," Luke remembered.

"Late the other night, she got up for water and came to talk to me out on the balcony. We talked about salvation," Clair looked up at him again. "She has a depth to her that few adults do."

"That's true; Sophie has insight," Luke agreed.

"I've been reading the Bible; I promised her I would. I'm going to look for a church. I want to be right with God. I don't know why I resisted for so long. I guess I was afraid I'd have to give up something," Clair said.

"You know that's not how it works."

"I do; the Bible makes it plain, Jesus did all the work, and we get all the benefit."

"I don't think I've ever heard it put quite so well," Luke smiled.

"I know Wes kept Sophie at arm's length at first, but he's come to realize how important the time is we have with her. He's reaching out to Sophie, Luke. I know you guys will never be friends, but I hope you know he will always treat her well."

"I know Wes is a good man, Clair," Luke said. Sophie came out of the theater looking for them.

"Mom, Dad, come on, the show is starting." Sophie grabbed their hands and pulled them up. They all hurried to get into their seats.

By the end of the third day, the group had ridden every ride and partaken in every vendor's food offering. If they missed any restaurants, it was only because they didn't see it. While they finished dinner at yet another restaurant, Luke spoke.

"I know we planned on spending most of our time here at Disneyland, but we've been through the whole park. What do you say we do Paris a little sooner?"

"I think that's a great idea," Anna said. The others agreed.

"We would love to join you for dinner some night while you're in Paris," Wes said.

"Yes, anytime. But only if you don't try to pay for all our dinners again," Jonathan insisted, smiling. Wes and Clair said goodbye to everyone and left.

On the first day, the group did all the mandatory sightseeing. They went to the Eiffel Tower, the Louvre Museum, the Hall of Mirrors, and Sainte Chapelle. The second day they rented a driver and a small bus to take them around to see some of the famous architecture. They drove by famous Cathedrals; walking through a few. They drove by parliament, and the Arc de Triomphe, among other famous sites.

Luke called Wes to see if he and Clair would want to join them that night on the Bateaux Seine River Boat Dinner Cruise. The boat had floor-to-ceiling windows. Luke remembered watching the light show on the Eiffel Tower with Marci as it cruised.

David was sitting next to Lance; the women took a trip to the lady's room. Lance spoke softly, so the others didn't hear.

"David, I've had so much fun with Pam. I'm getting pretty serious about her." David turned to him.

"Lance, that's what I was afraid of. You know she won't get serious with anyone who is not a born-again believer. She almost didn't come because she was afraid she was leading you to believe there was a future with her."

"Do you remember the interview with Mia Casale?"

"How could I ever forget it," David said. He lifted his coffee to take a drink, wondering what that had to do with this conversation.

"I went to church with you guys the next day, remember?" David nodded. "Pastor Ben's sermon talked about having peace in the time of trouble. I got to thinking about Mia. I wished she could have peace in her troubles. I came to realize you can't give yourself that kind of peace.

"Still, the next few days, that interview weighed on me. I needed peace too. So I made an appointment to speak to Paster Ben, and he led me through the sinner's prayer," Lance ended with a big smile.

"That is the best news, Lance. Congratulations," David patted him on the back.

"I'm not sure if I should tell Pam about it. I don't want her to think it's some sort of ploy to get to her. What should I do?"

"Lance, tell her your experience and then live the Christian life. Your conversion will be evident to all those around you. She'll see you are the real deal."

"Thanks, David. I'm hoping when I decide to transition out of the Army that we may all hook up again."

"I hope so too," David said ending the conversation because the women came back.

The kids were at the end of the table, sitting together. Duke was talking to CJ.

"'RC Racer' was so cool.," Duke reminisced.

"Yeah, I still like 'Tower of Terror' back in the States better, though. It has all those drops and turns."

"I liked Pirates of the Caribbean, the best," Sophie chimed in.

"I loved 'Thunder Mountain'," Lizzy added.

"I can't believe you went on 'Tower of Peril' without us," Sophie scowled at Duke.

"Don't make that face; it could freeze that way," Duke goaded her. She immediately changed her expression. CJ and Duke burst out laughing. Sophie was not amused and slapped Duke's shoulder.

"Stop teasing her, you guys," Lizzy insisted. David swiped a French fry from Sophie's plate. She slapped his hand.

"Eat your own food. I'm still mad you went on 'Tower of Peril' without us," Sophie pouted again.

"You didn't miss much," CJ admitted.

"Yeah, 'Tower of Terror' is much better," Duke added while stealing another of Sophie's fries.

"Stop that, Duke," Duke laughed as he stuffed it in his mouth.

"Are you guys getting along down there?" Zoey asked.

"Yeah, we're fine," they all chimed.

Their last day in Paris was reserved for shopping. They spent their time walking the Seine looking at all the book and art vendors offerings.

"Daddy, look, it's a sketch artist. We have to have a picture done." Sophie pulled him along. Everyone in the group wanted sketches too. The artist decided to take Polaroids of the different groupings. He said he would have the sketches done in two hours. When Sophie and Lizzy were posing for their Polaroid, Duke, and CJ photobombed them. The artist drew two sketches, one with and one without them. The men decided to get a caricature done like the one Sophie gave them years earlier.

That night, Wes and Clair came to the hotel to say goodbye to Sophie.

"Mom, don't cry. You're coming to see me at Christmas, right?"

"Yes, of course, darling. Austin feels so far away," Clair said.

"Can I still come to see you every summer, even though we're not in Turkey?" Sophie asked. Clair hugged her tight.

"Of course. I would want you to come even if you lived on the moon."

"Don't be silly, Mom. No one lives on the moon," Sophie laughed. Wes gave Sophie a big hug.

"I'm sure going to miss you, Sophie."

"I'll miss you too, Wes. Thank you for taking us to 'Beauty and the Beast'; I'll never forget it."

"When you come back, we'll go to the theater again. I promise."

Luke stepped over to Wes. "Wes, I want to thank you for being so good to Sophie. She had a wonderful time." He stretched his hand out to him.

Clair left in tears; leaving her daughter this time was so hard.

# CHAPTER TWENTY-ONE

R uby finally called the Military Families Support Services to send OCONUS over. She was ready to have them pick the boxes prepared to crate for shipment back to the States.

The kids routinely reopened the boxes, trading out items for their backpacks, so Ruby held off an extra day. She allowed Lizzy and Ricky to keep out only the personal things that fit in their backpacks. It would take a month or more for their belongings to catch up with them in Austin. Sophie and Lizzy spent hours the night before trying to figure out the right things to keep. Ruby quickly repacked their boxes and headed back to the kitchen to finish up there.

Ruby had stopped working as the Jag office receptionist the day before they left for Paris. Since they've been back, she spent her days getting everything ready for transport. Five more days, and they were on the plane to their new home. Her next call was to a moving company in Montana. The items she kept of her mother's were at her brother's home in Montana. Ruby hoped at least those items would get to Austin soon after they arrived. She was interrupted when the phone rang.

"Hello?"

"Ruby, I wanted to see if you needed any help packing?"

"Zoey, thanks, but I think I'm done now. I've had to redo the boxes in the kids' room several times, but they are sealed now," Ruby laughed.

"I'm expecting the same behavior with Liam. Ricky can stay here as long as you need if it helps."

"Thank you. Lizzy is at Sophie's. I thought it would be better if the kids weren't in the way when the workers came to take out all our boxes. I think the girls are helping Deniz sort through Sophie's things and pack her room. Deniz knows what fits Sophie better than Luke does. Knowing Sophie, she would give everything away," Ruby chuckled. "Deniz is going to take the clothes that are too small to her church so they can go to a needy family."

"That's good. Are you anxious about moving to a new city?" Zoey asked.

"A little, but I'm excited about seeing my new home."

"Last time we were home, mine and Anna's houses were the only ones built on our cul-de-sac," Zoey said. "Austin is a wonderful place to live. You'll love it there."

"I'll love having you as neighbors, for sure. I'm grateful that your husband and David made such a great offer to Manny. He is excited about his new job. Manny and I agreed to use part of my inheritance to live on until the office was open. But Emmett offered him a temporary job working with the construction company."

"I'm sure you packed all your kitchen items. Do you need Anna and me to bring you some essentials until you leave?"

"That is so thoughtful, thank you. But I have already requested kitchen supplies from the Housing Department. I do have one request; do you mind taking the clothes that don't fit Ricky and Lizzy anymore and taking them to the Turkish church where you and Anna volunteer? They are in excellent condition."

"Yes, of course. I'll be doing the same thing with Ricky and CJ's clothes," Zoey said.

"Thank you."

"If you are sure I can't help you with anything, I'll let you get back to work."

"Thanks for checking on me. I'll have Manny pick up Ricky when he gets done with his shift."

"Why don't you let him spend the night?"

"I'm sure he'd like that. If he's not in your way, that would be great. Talk to you later, Zoey.

The judge adjourned the court at 5 pm. Luke's last scheduled trial as lead counsel finished. For the next two and a half weeks, he would be the second chair for his replacement. There were still five trials scheduled before he left.

Luke had packed his personal items and what few household items he bought since he'd arrived. Except for Sophie's room, everything else belonged to the Army.

Luke couldn't help being excited about the new road his life was taking. The offer to join a firm this early in his career was not expected, and a partnership was unheard of. It would take him a while to earn the partner's buy-in, but he could do it.

As soon as he walked in the door, he heard Sophie and Lizzy giggling about something. Deniz must have heard him come in because she came out of the room and greeted him.

"Mr. Luke, I hope you had a nice day."

"I did, Deniz. What are the girls doing in there?"

"They are going through all the things Sophie had stuffed away and hadn't seen for a while. I'm trying to limit what she keeps for her backpack."

"I can see how that could be a difficult task. If you haven't started dinner, I'll take the girls out," Luke said. He put down his briefcase and hung up his coat.

"Time got away from me, Mr. Luke. I have not started dinner yet," Deniz said.

"Good, thank you, Deniz. I'll see you in the morning."

"Thank you, Mr. Luke; I'll be here." Deniz grabbed her purse and keys and stepped into the bedroom to say goodbye to the girls. The girls hugged her and went back to sorting through things.

Luke went into Sophie's bedroom. There were boxes open everywhere, but it was an organized mess. "Hi girls, how about I take you out to dinner tonight?"

Sophie turned when she heard her father's voice. "Daddy," she gave him a big hug. Lizzy did too.

"Can we go to the pizza place with the arcade?" Sophie asked.

"Pizza sounds good to me," he responded. The girls clapped their hands.

"You girls clean up. I'm going to change and call Lizzy's dad, so he knows where she is."

"Can Lizzy spend the night, please, please?"

"I'll ask. But you'll have to rearrange this room so you can get to the bed," he laughed.

"We will, Daddy," Sophie said smiling. He knew exactly what her plan was. She would take everything on the bed and place it on the floor in the corner. But that was a problem for tomorrow; it could wait. Luke changed and called Manny.

"Master Sergeant Diaz, speaking."

"Manny, sorry, I thought you'd be home by now. Do you have a minute?"

"Sure, Luke. I had to stay late to interview a suspected peeping tom."

"That's not something a father wants to hear. I can call Ruby if you're too busy?"

"No, I'm done. Go ahead, Luke."

"I wanted to know if Lizzy could spend the night with Sophie. I was going to take them out for pizza, the one with the arcade."

"Sure, I'll let Ruby know. I should be home pretty soon."

Luke asked for a few hours off so he could take the Diaz family to the airport. Sophie and Lizzy were in the third seat.

"Lizzy, are you going with your mom to check out the new school?"

"Yes, I'm so glad we are going to be together. I hate going to new schools."

"Me too," Sophie said.

"I'm going to miss you," Lizzy said.

"Me too."

Manny was sitting up front with Luke. "I'm a little anxious about this big move, but I know it's right for my family."

"I agree, Manny, it's a big risk; for all of us. At least we are taking it together," Luke said, taking his eyes off the road for a second to look at him.

"Did David and Jonathan decide to send their families home on the same flight as you and Sophie?"

"Yes, Anna and Zoey want to have the kids settled before school starts," Luke said.

"It was generous of Clair to upgrade our economy seats to first class. I didn't want to accept, but she insisted."

"She offered to pay for David and Jonathan's families too, but they said they had already upgraded."

"Well, I appreciate being able to have my family travel in first class," Manny smiled.

Luke pulled up to the airport drop-off area and pulled to the curb. Everyone exited the car; Luke and Manny grabbed the suitcases and backpacks out of the back. Sophie hugged Lizzy and Ricky, then hugged Ruby and Manny. She was crying by the time she watched them walk into the airport.

"Sophie, we will be with them in two weeks. Don't be sad," Luke hugged his little girl.

Sophie spoke with her mom and Wes every day on the phone or by Skype since they left Paris. Luke felt good that he settled the rift between him and Clair. Even he and Wes had an amicable understanding. His conversation in Disneyland Paris with Clair healed a lot of old wounds. He was genuinely glad she found happiness with Wes.

It had been almost two weeks since the Diaz family had left. Luke had spoken to Manny several times. Manny told him the section of Austin their homes were in was a safe, clean area and sent pictures. He and Ruby loved their home. The furniture Clair had sent for Lizzy was already set up in her room.

"Luke, your house is across the street. Lizzy is thrilled about that. Ruby said the private school is a former Catholic School property. They grew out of it and built a bigger school a few miles away. They were going to demolish it and sell the land, but Parkcrest Academy offered to buy it. The building was still in good shape; all they had to do was upgrade and remodel the inside. Now they have grades kindergarten through twelfth grade. Ruby temporarily registered all the kids and got the registration packets for all the families to fill out."

"Tell her thanks for me. Do they wear uniforms?"

"Yes, but only the first through sixth grades. They allow the older kids to wear what they want, within reason. Seventh, eighth, and ninth grades are considered junior high, and it is in a separate building, just across the parking lot. The high school is on the same property too."

"We'll be on the plane in two days. Can you pick us up?"

"Yes, Emmett and Jared are bringing cars too. We'll need them."

"Ok. I'll be glad to have this move behind me."

"See you soon," Manny signed off.

It was Deniz's last day. She came to help get Sophie ready and to say goodbye. Deniz was getting ready to leave when Sophie ran to her dad.

"Daddy, why can't Deniz come with us?" Sophie cried.

"Sophie, I would love her to come with us, but she has her family here. You don't want her mom, dad, and little brother to be sad, do you?"

"No, but I want her to come with us." Deniz took Sophie's hand and led her to the couch.

"Sophie, I love you very much, and I will miss you a lot. But I live here in Adana. I promise I will Skype with you all the time, and maybe I can visit now and then," Deniz said.

"You promise?" Sophie wrapped her arms around her and cried.

"I promise," Deniz started to cry. She got up and walked toward the door. She addressed Luke.

"Mr. Luke, thank you for paying me for the entire summer and the job. I will miss you both. I hope I can come to visit you someday in Austin."

"Of course, Deniz. You have been a blessing to us, and we would love to have you visit anytime." Deniz went to the door. Sophie ran to give her another hug and watched her leave. She had her arms wrapped around her dad.

It was the night before their early morning flight. David and Jonathan were taking them and their families to the airport. It was late, Luke had just repacked Sophie's suitcases, she was putting things in her backpack and duffle bag to take on the plane with her. Luke realized he hadn't fed Sophie anything for dinner. He looked in the cupboards and found one can of soup: Campbell's pea soup. He couldn't remember buying it but he heated it up and made grilled cheese sandwiches. He called Sophie in to eat. Sophie looked at the soup and spoke to her dad.

"What is this, Daddy?"

"It's soup."

"No it's not, it's green."

"It's pea soup, try it, it's good."

"No way."

"Sophie, please don't give me a hard time, it was all that was in the cupboard. Take a bite, you'll like it." He sat down with her and ate.

Sophie ate her sandwich, but still didn't touch the soup.

"Sophie, you are not leaving the table until you eat that soup. I won't put up with your picky eating tonight." Sophie took a tiny bit on the end of her spoon and put it in her mouth. She gagged.

"Stop that Sophie and eat."

"I can't, Daddy, it's awful and it's green."

"You can sit there until you do."

Luke cleaned the kitchen and still Sophie sat there. Finally, Luke said, "I'm disappointed in you Sophie, get to your room and get ready for bed." Immediately after he said it he felt horrible. He knew he was just taking his last-minute jitters about this huge move, out on her. Sophie moved to the kitchen entrance. She turned to look at him.

"Daddy will you still brush my hair." Luke turned.

"Yes, get ready for bed." Luke dumped the soup and washed the bowl.

Luke saw Sophie sitting on the bed in her pajamas, her head down. He sat next to her.

"Daddy, do you still love me." Luke gently moved her in front of him and lifted her chin with his hand to look in her eyes.

"Sophie, I want you to listen to me, not just up here," he touched her ear, "but in here," he tapped her heart. "There are going to be lots of times that I won't approve of what you do. And sometimes I will have to discipline you for doing those things, but you have to know that it will never effect how much I love you. Once a dad holds his little girl in his arms for the first time when she is born, he falls in love with her. From that day on a dad's love only grows. It can never diminish; it's not possible. Do you hear what I'm saying Sophie? Deep down in your heart, do you understand?" He tapped her heart again.

"Even when you are mad at me?"

"Yes, even when I'm not happy with something you do. I will always love you and don't ever forget that." Sophie threw her arms around him.

"You promise you will always love me more?"

"Always, I promise," Luke said. Sophie kissed his cheek.

"Alright, lets brush your hair." Sophie sat cross legged in front of him. All her belongings were gone; headed to Austin. The Army sent her over a cot to sleep on and Luke had brought a decorative mirror from the living room for her to use. He could see her face in the mirror. She was looking at him.

"Daddy, that stuff was really awful." Luke smiled.

"It really was, wasn't it?" They both laughed.

Once the plane was in the air, the kids switched seats so they could sit together. They had brought down the seat tables and were playing Chinese checkers. They would be changing planes in New York and again in Denver. Overall a twenty-hour flight with ground time between flights. They were all glad they had first-class accommodations.

**Paris**

Clair had spoken to Sophie just before she got on the plane. Wes came out onto the French balcony just before she hung up and was able to say goodbye to her too.

Wes saw Clair was upset. He sat down next to her on one of the padded rod iron chairs and set his coffee on the little table.

"Clair, love, don't be so sad. We will go down to Austin at Christmas and stay a week. Sophie can stay in our hotel with us and show us around Austin," Wes took her hand and kissed it.

"Thank you, darling; I don't know why I feel so lonely. I know it's just a plane ride away." Clair took her hand and ran it down Wes's face, then kissed him.

"You know that little church I've been going to?"

"Yes, Trinity over by Rue Jean Lantier."

"Yes, I would like you to come with me next time, Wes." She looked him in the eyes.

"Sure, love, I would like that," Wes nodded.

"Good. Now I am going to go get us some breakfast at the bakery across the street." Clair smiled. "Is there anything special you would like, Wes?"

"I like the smoked salmon and cream cheese with fruit, eggs, and avocado on a croissant and a Croque Madame."

"Sounds good." Clair stood up to leave. She called for Beau and went to get his leash.

"How about we take the day off and go for a ride in the country?" Wes asked.

"That sounds wonderful. I love you, Wes, and I am so glad you opened up to Sophie. I wanted that more than anything. Thank you."

"Clair, I was wrong keeping her at arm's length. But I plan on making it up to her," Wes smiled down at Clair.

"Do you want me to go with you to the bakery?"

"No darling, sit and enjoy your coffee," she said. Wes walked her and Beau to the door and shut it behind them. He went to his room and dressed, refilled his coffee, then went back to the balcony. The sky was blue and cloudless, a beautiful warm day.

It took twenty minutes to get to the front of the line and ten more to get her order. Finally, Clair was headed out the bakery door. She placed the food in her mesh shopping bag and put it over her shoulder. When Clair reached the corner to cross the street, she picked Beau up, as was her custom. As she waited for the light to change, she looked up and saw Wes watching her. She waved; he did the same. She smiled, thinking about how much fun she and Wes had with Sophie in Disneyland Pairs.

TO

BE

CONTINUED

# FROM THE AUTHOR

Thank you for reading 'The Promise'. I hope you are enjoying taking this journey with Sophie through her childhood experiences.

I hope you continue to read about the rest of her child and teenage years in the final installment of 'A Sophie Star Prequel'.

LJ